VULTURES AT TWILIGHT

VULTURES AT TWILIGHT

Charles Atkins

This first world edition published 2012
in Great Britain and in the USA by
SEVERN HOUSE PUBLISHERS LTD of
9–15 High Street, Sutton, Surrey, England, SM1 1DF.

British Library Cataloguing in Publication Data

Atkins, Charles.
  Vultures at twilight.
  1. Detective and mystery stories.
  I. Title
  813.6-dc23

ISBN-13: 978-0-7278-8141-0 (cased)

All Severn House titles are printed on acid-free paper.

Severn House Publishers support The Forest Stewardship Council [FSC], the
leading international forest certification organisation. All our titles that are printed
on Greenpeace-approved FSC-certified paper carry the FSC logo.

MIX
Paper from
responsible sources
FSC® C018575

Typeset by Palimpsest Book Production Ltd.,
Falkirk, Stirlingshire, Scotland.
Printed and bound in Great Britain by
MPG Books Ltd., Bodmin, Cornwall.

To Ida, Sue and Barbara

Prologue

Philip Conroy's dying thought was: *it's a beautiful day*. In truth, it was the kind of fall afternoon that brought leaf peepers and antique hunters in late-model Mercedes and convertible BMWs to picturesque Grenville where Philip – thirty-six, blond and movie-star handsome – had lived his entire life. Lying face up on a bed of freshly fallen leaves, with a bullet wound like a Hindu bindi mark in the middle of his forehead, the last images that shot through his blue-green eyes and into his brain were of a blazing red maple, surrounded by a sea of yellow ash. A breeze swept the deep ravine, and a fresh wave of leaves lost hold of their branches and danced on the currents. Philip's last sounds were the running water of the Nillewaug River, where he had swum and fished as a child, and the crunching of twigs underfoot. He heard something dull and metallic, but was fully dead by the time the hundred-year-old iron metal snips wrapped around the finger next to the one where he wore Tolliver's gold wedding band. He did not hear the single grunt as his murderer brought the handles of the heavy tool together and severed the finger or the clicking open of a Ziploc bag into which the digit was dropped.

The nerve fibers just beneath his skin registered the bracing cold of the river as he was rolled into the lapping waters. The pores of his skin clamped shut for a final time, trying in vain to preserve body heat, not yet understanding that this natural response would no longer be necessary.

As Philip Conroy's body eventually came to rest wedged between an outcropping of rock and the twisted branches of an active beaver lodge, two miles due west auctioneer, Carl McElroy, cursed under his breath. His meaty arms tugged at the bottom drawer of the antique dresser; this is not what he needed in front of a packed house. The tow-headed owner of The Maple Leaf Auction knew that the secret drawer, a standard feature on Empire furniture, had been hopelessly jammed by the clumsy hands of five hundred previewers.

With a forceful yank, it gave; the drawer skidded across the stage and its old-lady contents – bobbins, buttons, decades-old coupons – spilled, flew and rolled toward the front row of Friday night regulars.

'Knew I'd get it open,' Carl quipped, while shielding his fingers from the audience as they pressed back a two-inch hunk of badly cracked crotch-mahogany veneer. As he tried to restore order, and a semblance of his dignity, a murmur spread through the standing-room-only auction that was filled with dealers, townies and avid collectors of nineteenth- and early eighteenth-century furnishings.

The focus had shifted to Mildred Potts in her usual front-row seat. The teased-blonde owner of Aunt Millie's Attic picked anxiously at the folds of her voluminous red-and-white striped skirt where something had just landed. 'What is it? Get it off of me!' Her efforts impaired by the excited yapping and squirming of her white Shih Tzu, Taffy, who wore a bow that matched Mildred's dress. The little dog's tail twitched frantically and rapid snuffling noises emanated from her snout as she tried to free herself from Mildred, her focus riveted on what had landed in her mistress' dress.

Mildred shrieked, her rhinestone-crusted glasses fell, her *aren't they-darling?* dog earrings whipped back and forth, and her face contorted as she batted at her dress, while struggling to control Taffy. 'Get it off of me!'

Taffy yapped and Mildred, unable to rid herself of whatever had landed in her lap, pushed back in her folding metal chair.

'Get it off of me!' The rubber-tipped legs of her chair squeaked on the waxed wide-board floor.

Behind her the town's dentist – an avid collector of colonial-era firearms – and a pair of newlyweds in search of the 'perfect' Hepplewhite dining table, tried to clear a path.

'Mildred, Watch it!' Gustav Auchinstrasse, the morbidly obese proprietor of Eighteenth-Century Antiques, yelled as his doughy hands hung on to a tenuously perched soda and sausage-and-pepper hoagie.

He was too slow. With a piercing shriek, Mildred's legs kicked out, sending her chair toppling back. As she did, an unidentified object flew from her skirt and landed in the shadows beneath the stage. Fortunately for Mildred, rather than crack her head on the hardwood floor, she landed in the ample lap of Mister

Auchinstrasse and his warm sausage sandwich and icy cream soda, which now dribbled down the side of her face.

While extricating herself from Gustav – who she considered an uncouth and opportunistic pig – Taffy leapt from her arm, and with more energy than she had shown in five years of life, tore beneath the stage.

As Mildred picked bits of meat and sauce from her over-processed hair, Auctioneer McElroy tried to resume the auction, while keeping his simmering anger in control. 'I don't know what that was all about, but we've got over three hundred lots of fresh goods to get through. And time is money . . . All right, then, everyone back to normal?' he asked, waving his hands and trying to make light of the situation. He looked at the red-faced Gustav, and hoped he wasn't too upset to spend the copious amounts of money that he was known to. 'Let's get down to business.'

The audience attempted to oblige, when, from beneath the stage, high-pitched yaps and growls emanated.

'Taffy!' Mildred called out as she retrieved her retro-look glasses. 'Come to Mommy, Taffy.'

The yips accelerated.

'Come on, girl.' Mildred looked around anxiously. 'Why won't she come? Taffy, come to Mommy.' Mildred got down on all fours. 'Come on girl. Come on. Are you stuck? Come to Mommy.'

McElroy muttered, while plastering a good-humored smile. He hated that dog, and right now she was costing him money.

'Come on, girl,' Mildred pleaded. 'Come on, sweetie.'

Carl had had enough. He stomped his booted foot on the wooden stage.

The dog shrieked and with a flash of fluffy white, Taffy reappeared at the far end of the stage.

'Taffy!' Mildred called, getting to her feet and throwing out her arms. 'Come to Mommy.'

'Oh my God!' the dealer closest to the dog backed away. With eyes wide and finger pointing, he exclaimed. 'She's got something in her mouth!'

Mildred misheard and thought there was something wrong with Taffy's mouth. She raced toward the Shih Tzu; she stopped.

Silence spread as mistress and dog faced off. The dealers in the front row pushed back, trying to create space between themselves and the snarling dog. Because there, tightly clenched between the bared and bloodstained teeth of little Taffy, was something made of flesh: human flesh.

To those who would later be questioned by the female detective from the State's Major Crime Squad, it seemed as if time stood still. In reality, it was only a couple of seconds before Mildred found her voice, and, to the horror of the assembled, made the obvious connection – and with an unfortunate choice of words.

'Oh my, God! It's a finger! Taffy, give Mommy the finger.'

ONE

'Lil, this makes three funerals in three months; it's too much,' Ada whispered, while pretending to listen to the graying minister of Grenville's First Episcopalian's rambling eulogy. Ada Strauss is my best friend, but at sixty-two, and after decades spent in noisy manufacturing warehouses, her hearing has slipped, and she refuses to wear hearing aids. So what she thought discreet was overheard two pews in front of us. I squeezed her hand and said, 'They're dropping like flies.'

'Evie was lucky,' Ada persisted, looking like a gift from Tiffany's in a trim new robin's egg pantsuit, with fiery opal beads around her neck and dangling from her ears. 'Massive coronary in her sleep . . . Kind of like winning the death lotto.'

'Sssshh!' The black-suited woman directly in front of me shot Ada a pinched look.

'Sorry,' Ada responded, 'I'm a little hard of hearing.'

The woman shook her head and returned to the homily. I'd heard enough of these to realize that the minister's effort was sub par, a string of platitudes in predictable sequences. He said a lot that was nice, but it didn't get to the heart of who our friend, Evie, had been. More than that, it sounded like the one he'd given at Herb Neville's two months back.

'So who's next?' Ada whispered. 'I'd like to go a month without a funeral. It's not too much to ask, is it? And haven't we heard this eulogy before?'

The shoulders tensed on the woman in front of us; I silently dared her to say something. Who was she? I took in the cut of her suit, custom tailored, black like mine. I glanced at Ada, still not used to her ultra-short and spiky silver hair. She'd been a bottle redhead up until last Thursday. *'Too much bother, Lil,'* she'd said as we'd sat in adjoining chairs at Lucy's Salon. *'I like the way you just need to get your ends trimmed a couple times a year; this has got to go.'* The beautician had already mixed the dye for her monthly touch up and Ada had waved her away. *'No,'* she'd said, *'take it down to the roots; I want to see what's under there.'*

The change had been dramatic; instead of making her look older, it was surprisingly chic, and made it hard not to notice the incredible blue of her eyes, and wonderfully sculpted shape of her face and still-tight chin and jaw, like a lovely pixie. And not for the first time, I had to wonder: *why was I thinking these things?*

Ada caught me looking and smiled, she leaned up and whispered, 'This is the first time I've seen Evie's family in the flesh.'

'I know.' My voice caught in my throat, relieved that she couldn't possibly know what I'd been thinking about, and not sure myself what these growing feelings toward my friend were all about. Not wanting to think it, but what popped to mind – *Lil, you've got a crush. Stop it! Focus, what was she saying? Something about Evie's family.* I nodded toward the tensed-up woman in front of us. 'I kind of recognize her from some of Evie's pictures.' And it just struck me as sad. Lots of family who never visited, never wrote or helped with Evie's medicines or her cooking or her checkbook or her taxes, which she obsessed about endlessly as her mind drifted into Alzheimer's, losing pieces of herself with each passing day.

Ada was right; Evie – who was a good twenty years older than us, but who I'd known my entire life – had been lucky. Death was preferable. A chill shivered down my back. But lately, and certainly not helped by the horror of last night's auction, where a severed finger was discovered in a dresser drawer, I couldn't stop thinking about death . . . my death. Not that I'm in bad shape for fifty-nine. Aside from a couple teeth, my tonsils, and my uterus, Lillian Campbell still had her original parts. But sitting on the wooden pew, dressed in black and pearls, my still-natural blonde, albeit with a fair amount of silver, braided and up, and looking every bit Doctor Campbell's widow, death was on my mind. Not that I'm afraid of it; in fact I've always had a certain relationship with death – it's not a bad thing, just a part of things. Even now, it wasn't death that frightened me as I again pictured the bloody finger clenched between the pointy teeth of Mildred Potts' lapdog, but how it could come. Fingers don't just fall off and get stuffed into drawers. What should have been a fun night's entertainment had turned into something long and gruesome as Ada and I, along with over a hundred auction goers, had given brief statements to the local police before being allowed to leave. And now, less than twelve hours later, here I was at the funeral of a dear friend. It was too much, something evil had happened, and close to home; it frightened the hell out of me.

As the minister droned on about family and community, I stretched my neck and snuck a look at the assembled. It was easy spotting the players; Ada and I were experts.

As if reading my thoughts, she tilted her adorable chin toward me and whispered, 'Those are her sons . . . Which one is the alcoholic?'

The woman in front pretended not to hear; I wasn't about to let her spoil one of our games. I carefully considered Ada's question, while studying the profiles of the three dark-suited men in the right-front pew. They had all come from out of state – two from New York and one from California. As I recalled, from many conversations with Evie, it was the latter who had bounced in and out of three marriages and at least as many drug-rehabilitation programs. 'The tan one,' I offered, having made my selection.

'I think you're right,' Ada agreed. 'He has fleshy ears.'

'I thought that meant a bad heart,' I said, trying to remember what Ada had told me about her latest medical prognostic tool: earlobe signs.

'No, that's a creased lobe. They're very different. Although, he seems to have both.'

The woman in front turned. 'That's it,' she hissed between clenched nicotine-stained teeth. 'You two have no respect for the dead.'

'I beg your pardon.' I stared her dead on. 'We were both good friends of Evie . . . I can't recall ever having met you.'

She seemed taken aback. She squinted, appearing strangely constipated, was about to speak, and then turned away as Minister Ingram encouraged us to rise for a rousing, yet waspish, round of 'All Things Bright and Beautiful'.

As the service ended, Ada and I held back. We watched the mourners file past.

'Cemetery?' she asked.

I glanced to see she had worn appropriate shoes, as had I. This had been the rainiest year on record for Connecticut, where our normally dry fall had seen torrential downpours at least two or three times a week. The ground was marshy and it wreaked havoc on footwear. So while I had a closet of shoes – and isn't it funny how so many memories can be tied up in a pair of Ferragamo pumps or cork-soled mules, bought impulsively in St Martin's on one of the few vacations my Bradley had agreed to take? – now, we both wore sensible rubber-soled walking shoes; mine black, hers dyed-to-match blue.

We watched as Evie's sons exited. I couldn't say why, but something about them piqued my curiosity. I wanted to see more, to know why none of them had called or spent time with their mother in the last years of her life. 'Let's go,' I said, waiting for a break in the mourners and then stepping into the aisle. I made room for Ada, who at barely five feet is a head shorter than me. As I stood, I overheard the hushed conversation of the woman who had been in front of us.

'She promised me that ring,' she said to her companion.

'Yes,' he replied, 'but that was when you were still her daughter-in-law.'

'What difference does that make?'

'Carla, if it's not in the will, you won't get it.'

'It's not fair. After putting up with her bastard son for all those years . . . Well, it's one thing if she cuts me out, but if she leaves out Bobby . . . I swear I'll contest it.'

'Where is he?' the man asked.

'Soccer.'

'But his grandmother's funeral? He couldn't . . .'

'He hardly knew her,' she said defensively. 'Besides, I asked him if he wanted to come.'

As I listened, I thought of Evie and of her beautifully kept two-bedroom carriage house in the sprawling retirement community of Pilgrim's Progress, where Ada and I also lived. I thought about her jewelry, and the sapphire and platinum cocktail ring she so loved. Her great aunt Martha had given it to her for her twenty-first birthday. I suspected that was the object of Carla's desire. In Pilgrim's Progress, which catered to retiree New Yorkers and aging inhabitants of Connecticut's gold coast, we all had our accumulated treasures. Where most of us had downsized, the things we chose to keep were steeped in memory, and frequently, value as well. At fifty-nine and sixty-two respectively, Ada and I were two of the younger inhabitants in the self-contained gated community with its five thousand cedar-sided condos spread across seven miles of exquisitely maintained park-like grounds. We'd both been less than fifty-five, the lower-age limit, when we'd moved in eight years ago. But our spouses, now deceased, had been considerably older. Her Harry by eighteen years and my Bradley by twelve. Younger spouses – almost always wives – were the exception to the age restriction, all of which was carefully spelled out in the tome-like *By-Laws and Rules for residents of Pilgrim's Progress*.

Here, we had our own stores and restaurants, our own ambulance crew, two world-class golf courses, health clubs and bus trips that left daily for Broadway and the Indian casinos. Pilgrim's Progress nestled on the outer edge of scenic Grenville, Connecticut, where I've lived my entire life, with the exception of four years in Northampton, Massachusetts at Smith College where I majored in English and harbored dreams of one day becoming a journalist. Pilgrim's Progress is a romantic approximation of what the 'golden years', that greatest of fallacies, was supposed to be. But while designed with the 'mature adult' in mind, Pilgrim's Progress or PeePee – as Ada and I had started to call it for some unfortunate reasons – did not extend its bounty to those who could no longer care for themselves. It was common – and heart breaking – to see adult children pack up their aging parents' homes and move them to a more 'supervised' setting.

I shuddered as I thought about older friends and acquaintances that had slowly slipped into Alzheimer's, or had had strokes and been left unable to care for themselves. They'd been carted off to convalescent homes or down the street to Nillewaug Village, a pricey life-care facility. That would be the last we'd hear of them . . . until their name above a couple carefully worded paragraphs – *beloved wife and mother* – appeared in the obituaries.

I shuffled behind Ada and the other mourners toward the bright sun that filtered through stained-glass windows that I've looked at my entire life.

'Did you hear that awful woman?' Ada whispered, pulling out a pair of stylishly large sunglasses as a crisp October breeze rustled the changing leaves.

'Who?'

'In front of us, the one who kept telling us to shut up. Poor Evie, do you remember how she'd show us pictures of her grand-children? It makes me furious. They never visited; they never wrote. I hope she left everything to charity – serve them right!'

Not for the first time, I suspected that Ada's hearing was not as bad as she let on.

'She was one of the daughters-in-law,' I commented.

'The first one,' Ada said with authority. 'Evie said she slept around. Admittedly the husband was a lush, but still . . .' We headed toward the parking lot and my white Lincoln. 'Lil, you do realize this is the perfect car for funerals.'

'The black was better.'

'No. White is nicer.'

'Agreed,' I said, flipping up the automatic locks. 'Bradley always bought black.'

'That's because he was a doctor,' she offered. 'Black is more serious. But white becomes you.'

'It's strange, but I can't imagine ever buying a different car.' I pictured Bradley, how he'd look in the driver's seat, tall and thin, or his face as he'd turn to me to ask something, his smile, how he'd sometimes – for no reason – take my hand . . . touch my knee. He'd been dead nearly two years. I felt so guilty when I traded in his last car, like I was somehow going behind his back. Ada had gone with me to the dealer. I was all set to just get the same thing in black, but she'd asked one simple question: *Is that really the color you want?*

'I love your car, Lil,' she said as she nestled into the tan leather, the seatbelt's motor humming as it glided up to her side. 'More importantly, I love it that you drive. I so regret having never followed though with getting my license.'

'It's not too late. I'd be happy to teach you.'

'No,' she said. 'Although, it was one thing not driving in New York City, but out here . . .'

'The offer stands,' I said, thinking how much I'd like to roam the countryside with Ada, get away from all of these dying friends and chopped-off fingers.

'Let me think about it.' She gazed out her window as my cell chimed from my purse.

'Do you want me to get that?' Ada asked.

'Please.'

She fumbled through my black clutch, and retrieved the phone. 'Unknown name, unknown number,' she said. 'Should I pick up?'

'Sure.'

She pressed the accept button. 'Hello? Hello? Anyone there?' She waited. 'Hello? That's odd, it says "call ended".' She quickly pressed a couple buttons. 'And no number comes up in the history. Strange . . . you've been getting a lot of these.'

'I know, I just assumed it was a wrong number. But why would they keep calling?' *And why am I so nervous?* I flipped on the lights, and as the car in front of me started, I shifted into gear. 'You know, Ada . . . you were right about Evie.'

'That she was lucky to go when she did?'

'Exactly. How much longer could she have stayed in her condo? I wonder if we did her a disservice by helping as much as we did.'

'Lil, they would have put her away. She would have had to leave her home and all her things and share a room with some incontinent woman with no memory. People are always screaming in those places, they stink, and the nurses never come when you need them. We did right. Evie would have hated that . . . I'd do the same for you.'

'I know,' I said, not wanting to cry. 'What do you think they'll say when they find out we've been doing her checkbook and her taxes?'

'We do it for enough of the others. Her books are perfect. The real fight is going to be over her estate. She had enough to make it interesting.'

I looked at Ada, with her startling blue eyes and short spry frame that seemed dwarfed in the bucket seat. She'd know to the penny what Evie had. And her finances weren't the only ones she handled. For the forty years she'd been married to Harry Strauss, she had kept the books. If Harry were alive, he might argue the point, but it was Ada's savvy that had turned *H.S. Strauss*, which had started as a family business on the Lower East Side of Manhattan, into a twenty-store discount clothing chain. When they'd eventually sold out, they'd realized a tidy profit. My silver-haired friend stayed on top of changes in tax law and investment strategies. She was forever twisting my ear and getting me to invest in favorite stocks, mutual funds, and bond offers. She was even able to get us in and out of a couple IPOs; neither of us was hurting for money. At times it bordered on clairvoyance as she insisted I liquidate almost all my stock and shift into bonds, just a few short months before the financial crash of 2008.

As an unadvertised sideline, Ada helped the majority of our bridge and Scrabble clubs with their finances. It was because of this that she was the first one to diagnose Evie's Alzheimer's.

'How much longer do you think we could have kept her at home?' I asked.

'Another year. Maybe longer.'

I kept a steady distance behind the car in front of me as we turned into the Grenville cemetery. 'What about the will?' I asked. 'Any idea?'

'She never told me,' Ada said. 'She said she had taken care of it; I wonder if she did. Especially once her memory started to slip. She said that after Bill died she had the whole thing changed. I have no idea how she left things.'

'There'll be fights,' I commented as I parked and clicked open the locks.

'No doubt.' She opened the door and with cat-like grace pushed up from the bucket seat. 'It is a shame, though.'

'What is?' I asked, following her gaze toward the darkly clad mourners.

'That,' she said, hoisting her matching bag on to her shoulder. 'They all come now, a flock of vultures. But if they'd come before . . . when—' She stopped herself as a wave of emotion choked in her throat.

I put my arm around her shoulders, and looked toward the gravesite.

'Evie just wanted them to visit, and they never did,' she said.

'I know.' My tears started. I stood, not wanting to move, glad to have Ada beside me, and not caring who saw my grief. I was going to miss sweet Evie. But in truth, I'd already said goodbye as her dementia had worsened and taken away my sharp-witted friend.

'Vultures,' Ada repeated, looking toward the tent-covered grave, her head resting against my side.

There was such comfort in the closeness and I resisted the impulse to kiss the top of her head, which smelled faintly of green-apple conditioner. 'You're right,' I said, wishing we could just stay here and watch. 'So much greed, all jockeying to see what she'd left. All wanting their share.' Again I pictured that damn dog with her bloody prize, snapping and growling not wanting to give it up.

'Come, Ada,' I said, taking my hand off her shoulder, 'let's go,' and we tromped across the squishy lawn toward the grave.

Now I'm not superstitious, but as we neared Evie's family, I felt a chill. I took a deep breath, but the usually comforting smells of a fall day were tainted with the scent of decay, and all I kept thinking was: *something bad has come to Grenville*.

TWO

'**R**ude,' Ada muttered as she hung up on Graham Hennessy, owner of Epoch Antiques. Seated in front of her computer on the carved mahogany desk, from which she'd run *H. S. Strauss* for over thirty years, she typed *Gonif* – Yiddish for thief – next to Hennessey's name, then highlighted it and crossed it out. She fumed as she recalled the conversation.

'Well,' he had said, after she had described Evie's treasures, 'what you might think are valuable antiques, may not be worth much. But,' he'd quickly added, 'I'd be happy to come out and take a look.' His tone had communicated that he thought Ada was either slightly retarded, or headed to the dementia ward at The Hillside Convalescent Home.

This no longer surprised her, having been at this all morning. Why had Evie done this to her? Much as she had loved her friend – the first person in Pilgrim's Progress to welcome her and Harry when they moved in eight years ago – Ada wished she had picked someone else to be executrix. Or at the very least, Evie could have warned her.

One more, she told herself, scrolling down the list of dealers that she'd cut and pasted from the Grenville Antique Dealers' Association website, *and then a cup of tea*. Before she dialed, it rang.

'Hello,' she said, bracing for another interaction with one of Evie's sons, sons' spouses, or sons' ex-spouses.

'Hello,' a man's voice answered, 'I'd like to speak to Mrs Strauss.'

'This is she.'

'My name is Tolliver Jacobs; I was given your name by Attorney James Warren. He said you might need some assistance in liquidating an estate.'

The name was familiar, the accent slightly British, but she couldn't . . . 'I see, and you are with . . .?'

'I'm sorry,' he said. 'I'm one of the owners of Grenville Antiques.'

Ada glanced at her list. She hadn't planned on calling Grenville Antiques, mostly because of its reputation for being the most overpriced store in the Grenville constellation of dealers. While Evie had good taste and had accumulated a few better pieces of eighteenth-century furniture and Chinese Export porcelain, Ada had assumed that the scale of her estate was below what Grenville Antiques – a firm that put multi-page ads in *Architectural Digest*, and catered to high-end designers – would consider.

'Did Jim Warren give you some idea of the extent of the estate?' she asked, trying to keep excitement out of her voice. While she and Lil would never buy at Grenville Antiques, they loved to browse their well-stocked showrooms, identifying similar pieces that they owned, but had purchased at a fraction of the price.

'He wasn't at liberty to say, but we've handled a number of estates from Pilgrim's Progress. What most people don't realize is that we liquidate entire estates, everything from high-end Chippendale down to the chipped jelly glasses in the kitchen; we even broom sweep when we're done. It's quite a popular service, because we take care of the whole shooting match. You'd be amazed,' he said, 'that people are forever choosing the busiest person they know to be their executor.'

'Ain't that the truth,' she said, finding it hard to keep up her decades-thick New York wariness; there was something likable and familiar in his friendly tone and candid pitch.

'Anyway, the other reason we get a lot of business is price. We give top dollar for the better things, and if you're not under the gun time wise, we can take anything really good on consignment. That way the heirs can realize the maximum amount.'

'I had no idea.' Ada wondered if her search might not have come to an end. She liked this one, he wasn't too pushy and the British accent didn't hurt. And then it hit. 'You're on that show, aren't you? I love *Trash to Cash!*'

'I am,' he admitted. 'So would you like to set up a time?' he offered.

'That would be lovely. Of course,' she added, sounding slightly British herself, 'I will need to get quotes from at least three dealers.'

'That's wise,' he agreed. 'You'll be amazed at the range you'll get back.'

'Trust me,' she said, looking over her screen filled with crossed-out and annotated names, 'after a lifetime in New York, little amazes me.'

Tolliver Jacobs chuckled politely, and agreed to meet at Evie's condo in the morning.

Now, Ada thought, hanging up, *definitely time for tea.* She hummed as she left her office – the condo's converted third bedroom – and went to the galley kitchen that opened on to a light-filled living room/dining room combination. The furniture was a cozy mix of mahogany and walnut Chippendale reproductions that had followed her and Harry from their Brooklyn Heights brownstone, and all new couches, armchairs and a stunning cream and navy Persian carpet she'd purchased following his death three years ago. The man was a cigar smoker and nothing could be done to get rid of the smell.

Finally, she thought, *progress.* She was half tempted to take the first offer that Mr Jacobs might make. 'Sorry Evie,' she said as she spooned two heaping teaspoons of sugar into a mug adorned with a bright green cat, 'but your sons are a piece of work.'

As her fingers worked away at the lid on the four-pound tin of Danish butter cookies from Costco, the phone rang again.

'Pheh,' she said, picking up the kitchen cordless. 'Hello?'

'Mother, it's Susan.'

Ada wondered why her only daughter always felt it necessary to identify herself. 'Hello dear.' She cradled the phone in the crook of her neck, and continued to work away at the lid.

'Just called to see how you're doing.'

'That's nice. How are the kids?'

There was a pause. 'They're good. Aaron's starting to think about college and Mona's completely boy obsessed.'

'Well, she is at the age,' Ada said. And before she could stop herself, she asked, 'Is this one Jewish?'

'I haven't asked,' her daughter admitted. 'It would be nice, wouldn't it?'

'She'd make her grandmother very happy.'

'So you've told her,' Susan stated.

'What? I'm not supposed to talk about these things? Do you realize that the intermarriage rate is over fifty percent?'

'We did our part,' her daughter answered defensively. 'They both went to Sunday school, synagogue on Fridays. It just doesn't seem to matter. Aaron was in the youth group for a bit, but lately he's more interested in going on the Internet, skateboarding and hanging out with his friends at the mall. I can't think of the last time he went to services.'

'Do you ask him?'

'Of course I do. But he's at that age where everything is a potential fight. Sometimes I don't have the energy.'

As the kettle whistled, Ada asked, 'And how is Jack?'

'Busy. They're in the midst of another downsizing; he's convinced they're going to lay him off.'

'Didn't he say that the last time?'

'I know. He makes himself crazy. He always needs something to get mad about. Now he's convinced that there's something wrong with Aaron.'

Ada stopped, the creamer poised over her mug. 'Wrong? What do you mean?'

'I probably shouldn't say . . .'

'Susan, don't do that.'

Silence stretched. Finally, Susan blurted, 'Jack thinks Aaron might be gay.'

Ada poured her milk and stirred. *Why doesn't this bother me?* she thought, wondering if perhaps her daughter's words needed to gain momentum. *He could be gay.* 'What's so bad about that?'

'Mother! Did you hear what I said? Do you know what I'm saying?'

'You said that Jack wondered if Aaron was gay, and from your tone I'd say you were having the same thoughts. Not a big deal, as long as he's careful, plus he's only sixteen . . .' She was about to add: *how could he know?* And then stopped, her thoughts cata-pulted back forty-five years to a schoolgirl crush, and a name attached to a dark-haired beauty with laughing eyes – Miriam Roth. With the memory, a rush of feelings, longing, regret . . . She snapped back. 'Is this more than suspicion? Does he have a . . . boyfriend?'

'No,' Susan interrupted, 'I don't think he's done anything about it.'

'You have to talk to him about AIDS and condoms. Whether he's gay or not, I hope you've talked to him about safe sex,' Ada said.

'Mother, I'm not even sure he is gay. He probably isn't, but . . .' Susan stopped in mid sentence.

'But what?' Ada prompted, her knees rubbery.

'All right, but I didn't want to tell you this because I know you don't like Jack.'

'I have never said that I don't like your husband,' Ada corrected, picturing her balding ham hock of a son-in-law, who she frequently referred to as 'that right-wing Nazi'.

'Come off it, Mother. Whenever the two of you get together I have to pry you apart before there's bloodshed.'

Ada couldn't hold back. 'I just don't understand how you could have married someone so close-minded. Anyway,' Ada said, struggling to find her way back to the earlier conversation. 'What makes Jack think that Aaron is gay?'

'You can't say anything,' Susan cautioned.

'That's hardly fair, but OK,' Ada said, having no intention of holding her tongue.

'How much do you know about the Internet?'

'Some,' Ada admitted, glancing at the dancing red lights of the router on her kitchen counter.

'Well, Aaron's been spending a lot of time on the Internet. So Jack asked him what he was doing. And to be frank, I can't blame Jack because Aaron gave some sketchy answers. I mean schoolwork is one thing, but he's on it for hours every day.'

'So what is he doing?' Ada dunked her cookie in the tea.

'It's a lot of social network stuff; he's constantly on Facebook and My Space. But he's also in chat rooms where people of like interest talk about things.'

'How do you know that?'

'Jack went into his computer and pulled up the history of all the places Aaron had been going. Apparently a lot of the rooms he was in were for men looking for other men.'

'Oh,' Ada said, not liking the tawdry turn this had taken. 'I've read about that. But isn't that illegal, dear? I mean, he's only sixteen.' She thought about her beloved grandson, and her frequently red-faced son-in-law. 'What did Jack do?'

'What do you think?' Susan said. 'He exploded. Now, he didn't actually come out and accuse Aaron of being gay. He called his son a pervert.'

'That's ridiculous!' Ada was incensed. 'A lot of my friends have gay children and grandchildren. Your cousin Joanne is a lesbian! There's nothing wrong with it. Sure, it might cut down on the number of grandchildren, but I don't think that should be the issue. Besides, a lot of gay people have children, look at Rosie O'Donnell and Melissa Etheridge. He could always adopt. Or have a surrogate.'

'Mother, you amaze me.' Susan sounded annoyed. 'Here you get on Mona's case for dating non-Jewish boys, yet you don't seem to care if your grandson is gay or not.'

'Of course I care. And if he is gay, he should find a nice Jewish boy.'

'I give up,' Susan said, deciding it was best to get off the subject. 'So how are you? Any luck with the cholesterol?'

Ada eyed her stack of cookies. 'The doctor wants me on a high-fiber diet. I try, but a bowl of oatmeal every day . . . I just don't like the stuff, unless it's baked into cookies, but then I think the butter cancels the benefit.'

'It's hard,' Susan agreed. 'You could always use margarine.'

'Never touch it. Plus, it's probably genetic.'

'I hope not. Knock wood mine's been fine,' Susan said.

And Ada selected her favorite cookie with the chunks of crystallized sugar and popped it into her mouth and chewed silently.

'Otherwise, everything's OK, Mom?'

'Yes, dear,' Ada replied, wondering if she should mention the gruesome discovery at the auction, and then decided not to. 'Things are fine. Why don't you tell Aaron to give me a call? From the sounds of it he could use a friendly ear. If he wanted, he could stay the weekend.'

'You're not going in to see Grandma Rose?'

'No,' Ada said, feeling a guilty twinge at the mention of her ninety-one-year-old mother in her Lower East Side apartment. 'I went last week.' And not wanting to give Susan any more of an opening into a topic that was tearing her up: 'Tell Aaron I'll email him. I'd love for him to visit.'

'I don't know,' Susan said. 'He's gotten to be a handful.'

'Whatever you decide,' she replied, knowing that it wouldn't be what her daughter wanted, but invariably would rest with her bullying husband. 'I would love to see him.'

'Well, I'll let him know. I should probably get going.'

'OK dear, give my love to the kids.'

'Love you, Mom.'

'Love you too, dear,' Ada said and hung up. The call left her rattled, thinking about her grandson, her aging mother, but there was something else. She stared at her dated phone caddy, the kind where you move a lever over the letter and then press a bar to make it open. She moved it to 'R' and looked at the name. Without pause she dialed, half hoping a machine would pick up. Instead a woman answered on the second ring.

'Miriam?' Ada asked.

'No, it's Beth. Ada? Is that you?'

And Ada chatted with her friend's partner, quickly catching each other up on their respective lives. 'Hold on,' Beth said, 'I hear her getting out of the shower.'

After a couple moments: 'Ada! Dahling, how are you?'

'I'm good,' she said, picturing Miriam, with her curly salt-and-pepper hair, deep brown eyes and warm smile. 'I wanted to wish you *L'shana tova.*'

'And a sweet New Year to you, as well. So when am I going to break you out of that ghetto for old folks? Especially for a hot ticket like you. Last time I saw you, you didn't look a day over thirty-nine.'

'Your nose is growing and it's not that bad here.'

'So you say. I was sure that once Harry passed you'd come back to the city.'

'No,' Ada said, 'I like it. It's a bit geriatric, but it's beautiful and I've got friends.'

'So you've said.' Miriam's tone was questioning. 'Anyone special?'

'Oh, please. I'm sixty-two. I think that ship has sailed.'

'Are you serious? Sixty-two isn't old, and besides, you're still a fine-looking chick.'

Ada blushed. 'Yeah, but you should see the men out here . . . Slim pickings.'

'Dahling, not so interested in the men, and I hear those places have like three women to every one man. Maybe I should check it out.'

Ada chuckled. 'Actually it's more like ten women to every man, and I don't think Beth would appreciate your looking around.'

'True. You know we're going to New Hampshire next month to get married? Would love for you to come, maybe force you into some horrible bridesmaid dress.'

'Congratulations!' Ada said. 'But why not Connecticut? You could stay here . . .' she added, a weird mix of emotions tumbling through her head and her chest.

'Beth has family in New Hampshire, and good for you for keeping on top of this stuff. Wish it had gone through in Hawaii – oh well. Are you sure you're OK? Not that I don't love to hear from the girl that got away . . .'

'God,' Ada said, 'you still remember that?'

'And you don't? I thought I might get you over to my team.'

'No.' Ada smiled. 'I think you scared me into getting married at eighteen.'

'I hope that's a joke,' Miriam said.

'It is . . . and don't all jokes contain some truth?'

'Wow, this is unexpected. I don't know how I feel about that – scared straight. Shit! When are you coming in next?'

'Probably next weekend, I've got the ongoing mess with my Mom.'

'You want to meet up? Maybe grab lunch, or we could have you over for supper?'

'I'd like that,' Ada admitted, 'but I think maybe just the two of us, if that's OK.'

'Sure, give me a call when you know your schedule.'

After they hung up, Ada looked around her condo. Her thoughts were troubled, and she couldn't quite place what had her so bothered. She caught her image in a mahogany framed mirror. Her short hair still a shock, like another woman. *No, you don't look thirty-nine, but you could pass mid forties.* 'And what does that silver-haired woman in the mirror want?' she said aloud; and to herself: *is she brave enough to go for it?*

THREE

'It's odd,' Ada said, cueing into my mood as we surveyed Evie's condo and its contents.

'Almost like she never left,' I agreed, taking in the beige wall-to-wall, the raw-silk curtains and the dark-wood furniture that gleamed from decades of butcher's wax and lemon oil.

We had come early to Evie's home in the oldest part of Pilgrim's Progress, both of us in sweatshirts and jeans, to check things over before the cavalcade of antique dealers descended.

'What about this?' Ada balanced a fourteen-inch Chinese Export charger in the palm of her hand, like a game-show hostess displaying a potential prize. I smiled.

'What?' she asked.

'You're looking very Vana.'

'Please, if Vana were verging on a little person. But what do you think it's worth?'

'Hm.' It was one of Evie's favorites; around its border swam a herd of fantastical sea creatures and in the center was a fully rigged whaling ship. I looked at it objectively; it had no chips, was big, and was smack in the middle of the nineteenth century. 'Fifteen hundred to two thousand,' I declared, offering my ball-park quote. 'Double that in a shop, but we won't be getting that here.'

'That much?' Ada asked.

'I think so. What about the buttermilk blue step-back hutch in the kitchen?'

'Four grand, easy,' Ada shot back. 'Don't ask me why, but those things bring a lot. Personally, and I would never have said this to Evie, I think it's hideous.'

'It's shabby chic. People like things with distressed finishes and chipped paint. It's ironic, you spend all that money to have beat-up furniture.'

'It's a look,' Ada said, using her catch phrase for anything that veered from her gold standard of good taste: American Chippendale, preferably Philadelphia or Newport.

Ada had asked me to keep her company today when Mr Jacobs and the other dealers arrived. This whole executrix mess had her worried, and I was glad to help and just glad to be with her. Plus, although she'd never admit it, Ada was afraid of being taken advantage of. This was a pre-game warm-up.

As regular auction goers and visitors to the over one hundred and fifty antique shops in Grenville, we weren't novices. We'd even thrown around the idea of going into business ourselves. We both knew how and where to buy, and while everyone gets tricked into the occasional reproduction or outright fake, we could hold our own.

Ada came by it through all her years with Harry in retail. For me, born and bred in Grenville, I had lived with the antiques industry my entire life. Grenville was the antique capital of Connecticut, possibly the country. It was this fact that had saved the eighteenth-century flavor of the town. High Street, one of the most widely photographed roads in the world – a perennial favorite of calendars and coffee-table books with titles like 'Scenic New England' and 'Country Life' – was the epitome of well-maintained colonial America. Grenville is stunning and has the most rigid zoning in the state. Up until four years ago any house in the historic district had to be white, the only choice was whether you wanted black or dark-green shutters. But most of the wide-clapboard colonials and imposing federals, which were once private homes, had been converted into antique shops. Dealers and collectors viewed Grenville as Mecca. No buying trip to New England was complete without a day spent haggling at the open-air flea market, or haunting the upscale shops and auction houses for 'sleepers': undiscovered and undervalued treasures. The major risk to living here was the over-accumulation of stuff, especially for those of us who loved to collect, but had moved from large houses down to spacious, yet smaller, one-, two-, and three-bedroom condos in Pilgrim's Progress.

'What about doing it ourselves?' Ada asked. 'What if we did an estate sale and sold everything ourselves?'

'That's a lot of work,' I cautioned. 'We'd have to tag and cata-logue everything, collect sales tax, get a tax ID number. A huge headache. Plus, think about all the problems you're already having with her kids; they'd contest every sale. Much better have someone else do it.'

'You're right. I was thinking more like our yearly tag sale for the animal shelter, but that wouldn't work with this stuff.'

We startled as a brisk knock came at the door.

'Let me get that.' Ada strode through the airy living room and to the gray flagstone foyer.

I trailed behind as she opened the door on to a smiling and neatly pressed Tolliver Jacobs. I recognized him instantly. Not only was he a regular on the nationally syndicated antiques show, *Trash to Cash*, but years back my youngest had a crush on him; he had been two grades ahead of her. Now, his once-sandy hair was starting to gray, and with a start, I realized that this man I had known as a little boy was middle aged. His blue eyes twinkled pleasantly as he shook Ada's hand.

'Mrs Strauss?' he asked.

'Yes, please come in, and this is my friend Lillian Campbell. You know, you're much better looking in person than you are on TV.'

'Thanks.' He chuckled. 'And of course, I know Mrs Campbell. Her husband was our doctor for years.'

I laughed, charmed and a little confused by his faintly British accent; where did that come from? 'You and everyone else.'

'That was a different time, wasn't it?' he offered. 'I remember your husband coming to our house in the middle of the night when I had the mumps. They don't do that anymore.'

'No,' I agreed, feeling the surge of pride I felt whenever someone remembered Bradley. But as frequently happened, other feelings came; I fished a handkerchief out of my pocket and dabbed.

'I'm sorry,' he said.

'It's OK. I guess one never totally gets over these things.'

He looked at me closely. 'It's not,' he said, and there was an unexpected throb in his voice.

I found myself drawn to this attractive man, who, like my own children, was in his thirties. As he went through the condo he took notes and outlined strategies.

'Mrs Strauss?' he asked. 'How eager are the heirs?'

'Very,' Ada stated. 'That and they're contentious, which is why the probate judge ordered the estate liquidated.'

'That's different from the will?' he asked.

'Yes and no. The will had a provision where the heirs could take turns selecting items from the house, but one of the sons said he just wanted the money and the other two wanted the same item first and then there are the grandchildren who wouldn't know Sheraton from Shinola. The judge tried, but after two hours, he couldn't take the bickering and asked me – as the executrix – to go ahead and liquidate.'

'Out of curiosity,' he asked, 'which is the piece that the two sons wanted?'

'I'll show you,' Ada said, and we followed her into the living room.

There, behind a hyperactive philodendron and a potted palm,

hung a gilt-framed painting of three women in Victorian dresses and picture hats at a seaside picnic.

'Oh my!' Tolliver stared at the painting. He stepped over the plants to get a closer look. He ran the tips of his fingers gently across the surface of the large canvas. He pulled out a pair of half glasses and studied the red-paint signature in the corner. 'Unless they are in a huge hurry, we should consign this to either Christie's or Sotheby's.'

'What is it?' I asked, having never really given much thought to this particular painting hidden behind Evie's indoor jungle.

He sighed. 'It's an extremely desirable work of American Impressionism. The painter was a man named Childe Hassam. He was part of the artist community in Old Lyme, so it's not unheard of for one of his canvases to turn up like this. Still, this appears to be in pristine condition and was painted at the height of his popularity; it's spectacular. It has everything you want in a Hassam painting; beautiful ladies, the beach, gorgeous sky, lots of impasto. To get top dollar, it should go to one of the New York houses.'

'What's it worth?' Ada asked, cutting straight to the heart of the matter.

'Hard to say. I wouldn't be surprised if it brought three hundred thousand, maybe more. It's clearly the single most valuable thing here.' He smiled in our direction. 'Unless you know of any other American masterpieces hidden in the cupboards?' The corners of his eyes crinkled pleasantly and dimples formed in his cheeks.

It was hard not to like him, and I could tell that Ada felt the same. He knew his business, and thus far my antennae hadn't been alerted to any underlying fraud or attempt to put one over.

He finished his inventory, and as he set to leave, he handed each of us a heavy cream-colored card. 'You might want to do something about that painting,' he cautioned. 'I don't see a security system, and human nature being what it is, I've seen things like that go missing.'

'You don't think . . .' Ada started.

'It wouldn't hurt to get an insurance rider and put it in storage. Whether or not you decide to go with us, I'd be happy to show you how to do that.'

'That's good of you,' Ada said. 'I'll be in touch either way.'

We shook hands all around and then watched from the doorway as he headed out to a sporty black BMW convertible.

'He seemed respectable,' I commented.

'First of the bunch,' she said, checking the clock. 'Let's put some water on before the next one gets here.'

'You don't just want to go with Tolliver?' I asked.

She sighed. 'I'd love to,' she replied, heading to Evie's rooster-themed kitchen. 'But if I don't get three quotes, someone is going to raise a fuss. And don't have a fit, but number two is Mildred Potts.'

'You didn't . . . Oh, Ada, after the auction?'

'I know, but no one was returning my calls. I just pray she doesn't bring that dog. I keep thinking about how it went after that thing. Although a part of me,' she admitted, 'is dying to know whose finger that was.'

'Agreed,' I said. 'People don't go around losing fingers in drawers. And where's the rest of the person? It seemed fresh, like it had just happened, or maybe that was the dog's saliva? It's been giving me nightmares.'

Twenty minutes, and a good deal of speculation later, Mildred arrived. The mid-fifties blonde-headed owner of Aunt Millie's Attic blew into the condo, with her yapping Shih Tzu, Taffy, tucked under her arm.

I pasted a smile on my face as I jammed my hands, with all ten fingers, deep into my pockets. I watched as Mildred, with her orange and white polka dot dress swirling around her thick ankles, perused Evie's things. All the time making derogatory comments. 'You just can't get much for a lot of this stuff.' She pointed out chips and cracks; she clucked her tongue and shook her head, as if to say that if she took the estate, she'd lose money. But we could both see her ill-concealed excitement over Evie's collection of Chinese Export.

'What do you think this is worth?' Ada held up the whaling ship platter.

'It's pretty . . . if you like that sort of thing. I could probably get a couple hundred for it.'

'I see,' said Ada. 'Let me show you something else.' She led Mildred and the snuffling Taffy over to the Hassam painting.

As Mildred's skirt tangled in the potted plants, she and Taffy finally made it to the picture. They appeared to sniff its surface. Finally, she declared, 'It's sweet.' Her voice had the practiced sound of someone used to delivering bad news in what they considered a gentle way. 'But your friend probably bought it at one of those motel art sales. I hope she didn't pay too much. I always hate to be the one to say things like that, but I wouldn't be doing my job if I couldn't tell people the truth.'

She was there for over an hour, and the only other time she betrayed any interest was in the kitchen.

'Now that,' she said, practically squealing with excitement when she came upon the step-back cupboard, 'that is darling! I'd give you a thousand right now.'

Ada looked at me with her best bridge face. 'I had no idea it was worth that much,' she commented. 'It just looks like an old beat-up cabinet. I was thinking about giving it a good fresh coat of paint.'

'No!' shrieked Mildred, which elicited a round of yaps from Taffy.

My heart skipped and raced uncomfortably as I had a too-real flashback of the dog with the bloody finger.

'Whatever you do,' Mildred continued, petting Taffy while examining the surface of the cupboard, 'don't paint it! You'll destroy the value. People want the original buttermilk paint.' She ran a hand lovingly over the wide-plank construction. She examined the joinery. 'It's lovely.'

'Isn't that interesting, Lil. Who would have known?' Ada steered the dealer and her creepy white dog back to the front hall.

Mildred sensed her quarry slipping away. 'If you have any questions,' she said, turning in the doorway, 'don't hesitate to call. You have some charming things here.'

'Well, thank you,' said Ada. 'Why don't you get back to me with a quote. Obviously, I'm getting a few. So, not wanting to be crass, it will all come down to a question of money.'

'Oh.' Mildred's mouth twisted as if she'd just tasted something unpleasant. 'If you don't mind my asking, who else will be seeing the estate?'

'You mean dealers?'

'Yes,' said Mildred, nearly hissing between tangerine-painted lips.

Ada turned to me, smiling, clearly enjoying her role as the wide-eyed innocent. 'Do you think it's OK, Lil?'

I shrugged, not entirely certain what her game was, and eager to get Taffy, with her too-cute matching orange polka dot ribbon, out the door.

'Let's see.' She counted on her fingers. 'We just met with that lovely Mr Jacobs . . .'

'Tolliver?' Mildred asked. 'Did he make an offer?'

'No, but he said he would. And I must say that you and he had very different takes on things.'

Mildred tensed, her lips tightened and she gripped Taffy like a furry football. 'Well,' she responded, 'this is a highly subjective profession. Get any three dealers in a room and you'll get three different stories.'

'Yes,' said Ada, 'I see that.' And she showed Mildred and Taffy to the door.

'Two hundred dollars for Evie's charger!' Ada fumed after the dealer had left. 'I should report her to The Better Business Bureau.'

'People swear by her,' I commented, noting the flush in Ada's cheeks, and how her eyes seemed bluer – like sapphires – when she was angry. 'It does seem criminal. What if we didn't know? Most people don't, particularly in Pilgrim's Progress. I hate to say it, but if I were a criminal, I'd definitely focus on older people.'

'A lot of them do,' Ada stated. 'Since I moved here, I'm forever getting these awful phone calls from people telling me I've won something, but in order to collect I have to buy a water purifier, or something equally ridiculous. The worst part is, I know people who've bought those damn things, and half of them know they're being taken for a ride.'

'Me too. So why do they do it?'

Before Ada could respond, the bell rang.

'Contestant number three?' I asked.

'Enter and sign in please,' she quipped. 'I loved that show.' And she opened the front door.

Wafting in on the acrid stench of tobacco came Rudy Caputo, a potbellied man with a shock of white hair and a smoldering cigar glued to the corner of his unshaven mouth. He wore a well-loved black biker jacket and a pair of khaki paratrooper pants with pockets that tracked up and down his legs. I instantly recognized him as one of the major buyers at McElroy's auction. On a good night, Mr Caputo could buy up a third to a half of the furniture, making the other dealers squirm as Chippendale highboys and Queen Anne tea tables were hoisted to his truck. Often McElroy would joke: '*Well, guess that's heading to the West Coast,*' or '*California here I come.*'

'You Ada Strauss?' he grunted as he came through the door.

'Yes,' said Ada. 'And if you wouldn't mind putting out your cigar, I'd appreciate it.'

'No problem.' He flicked off the smoldering tip with his bare finger and then crushed the ash into the doorstep with his booted foot.

'Nice place,' he commented, sticking the unlit stub back in his mouth. He moved from the foyer to the living room, with its vaulted ceiling, skylights and abundant windows. 'Looks like some decent pieces, too.' He dropped on one knee and examined the underside of a Queen Anne style wingback chair. 'You know if this is all original?' he asked.

'No idea,' Ada admitted. 'My friend collected a lot of things, and some came down through her family. I'm not sure which are which.'

'You getting multiple quotes?' he asked.

'Yes.'

He mumbled something unintelligible. I thought I heard the words 'waste of my time', but I couldn't be certain. He was all business, tipping back chairs, running a flashlight over joints in the furniture and pulling out a tape measure when he came to Evie's spider-leg candle stand.

'You know this is a repro,' he stated, after measuring the top.

'Yes,' said Ada, 'but Evie knew that when she bought it.'

'It's good quality,' he conceded, pulling a magnet from out of a pocket and affixing it to a number of small metal statues and lamps.

'What's that for?' I asked.

He looked up. 'I'm trying to see what's bronze and what isn't. If the magnet sticks it's got iron in it, and it's definitely not bronze.'

'And if it doesn't stick?' I asked.

'Could be bronze, could be brass, could be copper, maybe pot metal. The magnet narrows it down.'

'Interesting,' said Ada. 'So how do you know for sure?'

'Bronze is solid, real heavy. If I want to know for sure, I'll scratch the base. If it's zinc alloy you get a silver streak; bronze looks bronze.'

'What about the mantel clock?' Ada asked.

'It's nice, but it's iron, not bronze. Pity.'

'If it were bronze, what would it be worth?' I asked, having some sense of the correct value.

'About four grand,' he said, coming close to the figure I had in mind. He then beat me to my next question. 'It's still worth something. A lot of people like these Victorian figural clocks. In a West Coast shop, you could probably get fifteen hundred.'

'What about in Connecticut?' I asked.

'A lot less, maybe half. Everything's cheaper here, that and the economy is in the toilet.'

'More stuff around,' Ada commented.

'Exactly,' he said, spotting the Hassam painting. 'But even out here, stuff is drying up. Everyone thinks they're a dealer and selling on eBay.' He pointed at the picture. 'You know what that is?'

'I think so,' said Ada, 'but you tell me.'

We watched as he sucked in his gut and squeezed through the plants. He looked back at Ada and smiled. 'You can't be too careful,' he commented dryly.

'No,' she agreed, 'you can't.'

'Mind if I take it off the wall?'

'Go ahead.'

He eased the painting off its hooks and maneuvered it overhead to the sofa. From his back pocket he pulled out his flashlight and ran the beam over the surface of the painting, both front and back.

'You got a honey here.' He wedged the light back into his pocket. 'This is a real good piece of American Impressionism. The painter used to live around here.'

'Childe Hassam,' Ada offered, sounding like she might know what she was talking about.

'Exactly. It's not my usual thing,' he said. 'It should go to New York, to one of the big houses, or else sell it directly to a dealer. If I were you, I'd take some pictures of it, bring them to the city and get a few quotes. If you want me to do it, I'd take a fifteen percent cut of whatever it brought.'

'That seems kind of high,' I said, quickly calculating his proposed cut of three hundred thousand dollars.

'Like I said –' and he chomped down on the cigar butt for emphasis – 'ask around. Bet the auction houses will take at least that.'

He took no notes, but seemed to be tallying values in his head.

'Do you have a shop?' I asked.

'Used to, too much overhead. Now I'm strictly a jobber.'

'What's that?' Ada asked.

'I wholesale to other dealers. Not around here so much, but up and down the coast, the Midwest, California. I have dealers all over.'

'Interesting,' I said, trying to reconcile his biker get up and rank cigar with the obvious care he took in handling Evie's porcelain. 'Do you like your work?'

He looked up from the eighteenth-century polychrome soup tureen he'd been examining. 'Been doing it for thirty years.'

'But do you like it?' I persisted.

'I suppose, but it gets to wear you down. 'Specially now where I'm not sure how much longer I want to lug around furniture . . . Rheumatoid.' He held up his hands, displaying a double row of swollen knuckles.

'How terrible,' Ada said. 'Would you like a cup of tea?'

'No thanks, I should probably get going.'

After a final look around, where he counted and weighted the pieces of Evie's sterling flatware and looked through her jewelry, Mr Caputo said goodbye and headed to his truck.

'That's three,' said Ada, closing the door behind her. 'What do you think?'

'I liked Tolliver best, although that Mr Caputo seemed to know what he was talking about. And that Potts woman is nothing more than a crook.'

'Agreed,' she said, sitting down at the dining room table. 'Let's see what they come back with.' She stared into the living room, deep in thought.

'What is it?' I asked, sensing something wrong.

'Well,' she started slowly, 'I didn't think I was going to tell you this, but you are my best friend.'

I braced for the worst.

'I have another appointment this afternoon.'

'What is it? Is something wrong?'

She looked up and smiled. 'No, I mean nothing aside from the usual. It's my mother, I'm getting a lot of grief from my brothers and sisters.'

'Because?' I asked, thinking of Rose Rimmelman, who I'd met following her cardiac catheterization and subsequent angioplasty last year when she'd recuperated at Ada's for six weeks. Small and feisty, Rose was fiercely independent, and her ability to care for herself had become an issue.

'Because she's over ninety; she's living alone and her visiting nurse says she's not safe in her own apartment and Mom adamantly refuses to move, or have a live-in aide. The nurse is threatening to bring in adult protective services if I don't do something. So I'm meeting with the administrator at Nillewaug Village. I can't keep running back and forth like this, and if my siblings had their way I'd have her move in with me, or vice versa; which, given a choice between living with my mother and having a sharp stick poked in the eye, I'd go for the second.'

'Do you think she'd go for it?'

'When pigs fly, but I have to try something. I was planning to take a cab, but I thought . . .'

'Of course I'll go with you,' I said. 'You know Bradley was their medical director when they opened that place.'

'You'd mentioned. But he didn't stay long.'

'No, and I could never get him to tell me why, other than he didn't agree with their business practices.'

'Great, so you're telling me that I'm about to try and put my mother into some kind of snake pit?'

'Ada,' I said, looking at the concern on her face, and feeling such affection, wishing she didn't have to go through this. 'We'll check it out. Like you said, you've got to do something. We just need to keep our eyes open.'

'I know. I hate to say it, but I've even thought of moving back to the city. Someone's got to look after her. And apparently as the youngest daughter . . . I just don't know what to do.'

Something caught in my throat at the thought of losing her, of not seeing her every day, and, if I were being honest, which I was trying to desperately not to be, I knew that the feelings I had for Ada had somehow passed the 'best friends' point. And how was that possible? I was a married woman for thirty-seven years, raised two children and had successfully stomped down any feelings I might have had for other women. But right now, looking at Ada and realizing she might move away, was more than I could bear. 'We'll figure this out,' I said, as much for her as for me. 'Let me grab my coat, aside from Bradley's issue – whatever it was – everyone raves about Nillewaug. I'm sure it's lovely.'

FOUR

Tolliver Jacobs' hands shook as he hung up. Philip had been missing since Friday, and now he knew why. Why he wasn't answering his cell. Why he hadn't called. *Dead.*

As he got up to shut his office door; his knees threatened to buckle. 'Oh God.' The information wormed into his brain. 'Oh God.' He sank to his chair. How would he be able to face the others, to face the day, to face anything? He thought of their employees, most of them had been hired by Philip, what would they say? What would they think?

Tolliver and Philip had lived with the gossip, the conversations cut short, the rolling eyes. He knew what they must be thinking, that he and Philip had a fight. But not this. He held his head in his hands. 'Oh God.' He pictured Philip with his perfect teeth and blue-green eyes.

'I think we may have found your partner,' the woman detective had said. Hope had surged only to be cut off by her next statement. 'We need you to identify the body.'

'Oh God. Oh God.' Tolliver tried to focus. What was he supposed to do? Maybe it wasn't Philip. But inside, he knew. Nothing short of death could account for the past five days. Not a word. After seventeen years, he and Philip had never been apart for more than a week. Since graduate school, the two men had been inseparable.

Tolliver tried to map a course of action. He took a deep breath, and stood. *Yes, just move.* Then, he was through the door with what he hoped was a normal expression on his face as he passed the desks of his buyers.

'I have to take care of some errands,' he told Gretchen, his secretary. 'If you need me, I'll have my cell.'

'Is everything OK?' she asked, her dark eyes searching out his.

'No, but . . .' He met her gaze, and then looked around at half a dozen faces, all turned toward him, wondering. 'Never mind.'

He pushed open the ancient iron-studded door, and stepped out into the cool October air and the crackling of fallen leaves. He walked across the beautifully landscaped grounds of Grenville Antiques, each specimen tree, each weathered marble sculpture, a tribute to Philip's eye and unfailing taste. *Keep moving*, he thought as he turned the key in his 5 series BMW. The powerful engine purred. But as he rode past their red warehouse, where Philip had painted a herd of whimsical Holsteins, his resolve faltered. He skidded to a stop, their last argument, more heated than any they'd ever had, played over and over. Philip storming out, his final words: 'I need space, Tolliver. Don't push me on this!'

Gasping for breath, Tolliver pulled off on to the gravel drive, and with his hands white-knuckled to the wheel, he sobbed.

FIVE

A s Delia Preston waxed eloquent about the virtues of Nillewaug Village, I grew increasingly anxious. I couldn't tell if it was the polished administrator's rapid-fire presentation, her too-red Chanel knock-off suit, her perfect ash-blonde upsweep, her flawless makeup, her stagey office with floor-to-ceiling windows that showcased the man-made pond and waterfall four stories below, or the hard fact that Ada was contemplating a move back to New York. I desperately wanted this to be the solution. Move Rose – possibly kicking and screaming from her fourteenth-floor rent-stabilized apartment on Rivington – to a light and lovely unit at Nillewaug. Problem was, everything that came through Delia's lip-sticked mouth was tripping alarms, and I couldn't tell why. Was it just that she looked like a woman trying too hard to stay pretty, like some ex beauty queen of indeterminate age, or was it more to do with the reasons why Bradley had stopped working here? *'It just doesn't feel right,'* he'd said, ten years back when he'd resigned after a very brief stint as their first medical director. At the time I'd not pressed for details.

'Every comfort and consideration has been taken into account,' she boasted. 'Nillewaug Village is the complete life-care community. We are committed to the Nillewaug Promise.' Delia paused, she made eye contact first with me and then with Ada. 'Once the Promise Agreement is signed, we will take care of everything. Absolutely everything. There's no need—'

'How does it work?' Ada interrupted.

'What do you mean?' The Administrative Director asked.

'I understand the basics. There's a one-time buy-in for your unit and then if you start to lose it, they stick you in the nursing home part.'

Delia looked at Ada, taken aback by her bluntness. I wanted to applaud.

Ms Preston deftly volleyed, spinning a more cheery light. 'I can see you've grasped the basics, but Nillewaug offers so much. The best way to show you is to take you on a tour.'

'Yes,' said Ada as she got to her feet, both of us still in jeans, sweatshirts and sneakers from the morning's marathon at Evie's. 'I suppose we'd better. Coming Lil?'

'Wouldn't miss it,' I said, entertaining pleasant thoughts of Ms Preston slipping in her elegant red pumps.

'Our first stop, the dining room. As you see –' the administrator waved her arm, like a game-show hostess displaying a new washer-dryer – 'it looks nothing like a cafeteria, but more like a fine restaurant.'

She had a point. The wood-paneled room was tastefully decorated with Queen Anne style furniture and sparkling brass chandeliers. Several diners, some engaged in quiet conversation, looked up as we entered.

I smiled, recognizing a couple faces. Apparently, we were not big news and after a cursory look, they returned to their meals. The air was heavy with the smells of beef Wellington and home-made rolls that steamed from inside linen-covered baskets. My mouth watered.

'Today we're having a choice of beef or scallops.' She looked at Ada. 'And for our Jewish residents we also have a kosher entrée. And people can certainly prepare their own meals in their apartments, but most of our residents come down for at least one meal a day. The socialization is so important, and we have a world-class chef.'

Ada wandered to one of the tables and examined its surface.

'Nice, aren't they?' Ms Preston said, trailing her prospective customer. 'It's hand-tatted Brussels lace.'

Sure enough, at each setting were exquisite doilies carefully protected beneath a layer of glass.

'We find they give you the feel of tablecloths without the need to do laundry. Everything wipes clean with a sponge,' Ms Preston gushed.

'Everything?' Ada asked, feeling the back of a mauve and gray upholstered chair.

'Yes.' Delia graced us with a dazzling smile. 'All of the fabrics are completely stain resistant. In fact –' she lowered to a whisper – 'they're guaranteed against all bodily fluids.'

'Bodily fluids?' I commented.

'Well,' she conceded with a tiny grimace, 'occasionally . . . accidents.'

I looked at Ada to see what effect that had on her. Apparently, she was a woman with a mission, and not to be deterred by placing her mother with some leaky neighbors.

'I'd like to see one of the apartments,' she said.

'That's a great idea!' Delia said. 'We have two bedroom, one bedroom and studios. Any preference?'

Ada exhaled heavily. 'I suppose the biggest you've got. My mother has a ton of stuff and getting her to part with any of it is a battle I'm not ready for.'

Delia prattled as electric doors slid shut. 'So you both live at Pilgrim's Progress. Many of our residents come from there. Of course we offer a number of conveniences that they are just not able to accommodate.'

'Such as?' I asked, noting how smooth and motionless Delia's forehead was. *Botox?*

'The full spectrum of personal care.'

Maybe I was being too critical, everything looked lovely. The halls decorated in contrasting shades of plum, gray and ivory. In the distance, I watched an elderly lady with Parkinson's shuffle toward her apartment. Each of her steps a small victory as she started and stopped, carefully gripping the handrail that ran the entire length of the wall. *Yes, for that woman this makes sense.* And I thought of Rose, who'd hate this place. But what were the options? I watched Ada as she was led into the model two-bedroom unit. Of course she'd put family first, and if that meant moving back to Manhattan or maybe having Rose move in with her . . . But I knew those long weeks of post-angio had been a nightmare for Ada. Because our mirror-image condos share an adjoining wall I'd heard it all. Embarrassing to admit that hadn't been the first time I'd eavesdropped. And here's where I go from nosy neighbor into stalker, I've actually listened at the wall with Bradley's stethoscope. We had both settled in Pilgrim's Progress eight years ago. It was part of Bradley's master plan to sell the big white house on High Street, with his increasingly frustrating medical practice downstairs, and retire to a life of golf, travel and reading. Like most of Grenville, we'd taken drives through the sparkling new condos, and he already had become a member of the golf club. But Bradley, who was twelve years older than me, wasn't ready to retire, regardless of what he'd said. After we moved to Pilgrim's Progress he became the medical director for half a dozen area nursing homes. His supposed retirement was mostly late-night emergency calls, very little golf, and then one night two years back . . .

If I could have erased a single memory from my mind, it would have been the night I woke to find him dead. The phone on his side of the bed had been ringing, and I wondered why he hadn't picked up. To this day, I can't understand how I slept as my husband died. For months, I tortured myself, wondering 'what if?' What if I had woken and given him CPR? Could I have saved him? Bradley would say that modern medicine had come miles in cardiology; that it was easier to keep people alive with bypass surgery and angioplasty. Why didn't I wake up?

As for Ada, she and Harry moved in to the adjoining condo three months after us. Harry, a lifetime smoker, had end-stage emphysema. My earliest impression was that they'd make fine neighbors, but really, what did we have in common? This red-headed Jewish woman with her largely silent husband and a house that reeked of stale tobacco. I'd made the snap assessment that ours would be a cordial, but reserved relationship. But then, a couple weeks after they'd settled, I'd overheard an argument through the connecting wall. Ada was being hounded by her visiting daughter and son-in-law. They were insisting that Harry be moved to a nursing home. 'Dad requires twenty-four hour care. The doctor says he needs oxygen and physical therapy. You can't provide that.'

Her son-in-law had called her foolish and had made it clear that he and Susan had enough to take care of with their two children. Repeatedly he had said, 'Don't look to us to bail you out when this doesn't work.'

I remembered thinking that Harry must have heard the whole

thing; how horrible. Later, as I came to know him, I learned that on top of his failing lungs and heart, he had Alzheimer's.

Ada had kept her voice low – which is why I simply had to use the stethoscope – as she'd stood her ground, and through the adjoining wall I'd heard: 'Susan, I will always love you, but right now I want you and Jack to leave me and your father alone. I vowed for better for worse and I intend to make good on it.'

With my ear to the wall, I'd wept and waited until they had driven off, and then, armed with an apple sour-cream coffeecake from the Pilgrim's Progress Bakery, I had called on Ada.

Now, as I trailed behind my friend and the Nillewaug director, I began to understand. Ada was at a crossroads. Her brothers and sisters – two in Florida, one in California and one in Arizona – were all much older and all had a shopping list of health issues. When Rose had her heart attack they'd all called, but not one was able to visit, citing various crises of their own.

As we wandered through the empty deluxe two-bedroom unit, I caught hints of its previous owner: a scrap of pink-flowered contact paper in the bottom of a closet drawer, a forgotten photograph of smiling, golden-haired children taped to the inside of a kitchen cupboard, and a series of stainless steel safety bars in the bathroom, kitchen and hallway.

My shudder had returned. Was the previous resident dead or had she declined to the point where they had taken her to one of the two nursing home portions of Nillewaug?

I listened as Ada questioned the director. 'So, how much does this apartment go for?'

'Well, they're not really apartments per se.'

'How much?'

'This very one?' Delia asked, her eyes fixed on Ada, something calculating and intelligent assessing her prospective client.

'A ballpark,' prompted Ada.

'Don't quote me, but when I last checked, this was five hundred thousand.'

Ada didn't flinch. 'Everything included?'

'Yes and no. There is a monthly fee.'

'How much?'

'Three thousand.'

'So, let me get this straight.' Ada looked at the ceiling as she figured the math. 'I'd have to pay five hundred thousand to buy in, plus three grand a month. I have to tell you, Delia –' she looked straight at the director – 'that seems high.'

'Well,' Ms Preston backpedaled. 'If you wanted to see something less expensive, like a studio, or one of our new convenience units . . .'

'Let me ask you,' Ada continued. 'There was someone else living in this unit. Will she get anything from the sale? That is, of course, if she's still alive. But even if she passed away, does her estate get the proceeds?'

Delia's jaw clenched while her mouth stayed fixed in a smile. 'The units go back to the Nillewaug Corporation.'

'So the estate gets nothing,' Ada said.

'If you want to think about it that way.'

'I don't mean to give offense,' said Ada. 'I just need to know what I'd be getting in to. Who makes the decision to send someone to the nursing home?'

'That's a question many prospective residents ask,' said Delia, clearly relieved to be on safer ground. 'At Nillewaug we make every effort, up to and including twenty-four-hour in-home companions, to keep our residents in their own units. We have in-home oxygen and intravenous therapy capabilities, and every other type of therapy: physical, occupational, even massage can be delivered within the campus.'

'That doesn't answer my question,' Ada persisted. 'Who makes the decision?'

'It varies,' admitted the director. 'Obviously, we take into account the preferences of the resident. But sometimes, if it's advanced dementia, or severe post-stroke paralysis, that may not be possible.'

'In which case?' Ada prompted.

'Then it's the families that help us decide, typically with the input of their physician and our medical director.'

'Who's your medical director?' I asked, remembering Bradley's veiled comments as to why he'd left the position.

'Dr Stanley. Gordon Stanley.'

The name was familiar but I couldn't place him. It bothered me. *Gordon Stanley, where do I know him from?*

'Well, I've seen enough,' Ada said as she moved into her I'm ready-to-leave-now mode.

I followed her lead and we edged toward the door.

Delia, sensing her prey was about to escape, launched the hard sell. 'If you're seriously considering this for your mother, and from everything you've told me about Rose, we'd love to have her. But you need to know that we have very limited inventory. The unit you just saw is our only open deluxe model.'

Ada shot her a look. 'Delia, we're talking about my mother and a tremendous amount of money. I will take all the time I need, and if you don't have a unit that suits, there are other facilities in this area.'

'Yes, but, you need to compare apples and—'

Ada interrupted, 'We'll be leaving now, but what you could get me is a copy of your standard contract that I'll have my attorney review.'

'As a practice, we don't release the Promise Agreement unless someone's actually buying in. It's proprietary and we—'

'Ms Preston, I don't enter into any business deal blind. If you want my business you'll fax me a copy of the tenant agreement, or promise whatever.'

'I assure you,' Delia said, 'there's nothing out of the ordinary. It's quite straightforward.'

'Then good, I'll take a look at it, and see if this is something that would work.'

'But I can't—'

'Then neither can I,' Ada said.

Delia's lower lip curled, and her forehead would have furrowed had it been possible. Her frustration was palpable as she tried to find a way around Ada's resistance. 'I'll have to speak with our CEO.'

'Who's that?' I asked.

'Mr Warren,' she said, clearly unhappy with the direction this was going.

'Jim Warren?' I asked. 'The attorney?'

'Yes,' Delia admitted. 'I'll have to check with him.'

'Then good,' Ada said, and she pulled out a card with her numbers. 'If you could either email or fax that would be great.'

When we finally freed ourselves from Delia, and were heading toward the car, Ada stopped. She turned and faced the towering Georgian brick façade of Nillewaug's central residential building. She ran a hand through her hair and took a slow turn. I stood at her side, taking in the stately outer buildings like spokes on a wheel, where the six hundred unit residential building formed the massive hub. All around lush and perfectly maintained landscaping with rustic stone walls, woods with walking paths and benches and the built to impress man-made lake and waterfall, where giant koi flashed beneath flowering lilies.

'It's nice enough.' Her tone was less than enthusiastic. 'Did you see how quiet everyone was? And why was she so squirrelly about letting us see the agreement? I don't know . . .' She sighed. 'I just don't know.'

SIX

As Mildred Potts punched in the security code for her shop, Taffy ran excited circles around her ankles. It had been a long day with a lot of *Lookyloos*, but no buyers. The end of the month was approaching, and even with her robust markups, if things didn't improve . . . Well, she wouldn't think about that. The down economy had hurt everything and the antique business was no exception.

She slid the deadbolt as Taffy started to yip. Mildred looked up and saw a lone figure at the end of the alley that separated Aunt Millie's Attic from the Grenville Historical Society.

She smiled. 'You came back to look at the cameo? Well . . .' She quickly disarmed the security system and unlocked the door. Normally she wouldn't have done this, but the cameo in mention was a spectacular Victorian lapis lazuli set in fourteen carat gold with large rose-cut sapphire and diamond accents. At ten grand it could go a long way toward pulling the month out of the crapper.

She ushered her late-afternoon customer into the showroom with its outstanding collection of antique jewelry and expensive bibelots, all purchased at a fraction of their value. Mildred Potts prided herself on never paying more than ten cents on the dollar. It had given her a reputation, but this was a tough business and considering how many of her colleagues had recently closed shop, or were in jeopardy of doing so, only the shrewd survived.

With Taffy under her arm, Mildred gushed, 'Now, I've been dealing in jewelry for . . . well, for more years than I care to say, but this piece is outstanding. You have a sophisticated eye.'

She unlocked the display case and lifted the jewel from its velvet-lined box. As she slid it toward the customer, her index finger lifted up the tag, letting her see the asking price, as well as her carefully encrypted code that told her what she had paid for it. The latter information she rarely needed. This piece in particular had been part of a major score. It was included in a liquidation she'd gotten on a low-ball bid, with heirs who were both eager and ignorant, a delicious combination. All said and done, the brooch had cost her less than a hundred dollars.

'Of course,' she offered, watching as the customer fondled the pin, 'I could do a *little* better on the price.'

'How much better?'

Mildred rechecked the price and inhaled deeply, as if experiencing sharp pain. 'I could go nine even, but I have a lot of money in that piece. I know I shouldn't have paid what I did for it, but sometimes you have to if you want quality.'

'Of course,' the customer said, and then uttered the one small sentence that was music to Mildred's ears, 'I'll take it.'

Taffy squealed excitedly, sensing his mistress' elation.

'Such a sweet dog,' the customer commented as Mildred wrote up the sale.

'Yes,' she replied, while figuring the six and a quarter percent sales tax. 'She's my little Taffy-waffy.'

'I'm sure she is.' And with that the customer pulled out a delicately engraved, Lady Beretta 21A and shot Mildred Potts at close range between the eyes.

As Mildred crumpled to the floor, still clutching a terrified Taffy, the customer snapped on disposable cream-colored latex gloves, grabbed Mildred's keys that dangled from the case where she'd retrieved the cameo, and systematically went through the shop liberating the jewels.

SEVEN

Tolliver waited numb and stiff on a scarred oak chair as the police conferred behind the soundproof glass of the interrogation room. Born and raised in Grenville, he'd only been inside the red-brick nineteen-twenties police station as part of a third-grade field trip. He felt unreal and disconnected, and in his chest a hollowness as if some vital part of him had just been ripped out.

Yesterday, at the Medical Examiner's office in Farmington, he had been shown a body and told that it was Philip's. He needed to be told, because the bloated and mangled remains in the refrigerated drawer bore little trace of the man who had shared his life for nearly two decades. Hours later, he still smelled the stench that had flooded over him as they'd unzipped the shiny black bag. He could still see his face, or what remained of it after three days in the Nillewaug river, the flesh ripped away in places, one eye puckered and closed, the other a hollow socket from where some animal – *fish, raccoon, crow?* – had dined.

Nothing made sense, but connections had emerged. It was now clear that the human finger found at McElroy's auction had been Philip's. They'd taken a print from the severed digit; it matched.

One day later and Tolliver still had to fight back waves of nausea. Who did this? Had Philip suffered? The coroner had assured him that the finger had been severed after he was dead. But why? And why plant it in an auction where any one of a hundred dealers could have discovered it? Nothing made sense.

'Tolliver?' Officer Kevin Simpson opened the door. 'You can come in.'

The small town irony was that Tolliver and the heavyset and balding Kevin had grown up together, classmates at different ends of the academic spectrum. Where Tolliver was second in the class, Kevin, with his even nature and dogged determination, had struggled to graduate.

Already in the small, windowless interview room was Detective Mattie Perez with the state's Major Crime Squad. Kevin made the introductions, and Tolliver felt the intensity of the detective's dark brown eyes as they shook hands. She was a squarely built early-forties woman with tightly curled black hair shot through with silver. She wore no makeup and her boxy navy suit and button-down oxford gave her a masculine feel. As soon as Tolliver sat, her questions began.

'Mr Jacobs, while you are not officially a suspect, you may have an attorney present.'

'I understand,' said Tolliver, noting the digital recorder on the table. 'I also understand that if I choose not to answer specific questions, that's within my rights.'

'Of course,' she replied, keeping eye contact. 'If you could start by telling me the nature of your relationship with Mr Conroy?'

'He was my husband.' The word was still new, after years of being *partners* and *significant others*.

'I see. Now when did you last see your husband?'

He didn't hesitate. 'Last Friday.'

'You're certain of that?'

'He didn't come home, or at least I don't think he did.'

'Wouldn't you know?'

'Generally, yes. But there was an auction that night and he had been out looking at an estate and hadn't come home. So rather than wait and miss the preview, I went to the auction myself.'

'The one where the finger was found?'

'Yes.'

'And if that finger belonged to your husband,' she continued, 'then I think it's safe to say he did not make it home, but in fact, was already dead.'

'Yes,' said Tolliver dully. 'That must be right.' He felt the room swim as memories of Philip – his first and only love – flooded his brain.

Kevin Simpson's pale blue eyes looked at his old classmate. 'You all right, man?'

'A little dizzy.'

'I'll get you some water,' Kevin said and left him alone with Detective Perez.

She eyed him coldly and silently jotted down questions.

As soon as Kevin returned with a cup of water, she proceeded.

'The Friday of the auction . . . You're sure you saw him that day?'

'We had breakfast together.'

'That would make it October the first?'

'Yes.'

'Forgive me for sounding confused, but today's the sixth. Didn't you wonder what had become of your husband, who had gone to look at an estate?'

'Of course.' He looked down at his hands.

'Well?' she prodded. 'Where did you think he was?'

'I wasn't sure.' Tears welled; he didn't want to cry in front of this woman. He hated that stereotype of the weepy gay man. 'We were having problems. I thought . . .'

'You thought what?' she prompted.

'I thought he might have gone away.'

'Was that something he did?'

'No.'

'Then why would this be different?'

'We were having problems,' he repeated. 'At least Philip was.'

'You said that before,' she commented tersely. 'Please be less vague.'

'He said he might go to the Cape. He wanted some time alone.' He looked up and met the dark-eyed gaze of the intense detective. And it hit him; he was a suspect. He looked at Kevin, who seemed sympathetic, but ineffectual in the face of this woman who had already tried and convicted him.

Finally, he spoke. 'I think I would like my attorney.'

Detective Perez nodded, and with what could have been a spark of compassion in her voice. 'Yes,' she said, 'that would be best.'

EIGHT

Ada fumed as she reread the bottom-line figure on Mildred Potts' handwritten offer that had arrived in the morning mail. 'Twenty-five thousand dollars! She should be shot!' Sitting at her kitchen table she reviewed the evaluation, wondering if a zero had been omitted.

It wouldn't have been so bad if either Mr Jacobs or Mr Caputo had gotten back to her. Neither had returned her calls, after assuring her that they'd get her at least a verbal quote within twenty-four hours. It was now Thursday and the twenty-four had turned into forty-eight. Caputo, she'd been told by his answering machine, was on the road and wasn't expected back till the middle of next week. *And he can't leave a cell phone number?* And Tolliver, who had seemed so pleasant . . . not a word. His secretary, probably sick of her calls, but promising 'he'll get back to you just as soon as he can.'

She wanted out of this mess, and the nasty calls from Evie's heirs. Each one more eager than the next to have the estate liquidated. She was sick of them, the subtle threats, and the not-so-subtle attempts to flatter and ingratiate. It nauseated her. *Is this what it's all about? Relatives fighting over the remains? Is this it?*

At least that Potts woman had gotten back to her. It would almost serve them right if she accepted the offer. She wouldn't, of course, but the thought gave her a needed chuckle. The worst part was now she had to get quotes from another dealer or two.

She thought of Delia Preston from Nillewaug, who had provided her with a list of antique dealers. 'I keep lists of everything and everyone,' she'd remarked. *Bet she gets a kickback*, Ada mused as she fished through her bag for Preston's card.

A knock came at the door. Followed by the bell.

'Coming,' she said, hoping it was Lil, but still checking the peephole. She'd lived in New York too many years to dispense with that basic caution. She was shocked to see her grandson, her attention riveted to an angry black-and-blue over his right eye. 'Aaron,' she said, opening the door. She hugged him tight, noting his black knapsack on the ground, how thin he felt, and the fact that it was too cold to not be wearing a jacket. 'What happened?'

He shrugged and winced. 'I ran into a wall.'

She grabbed on to his shoulders. He was a good head taller; she stared into his dark hazel eyes. 'Tell me the truth, Aaron Matthew. Who did this?'

'Grandma.' He stepped back. 'What do you think happened?'

'I don't know,' she said, formulating a number of hypotheses, most of which involved her son-in-law, Jack Gurston. 'But come in. And why aren't you wearing a jacket?'

'You talked to Mom?' he asked, ignoring her question.

'Yes.'

'What did she tell you?'

'That you and your dad weren't seeing eye to eye on some things.' As always careful to not let her true feelings slip about her son-in-law. *If he hurt you I'll kill him.*

'That's a laugh,' he said, then changed the subject. 'Got anything to eat?'

Ada smiled. *Yes, let's pretend everything's normal, but I will find the truth.* 'Come with me.' He followed as she went into her galley kitchen and foraged through the cupboards, looking for suitable sustenance for a sixteen, almost seventeen, year old. As she inventoried her on-hand food, she was struck by how erratic her dietary habits had become. Aside from large-curd cottage cheese, a head of iceberg lettuce, Danish butter cookies, cartons of blueberry and pomegranate juice – high in anti oxidants – and a half loaf of twelve-grain bread – which reminded her of eating birdseed – her pantry was bare.

'Wait a minute.' She opened the freezer. 'I have ice cream and . . .' She knew it still had to be there. 'Hershey's syrup.'

Aaron laughed. 'I'm not five.' But he didn't resist as she spooned out generous bowls of Ben and Jerry's and squirted bursts of chocolate syrup over the top.

'So what happened?' Ada asked, taking inventory of her tall, sandy haired grandson in his skinny jeans, sneakers and baggy tee. With his hazel eyes and even features, she had a moment's hesitation and surge of pride; *he's turning into a really handsome man.*

'I told you,' he insisted.

'You told me something. Are you hurt anywhere else? And how did you manage to *run into a wall*?'

'Jeez! You don't let up,' he said, avoiding her gaze and wolfing down ice cream. 'Dad and I were fighting, and I wasn't looking where I was going; I ran into the glass shelves in the living room. It's no big deal.'

'Hmm.' Observing how his story had just shifted from the wall to shelves, and that yes, somehow Jack was behind this; *you bastard!* 'Have things quieted down, or is that why you're here?'

'I had to get out of there, and Mom said you told her I could stay here.' He glanced up expectantly.

Ada swallowed back any criticism, any *you could have called first* or *does your mother know you're here?* Looking at his hand-some, albeit marred face, something melted; it's not just that she loved him unconditionally, but that in his eyes, the angle of his jaw, even the way he flicked his too long bangs off his forehead she caught traces of her own brothers at that age, and from certain angles her grandfather, Morris, a man who by all accounts was too handsome for his own good. 'Of course you can stay, but we'll need groceries.' Then she caught herself. 'Wait a minute; what about school?'

'I've got my car. I can drive.'

'Right,' she said, 'you're not five.' There were so many things she wanted to ask. *Are you really gay? How could you possibly know when you're so young? Did your father do that to you? What aren't you telling me?* Never one to hold her tongue, Ada was filled with trepidation. She pictured Lil, with her even features and soft brown eyes and how the feelings she had for her friend had progressed beyond . . . friendship. It had taken her decades to even entertain such a notion, how could he possibly know at sixteen?

'What?' he asked.

'It's nothing,' she replied, figuring if he were going to tell half truths about his father and whatever else was going on she'd do the same. And so they passed a companionable afternoon, playing Scrabble, finishing the ice cream and then taking a trip in Aaron's not quite vintage, and not quite restored blue Mercedes diesel sedan to Costco, Ada's favorite store.

NINE

Tolliver felt numb and not quite real as he pushed the unanswered stack of phone messages from one side of his desk to the other. A tsunami was overtaking his life; if he didn't put his business into order, everything he and Philip had built would be swept away. He imagined that the police would charge him with Philip's murder. After all, people are usually killed by those closest to them.

His attorney, Richard Thompson, III – Dick to his friends – had assured Tolliver there was nothing to worry about. 'There's no hard evidence,' he'd said. 'Nothing to connect you to the scene of the murder. I mean, hell, they're not even certain *where* he got killed.'

Tolliver fanned the messages over his leather blotter. He picked one at random; it was Ada Strauss calling to get his quote.

How long ago that seemed, but it had only been two days; Tuesday, almost a lifetime. He remembered the two women and the translucent Hassam painting with its idealized images of beautiful Victorian ladies in pastel dresses at a seaside picnic. It was worth a fortune, and not the kind of thing he'd normally let slip through his fingers. 'Just pull it together,' he told himself as he picked up the phone and dialed.

'Hello,' a woman's voice answered.

'Mrs Strauss?'

'Yes.'

'This is Tolliver Jacobs; I came by earlier this week to look over an estate.'

'Of course, Mr Jacobs. Not to be rude, but you'd said you'd get back to me yesterday. I'd begun to think you weren't interested.'

'I'm sorry.' His voice echoed in his head. 'Things have been a little crazy.'

'I hope everything's OK,' Ada remarked.

'It's good of you to ask. To be honest –' and he wasn't sure why he continued – 'things couldn't be worse. You see, my partner was found murdered.'

'In Grenville?'

'Yes.'

'How horrible for you.'

'It is. It's the most awful thing I could have imagined.' He held the phone to his ear and said nothing, having forgotten why exactly he had called. 'Oh right,' he said, looking at the pink message in his hand. 'About the estate . . .'

'Are you sure you want to do this now?' Ada asked. 'I hadn't realized. Obviously this can wait, or . . .'

'I don't know what I'm supposed to do,' he said, staring at the message slip. 'They can't release the body, and his parents couldn't get a flight till Saturday. I'm sorry, I'm rambling. I think work may be what pulls me through this. It's the only thing that feels half normal right now.'

'You could be right,' she agreed as she reeled from what he'd just told her.

'Good, let me look at my notes.' Finding comfort in the routine, he glanced through his three pages of jotted impressions. 'You'll have to forgive me, but usually I write these things up. I just haven't gotten around to it. OK, now without the painting, which I would strongly recommend consigning to a New York auction, I could go one hundred thousand for the entire contents.'

Ada paused. 'I know this is the wrong time,' she said, 'but I'm curious as to how people arrive at their figures.'

'Everyone does it differently. Basically, I add it all up and divide by four,' he said being more blunt than he'd ever been.

'So twenty-five cents on the dollar?'

'Yes. If it were all antiques I might go as high as thirty or even thirty-five cents, but where there's a lot of household goods, it takes more man hours to realize less money.'

'That makes sense,' she agreed. 'I was in retail for years. Let me ask you this: is your quote firm, or do you have anywhere to move?'

In spite of himself, Tolliver smiled. 'How much movement?'

'Well,' Ada continued, 'I was thinking more like one fifty, without the painting.'

'I'll go halfway,' he countered. 'One and a quarter, but that's it, especially with the economy being what it is.'

'That's close to what I was thinking, so yes,' Ada agreed.

After they hung up, Tolliver removed all three of her messages. It made the pile less bulky and he felt a small sense of accomplishment. As he flipped through the others, there was one among the dozen that caused his gut to churn. '*We had been having problems,*' he had told the intense detective, unable to tell her more.

He reread the message:

To: Mr Jacobs
From: D. Preston
Re: What we discussed.

He hated everything the message implied; all it meant, all of the changes that had crept into the business, a rot that he'd allowed to happen. He knew that he would have to get back to her; he was in too deep, both he and Philip; *is that why this happened?* Unable to think of any reason why someone would hurt his beautiful Philip.

Was it this? Over the last few years, the playing field of local dealers had changed. Strange affiliations and tacit agreements had sprung up creating questionable alliances as everyone jockeyed for shrinking inventory.

Yes, he thought – picturing Detective Perez – we were having problems. And motivated more by fear, than by anything else, he called Delia Preston.

TEN

I waited in Ada's front hall as she and Aaron got ready. Pretending to fix my face in the mirror – hair twisted up into its habitual bun, a bit of lipstick – I glanced into the living room, hunting for traces of Ada's face in her grandson's. His black and blue made that difficult, and I had the good sense not to ask questions. I also knew that Ada would fill me in on the details later.

It felt good to see her focused on something other than Evie's estate or her mother's proposed move to Nillewaug. She fussed over Aaron, trying to get him to put on a garish knit cap and scarf she'd made.

'Are you ready?' I asked, buttoning my chocolate brown leather coat.

'I am,' said Aaron as he joined me hatless in the hall. 'I'm not wearing this,' he said, stuffing the red, green and orange stocking cap into the pocket of his navy blazer.

'It's a little loud,' I agreed, 'but remember, there are few people in this world who will ever love you enough to actually knit you something.'

'I know,' he said, his voice low, 'but next time see if you can't get her to pick better colors. Black is good. And ditch the pompoms.'

'I'll see what I can do,' wondering why he thought I'd have input into yarn selection. We watched as Ada made the circuit of her condo, turning out lights and checking to make sure her electric teakettle and shredder were unplugged. I'd seen her do this so many times, it seemed dance-like, and bordered on obsessive.

'I know I'm forgetting something,' she said. 'You sure you wouldn't rather I fix something?'

Aaron shot me a glance, which let me know he had few illusions about his grandmother's culinary skills. Ada had many talents, cooking was not among them.

'No,' I said. 'We're going. My treat.'

'If you insist.' She joined us at the door. 'And don't you look nice,' she commented and proceeded to pinch her grandson's cheek. 'What did you do with that hat? It's Merino wool; I made it myself.'

'Grandma,' he complained.

'Sorry, but it's nice to see you in something other than jeans and a tee shirt.'

'You said I couldn't wear them to the restaurant.'

'True, and you look very handsome,' she said, taking in his blazer, chinos and button-down light blue oxford-cloth shirt.

On the way to my car, Ada stopped every few steps to uproot weeds that had grown through cracks in the cement sidewalk. 'You would think,' she commented, 'with the fees we pay, they could take better care of the grounds.'

'They used to. Things have slipped.'

'True,' she agreed. 'I wonder why? I mean yes, the economy tanked, but it's not like our fees have gone down. They raised them again last year. So what gives?'

'Priorities,' I offered as I clicked the button for the car locks. 'Let's face it; we're two of the youngest residents. This place is getting more and more geriatric. At the last homeowner's association everyone was focused on funding the ambulance and more ramps and handrails on the walking paths. Something has to give, like weeding the grounds.'

Aaron opened the car door and looked around. 'It is kind of weird that this is just a place for old people . . . like a ghetto.'

Ada sighed. 'It is, our own little Twilight Town.'

I slid behind the wheel and looked at her. 'You're really thinking of moving back to the city.'

'I don't know,' she replied, meeting my gaze.

I had the distinct sense she wanted to say more and didn't. I assumed because Aaron was there. And for the same reason I kept my thoughts hidden, like: *what would I do if Ada left? And why did the topic make me so sad?*

*   *   *

It was a quick ride to Pilgrim's Mall, the retail hub of Pilgrim's Progress. It houses several excellent restaurants and shops, a three-screen movie theatre and a series of elegant courtyards where venders peddle everything from sunglasses to vitamins. The design, which includes faux pushcarts, was lifted from Boston's Faneuil Hall Marketplace. It was scenic and safe and made it possible to take care of your shopping without ever leaving the community.

Tonight we headed toward Bayberries, an old Grenville restaurant that had relocated to the mall. It was one of my favorites.

'Let's look in the bookstore first,' Ada suggested. 'Our reservations aren't for another fifteen and I want to see the papers.'

As we meandered toward the Nutmeg Bookshop, Aaron spotted something dangling on a yew hedge. He went to investigate.

'Look at this!' he shouted, bringing over what appeared to be a piece of jewelry that glittered in the late-afternoon sun.

I looked over Ada's shoulder as she examined his find. It was a gold locket with a blue-enameled dove surrounded by concentric rays of diamond chips.

'Oh my,' Ada commented, 'someone will be missing this.'

'It's lovely,' I agreed. 'But what was it doing in the hedge? If it fell off its chain, it would be more out in the open.'

Aaron retraced his steps looking for the chain. We watched as he pushed into the tangle of sculpted yews.

'Watch out for your jacket,' Ada cautioned as he ferreted in the greenery.

When he emerged, he held two ladies' pocket watches.

Ada and I looked at each other as he handled the exquisite Victorian timepieces.

'Something's wrong,' I commented as I took one of the watches and opened the engraved case. I grabbed my reading glasses and saw that it was clearly stamped fourteen carat.

'Did you see anything else?' Ada asked, her expression worried.

'No, but it's really tight in there.'

Ada reached up and smoothed back her grandson's bangs, picking out small twigs and bits of leaf. 'We need to bring these to the security desk,' she commented. 'I have a sick feeling about this.'

'You think someone was robbed?' I asked.

'What else could it be? How sad. I hope no one was hurt.'

With Aaron's eyes peeled on the underbrush, we shifted directions from the bookstore and headed to the business office.

As we neared, I could see that the usually deserted storefront, where the community's activities and trips were posted on a wall of cork, was bustling.

'Marge,' I called out to a member of our book club, who was seated on a folding chair in a line that spread back from the door. 'What's going on?'

'Jewelry,' she said, pulling out a pair of jet earrings in the shape of teardrops. 'I found these by my mailbox.'

'Ada's grandson found some things, too. Nice pieces, actually.'

Another woman overheard our conversation and added, 'It's been like this all day.'

'Where's it coming from?' I asked.

'The police are taking statements. That's why we're waiting,' offered Marge. 'I've been here for over an hour. If I were a less honest person, I would have taken my earrings and kept them. They've been pretty insistent that we don't leave.'

'Who's been insistent?' asked Ada as she tried to look over the throng of gray and silver-haired heads that crowded the doorway.

'They know something,' Marge continued. 'When they took my name and address, I got the sense that this was part of something serious.'

'Who were the officers?' I asked.

'One of them was little Kevin Simpson, although I probably shouldn't call him that,' said Marge. 'He never was the brightest lamp,' she continued, drawing on her forty-two years of teaching third grade at Old Haven Elementary, 'but bless his little heart, he always tried. He was at least thoughtful enough to bring out chairs.'

She had a point; over the years Kevin had helped Bradley fix a number of minor scrapes for his patients. What Kevin may have lacked in IQ points, he made up for with a genuine caring and respect for those in his community.

'You said there were two,' I prompted, wondering who was with Kevin.

'There are,' she said. 'The other's a woman detective. She's not from Grenville. Or if she is, I've never seen her before.'

As if on cue, the door to the office opened and a short woman with dark curly hair in a boxy gray suit looked down the line. Our eyes connected for a brief moment. 'We don't have any women officers, let alone a detective.' I knew that for a fact, as I never miss a town meeting and I habitually review every line of the budget. Bradley was the same. While it may seem old fashioned, I was raised with the Jeffersonian philosophy, that citizens have a duty to be involved. In all the years that I had plowed through the police-force budget, I had never seen the name of a woman, aside from clerical help. 'She has to be from the state police. Why would they be involved?' Not liking the answer that came to mind. *Something very bad has happened here.* Which was a gross understatement, considering what Ada had told me about poor Philip Conroy. This had to be why the state was here, but what possible connection could there be between the murder of Philip and this jewelry?

'No idea. But if I were you,' Marge advised, 'don't let them know you're here and go get something to eat. At this rate, we'll be here for hours.'

'Well –' I checked my watch – 'we do have reservations.'

'Run away,' said Marge, with a smile. 'If anyone says anything, I'll cover for you.'

'Thanks.' And with Ada and Aaron in tow, we moved quickly and somewhat guiltily away from the crowded office.

'What is going on?' Ada muttered as she veered from the direction of the restaurant and back toward the bookshop.

'Where are you going?' I called out.

'Let's get a paper. Too many strange things. Something bad is happening.'

'Like what?' Aaron asked.

She looked at him and then at me. 'I'll tell you over dinner.'

I waited while Ada assembled a stack of papers. She grabbed everything: *The Grenville Weekly Buyer's Guide*, *The Pilgrim's Progress Reporter*, *The Hartford Courant* and *The Brattlebury Register*. Then, almost as an afterthought, she added a *Times*.

'Ada, you're not going to . . .'

'I just want to check a few things.'

Aaron chuckled. 'You still spread papers all over the table?'

'Rude, isn't it?' I commented.

'She's always done it,' he said. 'Mom says it used to drive Grandpa crazy.'

'I like to stay informed; is that a crime?' And with her papers tucked under her arm, she pushed open the double doors that led into one of the mall's covered courtyards. From there it was a quick walk to the buttermilk-blue clapboard façade of Bayberries.

Once inside, Curtis Simpson, proprietor and Kevin's older brother, ushered us past the wood-burning fire to our seats. 'Lillian, Ada, good to see you. Quite the evening, isn't it?' he commented, whilst handing us pseudo-parchment menus.

'You mean the jewelry?' I asked, savoring the warm smells of fresh-baked rolls, and slow-cooked meats and stews.

'That and two murders.'

I sat dumbfounded with a sick feeling in my stomach as he turned over our water glasses and motioned for the busboy.

'Philip Conroy I knew about,' said Ada. 'Who's the second?'

He eyed Ada's stack of papers. 'It's probably not in there yet, although if you have the late edition of *The Courant*, or *The Brattlebury Register*, there may be something.'

'Who? Who?' Ada persisted.

'I don't know if you knew her . . . Mildred Potts.'

'Oh my god,' said Ada, making a dozen connections at once. 'That explains the jewelry.'

Curtis stared at her. 'How could you know that?'

'She was robbed, right?' Ada asked.

'Yes, but you think that's her jewelry showing up?'

'Of course,' she said, opening her purse and pulling out the locket and pocket watches. 'My grandson found these in the bushes outside the mall.'

'I know,' the proprietor said. 'It's been like this all day. Like an Easter egg hunt.'

'When Aaron found these,' she continued, 'my first thought was that someone's apartment had been robbed. But if you look close –' she brought one of the watches up close to her eyes – 'you can see traces of some sort of adhesive, like they use for price tags. So that was one thing, and then both the watches and the locket are initialed, but they're all different initials, and not even close. See, this one is RRS, this is TLH and the locket has BT. Plus, they've all been recently cleaned. No one I know cleans their jewelry; too much bother. Anyway, it's clear they came from a shop. Mildred – who, now that she's dead, I will not say bad things about her character – did have the best antique jewelry in town.'

Curtis stared at her. 'You should have been a detective.'

'Yes,' I commented proudly, while trying to quell my darker thoughts; *this is Grenville, people don't get murdered here. This can't be happening.* 'Our very own Miss Marple.'

'Not her,' Ada said. 'Let me be the Helen Mirren one. She's still got some miles on her. And so do I.' And ripping off a piece of warm bread, and dipping it in the garlic-and-olive oil, she smiled at me. 'And so do you.'

ELEVEN

'One moment, Mrs Campbell.' Police Chief Hank Morgan's secretary put me on hold.

'I'll wait,' I told her, not certain that I would have the resolve to call again, but knowing that this was something I had to do, and not entirely certain why. After all, this wasn't any of my business. But Hank and his wife Joanne – who'd died of breast cancer some years back – were old friends. A soft-rock station played a watered-down version of 'Strawberry Fields'. The line clicked twice, and for a moment, I thought I had been disconnected.

A deep male voice boomed. 'Lil, how the hell are you?'

'Not too bad, Hank.' Which wasn't the truth considering two people I knew had just turned up dead. I pictured the robust, silver-haired Chief of Police who had headed up our diminutive force for the past twenty-five years, and who'd been a frequent golf partner of Bradley's.

'What's on your mind, Lil?'

'Hank, I know this is pushing it, but I wanted some information on the murders.' As the words left my mouth I realized how ludicrous and inappropriate this must sound to him. But I needed to know: *what the hell is going on in my home town?* And more importantly: *what are you doing about it?*

His tone shifted from hail-fellow-well-met to something more serious. 'Why would you want to know that, Lil? Taking on a new career as a reporter?'

'Call it a favor, but I knew both of the victims. In fact,' I continued, trying to spark his interest, and wondering if I'd ever told him about my long-put-to-bed dreams of becoming a journalist, 'I saw Mildred the Friday before she was murdered.'

'You don't say? In her shop?'

'No,' I said, and I laid out the ongoing saga of Evie's estate. 'Why would someone kill her, rob her, but then throw out, or give away all the jewelry?'

'That's the big question, isn't it?' He paused. 'But you're making a number of assumptions that could be wrong.'

'Like?'

'For starters, we've recovered less than fifty pieces of jewelry. According to her daughter . . . and Lil, I'm telling you this as a friend; it's not for general consumption.'

'My lips are sealed.'

'Good. Supposedly, over five hundred pieces were taken. Whoever did it made a clean sweep. So either there's a lot more hidden around town, or someone stands to make a tidy profit.'

'Hard to fence, don't you think?' I asked. 'Mostly antiques and a lot of it has initials. You'd think it would be easy to trace.'

'True, at least locally. But if you brought it to a different market – say New York or Boston – no one would be the wiser.'

'It has to be someone who knows antiques,' I offered.

'Stands to reason.'

'Do you think there's a connection to Philip Conroy?' Not wanting to picture the handsome man, who I'd often see at the grocers or the Brantsville flea market.

'It's not clear,' he said. 'We haven't had a murder since Billy Paddock shot his wife, and that was a good five, maybe six years ago. To have two together, makes you wonder.'

'That, and they were both high-end dealers.' I was trying to keep the anxiety out of my voice.

'Correct. Lil, I've got to put you on hold, I've got another call.'

Before I could respond, I was back with the mellow melodies. It was all Beatles tunes, songs I'd played over and over as a teen, wearing down 45's on a cheap mono player and dancing like a fool. As a sanitized 'Twist and Shout' played I thought about connections between the deaths of Philip and Mildred.

It had been the major topic of discussion when Ada had popped in earlier to show me a small blurb in this morning's *Brattlebury Register* about Philip Conroy:

Local Antique Dealer Slain

The partially decomposed remains of Grenville antique dealer Philip Conroy were discovered earlier today by a local gamesman. Clarence Hathaway, of Grenville, who had been fishing in the Nillewaug River, stated, 'My dog caught wind of something, and before I could stop him he started to drag a body out of the river.'

Mr Conroy was positively identified through fingerprints and DNA matching. The exact cause of death has not yet been determined, but the Medical Examiner's office has deemed it a homicide.

When asked to comment, state authorities reported that they were following a number of leads, but had not yet made an arrest.

Tolliver Jacobs, a local television celebrity and Mr Conroy's partner at the world-renowned Grenville Antiques, was unavailable for comment.

Mr Conroy is survived by his parents, Estelle and James Conroy.

Ada had read and reread the article trying to glean any information from the vague text. 'There is nothing here we don't know,' she'd fumed. 'They almost make it sound like Tolliver had something to do with it.'

'Well,' I had said, 'he was the closest. They have to follow up with that. And you noticed how they didn't call Philip his husband.'

Ada had become quiet. 'That poor man. I just wasn't thinking.'

'What are you talking about?'

'I just wasn't thinking,' she'd repeated. 'That poor man is probably the focus of the investigation. I wonder if I shouldn't make other arrangements for Evie's estate?'

'You said that he wanted to work. That he needed to try and get his mind on other things. When Bradley died I think staying busy was the only thing that kept me from losing my sanity.' I'd looked at her. 'And that was a lot of your doing.' I was remembering how, after Bradley's death, Ada would come over or call multiple times a day. Like a childhood friend: *can Lil come out to play?*

'It's not good to be too alone,' she'd said. 'Maybe we should invite him to lunch.'

'What are you up to?'

'Nothing,' she'd said with a chuckle. 'But you have to admit the mystery is delicious.'

'No, it's ghoulish. Doesn't it bother you that we saw Mildred, and a couple days later she was dead? I wonder who's taking care of her dog.'

'Her daughter,' Ada had responded without hesitation.

'How do you know that?' I'd asked, wondering what other pearls she might have accumulated, and not certain how I felt about this side of my wonderful friend.

'While you were handing in the jewelry this morning, I made some phone calls. Isn't it something how the papers give such little information?'

The line clicked and the music stopped. 'Sorry about that, Lil,' Hank said. 'My phone hasn't let up.'

I felt guilty taking his time, but then again, Bradley and I had always supported Hank and the Grenville Police Department; if I wanted a little information, I didn't think he'd begrudge me. 'I don't want to keep you long, but the paper said that Philip Conroy had been missing since Friday. Ada and I were wondering . . . Remember the McElroy auction?'

'Yes,' he said, already knowing where I was headed. 'The finger *was* Conroy's. But that can't be shared, Lil.'

'Of course, but it's not that hard to put together. The question is why? Were there other fingers missing?'

'Lillian Campbell, I had no idea you had such morbid interests.'

'I didn't either,' I admitted, confused by the flirtatious lilt in his voice. 'So was it just one finger?'

'Yes.'

'Why just one?' I asked.

'Sixty-four thousand dollar question. I suspect you have a theory.'

'Of course. Which isn't to say it's right. But a lot of us had gone though the auction preview. At least half of us opened that drawer.'

'Did you?'

'No, I don't care for Empire furniture. Pretty, but impractical. The veneer is forever chipping.'

As a true Grenvillian, Hank knew exactly what I was talking - about. 'You're more of the Chippendale set.'

'Exactly.'

'Do you still have Bradley's Philadelphia bookcase?'

As he spoke, I glanced across my dining room table at the gleaming mahogany bookcase with its flame finials and sunburst drawer fronts. 'Yes, and I'll be hanging on to that until they cart me off in a box.'

'Can't blame you. If it was mine, I'd want to be buried in it. Anyway, you were saying about the auction . . .'

'You probably know this, but the preview went right up until fifteen minutes before the auction. Someone had to be there to put the finger in the drawer.'

'Which narrows it down to about four hundred suspects,' he commented. 'If indeed it was planted at the auction.'

'Had to have been. Didn't it?' I asked.

'Probably. Still, it's too soon to throw out possibilities.'

'And not to question your judgment, but why in God's name is Kevin Simpson involved in the case?'

'Lil,' he said, laughing, 'you must think I'm a complete idiot. He's peripheral; we both are. Whenever there's a homicide the state police step in. It's for the best, as long as they don't step on too many toes. They sent a Detective Perez who strikes me as capable. Ever since the finger was found she's been over everything. Now, with two murders, they've added a second team of detectives. As for Kevin, he knows everyone and people like him, don't have trouble talking to him. All said and done, they'll be able to take care of things.'

'Are they?' I asked, hoping for a bit more detail.

'I think so.'

'Close to an arrest?'

'Possibly.'

I was wading into dangerous waters, but I wanted to know. 'Tolliver Jacobs?'

'Lil, I can't say.'

'For what my opinion is worth, Hank, I don't think he did it.'

'What makes you say that?'

'I've known him his entire life. Not a violent bone in his body. Someone doesn't just wake up a killer.'

'No, they don't, but basically all you're going on is intuition.'

'Pretty much.'

He laughed. 'Well, if you can nail it down any further, give me a call.'

'Of course,' I said, feeling my private interview coming to a close. I tried to think if there was anything more that Ada might have wanted to know.

'Lil,' Hank said, 'it's been good talking. I've missed seeing you . . . and Bradley, of course.'

'Likewise,' I said, not wanting to overstay my welcome, and getting a funny feeling like he was about to ask me out. But then it hit me. 'It was a warning,' I blurted.

'What was?' he asked.

'The finger. It had to be a warning, and it had to be planted by someone who knew McElroy.'

There was a pause. 'OK, I'll bite.'

'You don't go to the auction, do you?'

'Nah, I'm more the car-show type.' Referencing one of Grenville's other pastimes, vintage and antique car shows, from the June bonanza to Thursday night gatherings of enthusiasts in the high school parking lot.

'Right. I've been going to McElroy's since his father ran it. Anyway, Carl has a thing about getting every single door and drawer open when he shows a piece of furniture. Someone was counting on the finger being found . . . by him.'

'But they couldn't have predicted on it flying out into the audience.'

'True. In which case, the only person who was supposed to see it was Carl. You see what I'm saying?'

'Someone was trying to scare McElroy . . . Interesting, Lil. I'll have the kids check on it.'

'Hank, if something comes from it, you'll let me know?'

'I can't make a promise like that.'

'How about I have you over for lunch?' I suggested, wondering what I was getting myself into.

'Let me think about it.'

'How about tomorrow?'

'Lil!' I heard the laughter in his voice. 'I'll get back to you.'

'Thanks, Hank.'

'You take care, Lil.'

'You too.' And he hung up, just as my cell buzzed from my purse. I wasn't even going to pick it up, knowing there'd be no answer, and unknown name/unknown number in the readout. They'd been coming more frequently, at least one a day, sometimes two or three. I tried to tell myself it was a telemarketer, which made no sense because the few times I did pick up no one spoke, just a pause and the sense that someone was on the line before it clicked dead. I thought about calling back Hank and asking him if there was anything I could do to track down my mystery caller.

But I figured with two murders on his hands, my hang-up caller wouldn't rate. *It's probably nothing*, but I couldn't shake the creepy feeling that someone was checking on me, and for the life of me, I could not imagine why.

TWELVE

C arl McElroy sweated as he fidgeted with the ledger. Despite knowing Hank Morgan for years, having two law officers crowded in his small, unfinished office at the back of the auction house, had his adrenalin pumping. *What did they know? What did they suspect?* 'It was pretty shocking,' he said, trying to stay composed. 'You say it was Conroy's finger?'

The female detective eyed him closely. 'Yes, had you considered that yourself?'

'No,' he lied, watching his own fingers slowly shred the edges of the ledger. He pushed it away, and thought longingly of the bottle of Canadian Club in his bottom right drawer.

They said nothing; the silence stretched.

'How could I have known?' he blurted.

'That's what we're here to find out,' Detective Perez stated. 'You seem nervous, Mr McElroy. You always sweat like that?'

'Well –' pools of warm liquid under his arms soaking the fabric of his plaid shirt – 'two people I know have been murdered.'

'Yes.' The boxy detective leaned on the desk, and stared down; she said nothing until he finally looked up and met her gaze. 'Two people you knew; two people in . . . your business . . . Two customers . . .' Her voice trailed.

'So? What does that mean?' he asked.

'An observation,' she stated coldly.

Hank Morgan smiled, his gaze on the no-nonsense detective maneuver. 'She has a point, Carl. If I were an antique dealer in Grenville, I might be getting nervous.'

'No kidding.' He was relieved to hear a friendly voice, and wondered how much longer they'd be there. *God, I need a drink.*

'So that's why you're so nervous,' Detective Perez commented, deftly picking up Hank's opening. 'Look at you, your hands are shaking.'

'Yes, that's right,' the auctioneer agreed, glad for the pat explanation.

'It wouldn't be something more immediate?' Her dark eyes bore into his blood-shot blue. 'Some say the finger was a warning.'

Carl's breath caught.

'In fact,' she pressed, 'some say it was a warning for *you*.'

The pale auctioneer sputtered, his cheeks turned red. 'A warning for what?'

'Good question. Any ideas, Carl?'

'No! Why are you doing this to me?'

'Carl.' Hank stepped in, cooling things down. 'Just trying to look after your interests. Can you think of anyone who might have it in for you? After all, yours can be a tricky business. There was that unpleasantness a few years back with Katherine Williams . . .' He let the statement trail.

'They never proved anything,' Carl said.

'But if someone held a grudge,' Hank continued. 'How does the saying go, "Revenge is a meal best eaten cold"?'

'What *unpleasantness*?' Detective Perez asked, having already reviewed the charges that had been filed, and then dropped, against Carl some five years earlier.

'It was nothing,' Carl said, unable to meet her gaze. He stared at the grain of his oak desk. 'Consignors always think they should have gotten more than their stuff is really worth.'

'And sometimes mistakes happen,' Detective Perez prompted.

'I'm not saying anything, but on a Friday night we run through over three hundred lots. There are bound to be mistakes.'

'I bet,' the detective said. 'And the particular *unpleasantness* we're talking about involved about two dozen "mistakes", or so the consignor alleged.'

Carl looked crushed.

'How did the charges get dropped, Carl?' she asked.

'I . . .' He couldn't find the words, and he gripped his left hand over his right to keep them from shaking.

'Let me help,' Hank said. 'I encouraged Carl to settle. By and large it seemed to take care of all the involved parties.'

Detective Mattie Perez looked at the local police chief and smiled. 'Neither side wanted publicity?'

'Basically,' Hank admitted.

'So, Carl, who was the aggrieved party?'

'That can't have anything to do with this,' he spluttered, struggling to keep his temper in check.

'Why is that, Mr McElroy?' Detective Perez asked. 'Could that be because the plaintiff is no longer living?'

'Yes,' he admitted.

'In fact,' Perez continued, 'Katherine Williams never lived to receive her settlement.'

'No, it went to her estate . . . to her son.'

'Sad, isn't it,' the detective said. 'An old woman consigns her prized possessions to an auctioneer, someone she knows . . . trusts. And then that auctioneer repeatedly records inaccurate sales figures for her possessions. And curiously enough, the discrepancies always came out in your favor, Carl.'

'It got settled. It never went beyond the civil suit,' he persisted.

'Yes, and more's the pity. So what we need to know is,' she continued, 'how many Katherine Williamses are out there? A dozen? A hundred? More? You have quite the dossier at the licensing board.'

Wisely, Carl kept his mouth shut.

'You have to wonder,' Mattie Perez continued, pacing slowly in front of Carl. 'Is someone dishing out just desserts to the local dealers? And, Carl, I suspect there are one or two little details you've left out. If I were you –' she stopped and leaned over his desk – 'I'd cough up everything now.'

'I want my lawyer,' he said.

'Whatever for, Carl?' Hank asked. 'No one's charging you with anything.'

'She's badgering me. I don't have to take this,' he said, whining like a schoolboy, his thoughts fixed on the waiting bottle, needing it desperately.

'We're trying to look after you, Carl. While Detective Perez may come across a little hard; we don't want to see you turn up dead.'

McElroy blanched. He gripped his hands tighter; he couldn't make the shaking stop. His entire body felt like it was vibrating, a darkness closed in on his thoughts, making it hard to think; *just keep your mouth shut. They've got to leave some time.*

Mattie and Hank watched and waited. The silence was complete.

Finally, Carl spoke. 'I have nothing to say; I'd like you to leave.'
Hank wasn't surprised. They'd pushed too hard.

Disappointment flashed across Detective Perez's face.

'Have it your way, Carl,' Hank said. 'Think about it, though.
Whatever you're sitting on is going to come out. Better sooner
than later. And, Carl –' his words dropped slowly – 'whatever you
do . . . lock the door, set the alarms, be careful.'

Carl peered through a dirt-streaked window as Hank and the woman
detective got into the Grenville police cruiser. His hands shook
and his knees felt like if he tried to stand they'd give out. Half
moons of sweat soaked his shirt from armpit to waist. *Sure*, he
thought, reaching down for the liter and a half bottle of CC, there
were a couple things, but what good would it do to talk about
them? Just get him in trouble. It wasn't worth it. Mildred was
robbed and that's a shame. And Conroy, well who knew what sick
stuff he was up to? Probably a lover's spat. *Nothing to do with
me*. But what if they were right? He'd thought it himself; Conroy's
finger was a warning. But from who? Faces of angry consignors
flashed in front of him. Dozens over the years, most of them
backing down, a few he'd had to buy off. He took three long,
grateful swigs; the liquor burned the back of his throat and spread
warm into his belly. He looked at the bottle, two-thirds gone; it
had been new yesterday; *you're gonna have to cut down, just not
now.* He listened into the darkness, and spooked, he got up and
switched on the security system.

Slowly, he reined in his racing thoughts. And as darkness fell
over a red-streaked October sky, he settled down to sipping whiskey
straight and the familiar task of reviewing the catalog for tomorrow
night's auction, never once considering it would be his last.

THIRTEEN

I watched as Ada lit the Sabbath candles. She waved her hands
in front of her face, and in a rich beautiful alto sang, '*Baruch
atah Adonai . . .*' The flames cast a golden glow on her skin
and her eyes sparkled. She looked absolutely lovely in a dark gray

silk blouse, black slacks and iridescent peacock pearls around her throat.

Aaron hummed the melody as his grandmother blessed the candles, and we both chimed in with the 'Amen'.

It was Friday night, a time that Ada and I had shared ever since Bradley died. It was a week after his death, she'd invited me over, and after that it had become a part of the rhythm of my life. Aaron's presence changed things, as did my growing unease about the two murders. She bustled around her condo as smells heretofore unknown emanated from her kitchen.

The oven timer clanged. 'My kugel!' exclaimed Ada, sprinting to rescue the steaming concoction from the oven. I trailed after her, noting her dismay as she removed the slightly charred contents of a Pyrex casserole dish.

'Oh well.' She chuckled, moving toward the sink. 'I'll cut off the burned bits.'

Her stovetop was cluttered with saucepans, skillets, opened spices, mixing cups and measuring spoons. The comforting smell of chicken soup wafted through her condo; I peeked under the stockpot lid and got a strong whiff of that most primal brew.

'I made *k'naidlach*,' she beamed.

'Those are the dumplings?' I asked as I watched several pale objects bob in the soup.

'You bet,' she said. 'My mother makes the best *k'naidlach*; "light as air" my father used to say, although legend has it that the very best were made by my grandmother.'

'What was her name?' Aaron asked, having followed us into the cramped kitchen.

'Rachel,' said Ada.

'And Great-great-grandpa?'

Her smile evaporated. 'Morris.'

'They came from Russia, right?'

'Poland,' she corrected. 'A little town outside of Krakow.'

'Did you know your grandparents?' Aaron asked.

'No,' she said, while stirring the soup. 'They were both dead when I was born. Here, are your hands clean?'

He held them out for inspection.

'Wash them in the sink,' she bossed. 'Then cut up some tomatoes for the salad. So your mother never told you about your great-great-grandparents?'

'No, I don't think she knows a lot about them.'

'I wouldn't bet on that. Our family is filled with stories; she's heard them, but some she might not want to repeat.'

'Good dirt?' he asked as he quartered tomatoes.

'You might say that,' she agreed. 'Your Great-great-grandpa Morris was something of a bastard. And sadly, you're getting to look like him.'

I choked and Aaron laughed. 'Why? Was he ugly or something?'

And the look she gave her grandson was so filled with love. 'No, the opposite. Too good looking for his own good; he got away with murder. I've got some old photos of him I'll pull out for you later.'

'OK,' he said, 'you've got to tell me.'

'Do you want to hear this, Lil?'

'You know I do,' I said. I had always been fascinated by the anomalies that Ada embodied. I was daily struck by the improbability of our friendship, how two such different people could find so much in common.

'Let me be the *Bubba Meiseh*,' she said, ladling broth into her good Rosenthal china.

'Can we ask questions?' I laughed.

'Of course.'

'What is a *Bubba Meiseh*?' I asked.

'An old woman who tells stories.'

'This is great,' said Aaron as he carried the fresh-baked challah bread that Ada had whipped up in the bread maker that she'd bought at Costco over a year ago, but had never taken out of its box before today.

'First the blessings,' she said as we settled around the linen-covered table.

Usually, Ada and I have Chinese takeout for our Friday meal, and while she does say the blessings, it's always to herself. Today was different. She blessed the wine and the bread, and I sensed her listening to Aaron, to see if he knew the words.

'Now,' Ada began, 'my mother – your Great-grandma Rose – was a little girl when she came to this country. It was her, your great-great-grandparents, and your Great-great-uncle Ben. My mother was five, but to this day, she's not certain how old she really is. She has no birth certificate.'

Aaron and I quietly sipped soup and nibbled at the edges of

the strange dumplings, which, while not "light as a feather", did have an appealing dense texture that held the flavor of the rich oniony broth.

'She could be ninety, maybe ninety-one, maybe older, maybe younger.' She tore off a hunk of challah and dipped it in her soup. 'They were the greenies, the last ones to come over. Which was how it was done. My Great-uncle Natie and his wife Esther came first, and one by one they sponsored the rest of the family. Not everyone came, and you should know this, Aaron, but there are whole lines of our family that were murdered by Hitler.' Her voice caught. 'I can't believe your mother never told you these things. I have pictures of some of the relatives who were killed. I think it's important that you see their faces. I used to look at them and wonder what were they like. How did they live? Why didn't they leave?

'Anyway, my grandparents, your great-great-grandparents Rachel and Morris came to New York, the Lower East Side. All of them crowded in with aunts and uncles, Grandma pregnant – again. So many cousins, and people who weren't even related, but had come from the same village. They spoke Yiddish, and lived in two different worlds. There was Delancey and Orchard, and then there was the other world. They stuck together,' she said, looking at Aaron. 'It was important because family was everything. That's how it worked back then. My grandfather got a job working in Uncle Natie's store.'

'What kind of store?' Aaron asked.

'*Shmatehs*.'

'Excuse me?' I said.

'*Shmatehs*, rags. The clothing trade. It was *Shmatehs*. My uncle Natie had a good store, first on Orchard Street and then he opened a second with two floors of seamstresses on Eighth Avenue.'

'So they were doing pretty well,' Aaron commented.

'Eventually, but not at first. Every cent they earned went into bringing over family and building the business. And almost every year my grandma had a new baby.'

'How many?' Aaron asked.

She stopped to think. 'Nine.' She counted on her fingers: 'Ben, my mother Rose, Bette, Lewis, Abe, Mortie, Pearl, your Great-uncle Hector who died of influenza, and finally, Adele.'

'Mom said Grandma Rose ended up raising them all.'

'That comes later, and is part of why my Grandfather Morris

was such a bastard. Was the soup OK?' she asked, obviously pleased that both of our bowls had been emptied.

'Excellent,' Aaron said, and I heartily concurred.

'Bet you didn't think I had it in me,' she quipped and winked at me while gathering our bowls.

We watched as she disappeared back into the kitchen.

'She's pretty amazing,' Aaron said.

'Agreed,' I replied, finding myself inexplicably close to tears.

'Did you know all that stuff about my family?' he asked, fixing me with his intelligent eyes. The bruise around his right eye and cheek had faded, mostly yellow now. I found myself thinking about my own grandchildren. How far away they were, how seldom I saw them. I realized that part of what I was feeling had to do with the ease with which Aaron had found his way to Ada. I was jealous, and wondered if in a time of need my grandchildren would look to me as a safe harbor. *And is that it, Lil? Are you also jealous of Aaron? Of how she so easily loves him. What is wrong with you?* 'She doesn't talk much about her past,' I said.

'It's cool, isn't it?'

'It is.'

When Ada reappeared she held a white ironstone platter with a steaming roast surrounded by small white potatoes and slices of carrots. From her pleased expression, I knew that whatever it was, it had turned out close to her goal.

'It's brisket,' she declared proudly. 'I haven't had this in years.'

'What's brisket?' Aaron asked.

'I'm not entirely certain,' she replied, slicing the steaming roast and giving us each a potato, two carrots and a ladle full of juice. 'It has to be some part of the cow, and because it's kosher we know it's from the front half. But it's cured. It's really good, though.' She popped a bit of end-piece into her mouth. 'Just scrumptious.'

It was delicious. 'A regular Julia Child,' I commented, enjoying the melt-away meat with its savory flavors. 'I had no idea you could do this.'

'Hidden talents, Lil. Although, to be honest, I wasn't quite sure how it would come out. I did this once before and got distracted with something for the business; the whole thing came out like shoe leather with a side of burnt potatoes. It's funny, all this talk about family, but as I was cooking I kept picturing Mama, and my Aunt Esther in the kitchen. Oh, the things we would make. The Sabbath was very special, but the holidays, now that's when you saw cooking.'

'Were you very religious?' Aaron asked.

'We were observant, but everyone was. There was none of this Orthodox, Conservative and Reform. We were all observant, everyone went to shul; the women up behind the screens and the men downstairs carrying the Torahs and *davening*.

Aaron and I shot each other looks.

'This is terrible,' Ada said, catching our confused expressions. 'Lil, you have an excuse, you're not Jewish. But Aaron don't you know what *davening* is?'

'That would be a no.'

'Oh my. It's the style of praying, where the men wrap themselves in their *tallisim* and sing the prayers and the responses to the scripture. While upstairs, we'd look through the screens and follow along. I was always jealous of the boys, who every day after school went to study with the rabbi. That was just for boys. And unlike your sister Mona, who had a bat mitzvah, there was none of that when I turned thirteen.'

'Kind of a rip-off,' Aaron commented.

'It was disappointing. But you wanted to know about your great-great-grandfather.' She bit down on a flavorful morsel. 'Hmm,' she said, letting the taste of another time send her back. 'They moved to Queens, to a big three story house, and that's when things started to fall apart. My grandmother got sick with cancer and Morris apparently had a roving eye.'

'Really?' Aaron's expression lit at that scurrilous bit of history.

'It's true. Growing up I'd catch snippets from the aunts and the uncles. It was always, "Poor Rachel" this and "Poor Rachel" that. I just assumed they were talking about how hard it must have been to have nine children. She died before I was born, leaving my mother to raise her brothers and sisters. She was probably twelve or thirteen, had a huge house to run and a father who would disappear for days at a time. Adele and Hector weren't even toilet trained when my grandmother died.'

'This is like TV,' Aaron offered, while helping himself to seconds.

'And then Morris moved out altogether,' Ada said.

'How could he do that?' I asked. 'He abandoned his family?'

'Yes, he had another woman, one of the seamstresses. She was an Irish girl who wanted nothing to do with a house full of children. She was supposedly quite pretty, and he gave her expensive gifts, while his own children wore hand-me-downs from the cousins. Things got very bad. There were no child-support laws in those days. Morris had no obligation, other than the ethical one, to care for his children. The family tried to pressure him to make sure there was at least coal for the furnace. My mother would tell me how she and her brother Ben would go scrounging among the neighbors. Or how she'd dress the little ones in rags and take them down to the welfare office to try and get some money. I also think – no, I know – that's why she married so young.'

'What do you mean?' I asked, trying to reconcile this history of Ida's mother with Rose Rimmelman, the cantankerous nonagenarian who'd stayed here last year.

'She was fifteen when she got married; my father Isaac was twice her age, and was managing his family's store. I think the idea of having someone to support all those children and that house must have been hugely attractive. And then, just like her mother, the babies started coming.'

'Sort of like you,' Aaron interjected. 'Weren't you married super young?'

'Eighteen, and yes, I also married back into the business. Although Harry had his own store. Oh my—' She stopped short. 'What time is it?'

I looked at my watch. 'Nearly seven.'

'Where has the time gone? Services start in half an hour.'

'Services?' Aaron asked warily.

'Yes,' said Ada, in a tone that made it clear attendance was mandatory. Even though more often than not – depending on what we saw at the preview – we'd typically end up at McElroy's auction instead of Grenville's tiny synagogue.

'Are you going?' he asked me.

'Yes,' I said with a smile.

'But you're not Jewish.'

'Episcopalian.'

'Then why?'

'I like to,' I said.

'She goes out of pity,' Ada responded.

'I do not. I like going.'

'You just don't want me to be taking cabs everywhere.'

'Ada, sometimes you say the meanest things.'

'You're right, that was unfair of me.'

'Yes, it was,' I said, feeling a little hurt. 'I go because it's different from what I'm used to. It's small and everyone seems interested in trying to keep it going. And besides . . . you come with me to church.'

'Grandma!' Aaron sounded shocked. 'You go to church?'

'So what if I do? God is God. Besides, we go to The Greenery afterwards for lunch.' As though eating in the two hundred-year-old inn was justification for her religious infidelity.

'You two are kind of like a married couple,' he offered, while helping to clear the dishes.

Ada looked at me; I felt the room start to spin.

'And what if we were?' she asked. 'Would that bother you?'

I was mildly shocked at what she'd just said, and apparently so was Aaron. An uncomfortable silence followed. I needed to say something, but my mouth was dry and a vein pulsed on my forehead. *Does she know what I feel for her? Could she possibly feel the same?*

Instead, it was Aaron that broke the silence. 'You're just saying that because of what Mom told you. Although –' and a smile crept across his face – 'it would be pretty cool to have a lesbian grandmother. It would just kill dad.'

'Seriously?' Ada flashed a wicked grin. 'Then Lil, it's definitely something to consider.'

I knew that she was making a joke and it bothered me. Because deep down, and there was no getting around it, I wished she weren't.

FOURTEEN

Carl McElroy looked over the night's auction receipts, and took a much-needed swig of whiskey. All said and done, not too shabby. Although, spotting that woman detective in the audience gave him pause. *Nosy bitch. Who the hell does she think she is?* Conroy got what he deserved and Mildred was robbed, tough break, but it happens.

He thought about Hank's warning, and felt an uneasy tingle. He listened hard to the creak and whisper of the ancient floorboards and weathered wood siding that comprised the shell of his auction house, which stood alone on the country road a couple miles from the center of Grenville. *It's nothing,* he thought, and he reached down for the new bottle of CC, and filled the tumbler. *You deserve it, long night.*

At least he'd been able to warn off Pete and Sal. It wouldn't have been smart to have them buying back any of their furniture with that detective nosing around. Years back that's what caused the trouble with the Williams bitch. Although if her son hadn't made such a stink no one would have known.

In the end, it didn't make a difference. Tonight had been a good night, although lately, they'd all been good, especially for the high-end stuff and precious metals. The influx of fresh dealers and the increasing desperation among the old-timers had pushed prices to exhilarating highs. All the smaller lots were now simultaneously posted on eBay, so if someone in the audience didn't feel like coughing up thirty grand for a Tiffany tea service, you could bet there'd be some fool in Tokyo who just had to have it. New phrases had seeped into his tried-and-true auction patter; he fed on their fears. 'Aren't going to see another one like this,' he'd warn, whipping them into a frenzy over a tiger-maple Connecticut highboy. 'Stuff's really drying up.' Or: 'Stocks crash . . . Chippendale never does,' he'd commiserate, while bumping up the bid and inciting all the petty rivalries that got dealers and collectors, particularly the newbies, to bid with their hearts and not with their heads.

He'd listen to the dealers as they'd bitch. 'There's nothing out there anymore,' one had said, echoing the general belief. *Yes and no*, Carl thought. Sure, he had to look a little further, and make deals he had never done before, but every Friday night, like clockwork, he auctioned off over three hundred lots of quality goods.

But in truth, it was drying up. He looked at his ledger, at how incredibly complicated it had become, what with the finder's fees and other costs that had to be massaged into the figures.

It made him nervous the way the detective had so blatantly recorded the selling price of every item that crossed the block. What was her game?

Hank at least turned a blind eye. Hell, why not? It wasn't like anyone got hurt, and by and large the deals he cut kept the merchandise flowing. If you thought about it, the auction house was a public service, part of Grenville's lifeblood. It amused Carl to walk though the shops and see how much had passed across his auction block.

He eyed the locked cabinets where he kept the second set of ledgers. 'Tomorrow,' he muttered, emptied half his glass and pushed back from his desk; a floorboard groaned loudly behind him.

His head whipped around at the sound; his eyes bulged. 'You! What are you . . .'

'Surprise!' the gloved assassin whispered, while squeezing a single shot from the delicately etched 22mm Beretta.

A small dark hole, like a third eye, appeared in the center of Carl's forehead. His mouth continued to move, but no sound came. Blood slowly blossomed around the entry wound as the dying auctioneer recognized his fate, and, with a final angry surge, he lunged from his chair, spilled his drink and crumpled to the ground.

A gloved hand moved to Carl's carotid. Beneath the thin latex glove, the killer felt the last few spurts from the dying heart grind to a sluggish halt.

With an efficiency of movement the killer found Carl's keys next to his bottle of whiskey and unlocked the filing cabinet. Out came the ledgers and McElroy's fiercely guarded address book. Everything was just where it was supposed to be, and working fast, the shooter set about their intended tasks.

FIFTEEN

News of McElroy's murder spread fast, and with it hysteria. Ada and I overheard whispered rumors and speculation in our Sunday morning pew at St Luke's Episcopal:

'*Who's next?*'

'*Who's behind it?*'

'*I won't go out at night.*'

'*For the first time in my life I'm locking the door and checking the windows.*'

Hattie Cavanaugh, the police chief's sister, leaned over to let me know. 'Lil, Hank said McElroy's body had been mutilated. We've got a serial killer in Grenville. Although,' she continued, keeping her voice low, 'I've always thought a lot of the dealers are just out-and-out thieves.'

Ada, in a stunning green pantsuit with an ice-blue blouse, cut her a look.

'Well,' Hattie persisted, 'they are.'

'I didn't say a thing,' Ada whispered, although I knew she was dying for the details, and sickly, so was I.

After church, we walked across Town Plot to The Greenery, one of the oldest continuously operating inns in the United States. Like most after-church diners we had standing reservations. Frieda Auchinstrasse, the proprietress, led us straight to our table with a mullioned window that overlooked High Street.

'Isn't it terrible,' she commented, handing us our menus, while shooting a glance at the Channel Eight news truck parked across the street.

'Yes,' I agreed, knowing that she wasn't referring to the notoriously leathery rack of lamb on today's handwritten special board.

'It's all people are talking about,' she continued, puffing up her tightly curled Lucille Ball perm. 'You just never think it could happen here.'

'We've had murders before,' I reminded her, staring out at the news truck and then noticing a second parked at the distant end of Town Plot and a third with the CNN logo in front of that one.

'Doesn't it scare you, Lil?'

I looked at Frieda with her billowy mess of dyed hair. I had to remind myself that she and her husband Gustav – who ran the antique shop in the colonial next door – were relatively recent additions to Grenville. To my way of thinking, The Greenery was eternal; it had stood and functioned as an inn and restaurant for over two centuries. Its owners, however, seemed to come and go with the seasons. The Auchinstrasses had been in Grenville for less than twenty years. In that time they had systematically bought up High Street real estate, and last year had taken over The Greenery. They had mostly left things unchanged and, to their credit, had attempted to revitalize the sagging cuisine, which had deteriorated into glutinous gravies and over-boiled vegetables. The food had never been the selling point; why we continued to come was hard to define. Yes, the dark ambience, with the open hearth and hand-wrought tools, like stepping back into the eighteenth century was a treat. But something else, looking first at Ada, and then at all the familiar faces at their regular tables; this was my community, and this inn was a part of its rhythm.

'Why should it scare me?' I asked, and yet I was anxious. 'I don't fit the profile.'

'But what about me?' Frieda asked, her eyes comically wide. 'I have two shops on High Street.'

'She's got a point,' Ada chimed in maliciously.

As she did, a stocky dark-haired woman in a green turtle neck and khakis eating by herself at the next table looked up. She gave an enigmatic half smile.

I smiled back, recognizing the state detective.

'She's right, you know.' The woman said, seemingly weighing each word as she made eye contact first with Ada and then with Frieda. 'There is a pattern.'

Frieda shook her head, sending her curled tresses into a spasm. 'I don't want to talk about this. I'll have Annie get you your drinks.' Clearly spooked, she scurried off to greet and seat the diners who were backing up into the foyer.

'Detective Perez, isn't it?' I asked, not about to let the opportunity slip.

'Yes, and you are . . .?'

'Lillian Campbell.'

Ada looked at me for an explanation.

'This is the detective working on the murders,' I told her. Taking in details of this intense woman from her tightly curled hair, with touches of silver, to how she wore no makeup and the two little gold stud earrings that seemed more part of a uniform than any conscious stab at adornment.

'Oh, please join us,' Ada said.

I looked across at the detective. 'Please'.

She paused as though weighing some internal question. 'I'd love to,' she finally said. 'If you're sure it's all right?'

'Are you kidding?' Ada said, moving her chair to make space.

'I hate eating alone,' the detective said as she grabbed her cutlery and water glass. 'Mattie Perez,' she said to Ada as way of an introduction.

'Ada Strauss, and I have something to confess.'

'Not to the murders, I hope. We've already started getting a bunch of those.'

'Augie Taylor?' I asked.

'Yes, but how . . .?'

'Augie confesses to everything in the police blotter. He's not right in the head. His sister told me it's some form of obsessive-compulsive disorder. That he's forever thinking he's guilty of crimes he didn't commit. He's supposed to take medication . . . Usually, he doesn't.'

'You know this town well,' Mattie said, dipping a breadstick in the crock of port-wine cheese. The detective glanced out the lattice-framed window. 'It is lovely, isn't it? All the old houses and storefronts; it looks like nothing has changed in hundreds of years.'

'Strict zoning,' I replied. 'That, and a historical society that has become increasingly fascistic over the years.'

'Keeps the rabble out,' she joked dryly.

'Exactly. We don't want people painting their eighteenth-century colonial in colors not anticipated by the founding fathers.'

'Or worse still,' Ada said, 'vinyl siding.'

'Heaven forbid,' the detective replied. 'So what was your confession?'

'I didn't stay to turn in the jewelry we found the other night. Lillian did it for me the next morning.'

'No harm. We could have handled that better; thank God Kevin thought enough to get chairs. We got a lot of complaints, eighty and ninety year olds waiting for hours; I feel awful about it. So the two of you live in Pilgrim's Progress? If you don't mind me saying, you look kind of young for that.'

'But we do,' I offered. 'Adjoining condos. So did you recover all the jewelry?' I asked, remembering Hank's comment from the other day.

'No,' she admitted, and then quietly added, 'unfortunately.'

'Yes,' said Ada, deftly catching her thread. 'It clouds the motive, doesn't it?'

'How do you figure that?' Mattie asked, her dark – almost black – eyes giving Ada an appraising look.

'If the motive was purely revenge, then giving away all the jewelry makes sense. Pretty creative if you ask me. Mildred Potts – God forgive me for saying this – was a crook . . . I'll get to that,' Ada added, sensing that the detective was about to ask for clarification. 'Anyway, if the majority of the jewelry is not recovered the possible motives are greater. The recovered pieces could be a smoke screen for a crime that was purely profit driven. I'd have to wonder if Mildred might have had one or two large-stone diamonds, or something else of great value that could make all the lovely trinkets pale in comparison. Especially if it was something that could be readily sold.'

'You've given this some thought, Mrs Strauss.'

'It's Ada.'

'Mattie,' offered the detective.

'Well, Mattie,' Ada continued, 'you've probably already gotten this piece of information, but I can't stress how upset people can get if they're being taken advantage of. Personally, if I feel that someone is lying or trying to cheat me, it makes my blood boil. And Mildred was shameless.' Ada recapped the saga of Evie's estate and how Mildred had tried to pay pennies on the dollar. 'Now it is possible,' Ada mused, while buttering a roll, 'that she really didn't know the value of the Childe Hassam painting. But what really gets my goat is the comment she made that Evie had bought it at one of those "starving artist" motel sales. It was too much.'

'Not an honest mistake?' Mattie asked.

'Please, the frame alone is worth a few thousand dollars. Someone who knows nothing about art could tell the picture has value. Mildred knew what she was about . . . Her behavior speaks volumes of her character and business practices. She thought nothing of cheating people. So what do you think about McElroy's murder?' she asked, switching back to the topic that had the town buzzing.

The detective shook her head.

'What is it?' I asked, figuring Mattie to be in her late thirties, maybe early forties.

'It's been a long and gristly morning,' she admitted. 'After I finish here, it's back to work.'

'On a Sunday?' I asked.

'That's the nature of homicide. Even taking lunch isn't something I normally do. I just wanted to clear my head, and also try to get a better sense of this town. You two are actually being quite helpful with that.'

'You just do murders?' Ada asked.

'Yes.'

'That's amazing,' I said, and then I don't know why, but I blurted. 'Not the most girlie of professions.'

'Yeah.' She laughed. 'It's still mostly for the boys, but that's changing.'

'Men get upset,' Ada interjected, 'when we move into territory they think is theirs.'

'Exactly.'

'But, Ada,' I said, 'you managed Strauss' for years.'

'Yes, but Harry got the credit. I was the woman behind the man.'

'Are you talking about the department store?' Mattie asked.

'Yes, although it's no longer Strauss',' Ada explained.

The detective tucked a stray curl behind her ear and looked at Ada. 'My mother used to take us back-to-school shopping at Strauss' in Hartford. That's a blast from the past. She'd have us all wear matching red knit hats so that we wouldn't get lost.'

'Our back-to-school sale,' Ada said, 'was a major event. We'd hire extra security guards. More often than not fights broke out over the silliest things. That and the yearly wedding-gown sale. Both of which, I might add, were my ideas. And I don't mean to sound bitter, but Harry always took the credit.'

'That sucks,' said the detective, and then, with a sheepish smile added, 'sorry.'

'Don't worry,' I assured her. 'We're not as genteel as we look.'

'Yes,' said Ada with a twinkle that warned of an impending pun. 'Some of us aren't gentile at all.'

We all ordered the prime rib with assorted sides. Considering her cholesterol issues I wanted Ada to have the roast chicken, but she would have none of it.

'Pheh,' she said. 'I can have chicken at home, and if a piece of prime rib is going to tip me over the edge, then it's time to go.'

'You don't look like you're ready to go anywhere.' Mattie said. 'In fact you two don't really look like the rest of the residents I was meeting at Pilgrim's Progress. They all seemed much . . .'

'Older?' I offered. 'It's a retirement community, supposedly for the "active adult". At least that was the idea when they developed it some thirty years back.'

'So what happened?' Mattie asked.

'The people who bought in twenty and thirty years ago never left.

And there's a huge difference between a group of people in their mid to late fifties and sixties and those in their eighties, nineties and beyond. So the targeted "active adults" are getting increasingly less active.'

'Interesting, and what happens when someone can't take care of their own place anymore, is there like a nursing home piece?' Mattie asked.

'No,' I explained, 'you're thinking of a life-care facility, or even assisted living.'

'The difference?'

'In a nutshell,' Ada said, 'and I've become something of an expert on the topic, if you get sick at Pilgrim's Progress, you're on your own. In a life-care facility, if you get sick, they move you from your apartment to a nursing home within the complex. Right now I'm thinking about buying into one for my mother, and it is hugely expensive, and on some level I think it's a giant rip off.'

'Local?' she asked.

'It's down the road from Pilgrim's Progress: Nillewaug Village.'

'Is it nice?'

'Very,' Ada said. 'Kind of like a tarted-up nursing home, where people get the illusion of having their own apartment.'

'Do a lot of people move from Pilgrim's Progress to Nillewaug?' Mattie asked.

'A fair number,' I admitted.

The detective stared at her plate, clearly following some inner trail. 'And they can move all their stuff with them?'

'To an extent,' Ada said. 'The apartments are small, so down-sizing is almost a given.'

'Interesting,' Mattie said. 'So how would someone trim down?'

'Are you kidding?' I asked. 'This place is antique central. You have dozens, maybe hundreds of dealers hungry for fresh merchandise. And then there's always McElroy's auction; of course you'd better be in the room for the sale.' I winced as the words left my mouth. 'Of course, now . . . I don't know. Oh, God!'

Mattie caught my gaff, her look was intense. 'McElroy wasn't honest?'

'McElroy has . . . had a bit of a reputation,' Ada interjected. 'I don't know if it was true, but an ounce of prevention . . .'

'So if you were at the auction, there was no way he could underpay you?'

'Exactly.'

'Did many people know this about him?'

'It's endemic,' I said, realizing how little Mattie knew about our local antique industry. I also felt a wave of sadness and loss, not that I particularly liked Carl McElroy, but his auction, which had been started by his father was part of the rhythm and lifeblood of Grenville. 'Auctioneers have a reputation for not being the most scrupulous people. Although I am sure there are exceptions. In some ways, it's one large horse sale, where the message of the day is "buyer beware".'

'And seller beware too, apparently,' Mattie added. 'But other than misrepresenting the merchandise, or out-and-out underpaying the consignor, are there other scams?'

'You have all afternoon?' I asked. 'After a while you pick up on the various games; it's like theater.'

'Give me a for instance.'

'OK, there's something called an auction reserve, and basically that's a price below which the consignor doesn't want to sell their item.'

'That seems fair, sort of a stop-gap.'

'It's perfectly fair, if you tell everyone that there are reserves. But what a number of auctioneers do, including McElroy, is buy back items using plants in the audience if they think the prices are too low. The shills keep bidding until some agreed upon price is reached, and then they stop.'

'How can you know that?' she persisted.

'You get a feel for it. That, and you see an item that supposedly sold the week before going back across the block a couple months later. McElroy would make some lame excuse like the buyer never paid for it, or they wanted to flip it for a quick profit, but you know it's not true. Most of the time he wouldn't say anything.'

'But why do that for some pieces and not for others?'

'That's easy,' I explained. 'If it *was* a consignor's piece, he wouldn't do it; he gets his fifteen or twenty percent cut, regardless. But a lot of times McElroy would gamble with his own money and buy out estates. So he owned the merchandise outright.'

'I see, but wouldn't people get suspicious?'

'I'm sure the dealers knew what was going on, but as long as it was only a small portion of the merchandise, no one would say anything. McElroy was a major supplier. If you raised a fuss, he

might cut you off. Auctions are funny things. There is a lot of
room for *mistakes*. Maybe he didn't see your bid, or maybe he
says, "sold", right as you're trying to get your hand up.'

As we started in on our meals, I could see Mattie mulling the
information. She stared at her thick slab of prime rib and poked
at its center with her knife. I suppressed an urge to tell her not to
play with her food.

'What is it?' I finally asked, thinking how in many ways she
reminded me of my no-nonsense daughter Barbara.

'You said McElroy used plants to buy back merchandise.'

'Yes?'

'You're sure of that?'

'Fairly, but I couldn't say a hundred percent.'

'Who would he use?' she pulled a small spiral notebook from
her back pocket.

Suddenly, I became aware that our table was the focus of much
interest. As I looked around, I caught a number of speculative
looks from the post-church crowd.

'Like I said –' lowering my voice – 'I can't be certain, but there
was something going on with Pete Jeffries and Salvatore Rinaldo.
I couldn't say exactly.'

'Don't forget Rudy,' Ada added.

'Rudy?' Mattie asked.

'Rudy Caputo,' Ada clarified. 'You know he still hasn't gotten
back to me. He was supposed to give me a quote sometime in the
middle of the week.'

'So how was this Rudy involved?' Mattie asked, while scribbling names and bits of ideas.

'Whenever Rudy was at the auction,' Ada explained, 'he would
leave with a good hunk of the furniture.'

'You think he was buying back his own things?'

'No, not that,' she continued. 'But I did wonder if he might
have had some special arrangement with McElroy. In retail, if you
want to beef up your profit margin, buy in bulk. Maybe McElroy
gave him a kickback at the auction . . . or what if Rudy gave him
a percentage of his sales?'

'And you say he hasn't gotten back to you?'

'No,' Ada remarked, a horrified look on her face. 'You don't
think . . .? Oh, God! First that Potts woman and then . . .'

'I don't know,' Mattie commented and then pushed back from

the table. 'Ada, Lillian, I've really enjoyed meeting both of you, but I should get back to work.'

'You've barely touched your meal,' Ada protested.

'I don't seem to have much of an appetite.'

'Occupational hazard?' I asked, finding that the bloody slab of meat in the center of my plate was looking less and less attractive.

She pulled out her wallet and left a twenty under her plate. 'That should cover it.'

'Don't be silly,' I said. 'We'll take care of it.'

'I can't do that,' said Mattie. 'You two have been very helpful. Would it be OK if I called on you if I had any questions? And please, call me immediately if Mr Caputo calls.'

'Of course,' Ada said, speaking for us both.

'I'd appreciate it,' she said, her voice low. 'I find myself on the outskirts here.'

'Grenville is very pretty,' I said, matching my tone to hers. 'But don't let that fool you. There's a lot below the surface, and we tend to be careful around strangers.'

After Mattie left, we had them doggy bag our mostly uneaten entrées, and ordered crème brûlée and tea.

'Nice woman, Hispanic, I think.' Ada commented, while breaking the caramel topping. 'No wedding ring, either. I wonder if she's out of her element in Grenville.'

I was about to respond, when I noticed a look of consternation on Ada's face. 'What's wrong?'

'Oh no,' she muttered while twisting up the right side of her mouth.

'What?'

'I don't believe I just did that.' She produced something small and white on the tip of her tongue.

'A tooth?' I asked.

'No, I should know better than to eat caramel; it's a cap.' She put her hand to the side of her face, 'and now I've got a little nub in there that in any second will start throbbing.'

'We need to get you to a dentist.'

'On a Sunday, good luck. I'll take a couple aspirin and see someone tomorrow.' She examined the porcelain cap in the palm of her hand. 'At least it seems intact. Maybe they can just glue it back. Ow!' She winced. 'There it goes.' And she pressed her ice-water glass to the side of her mouth.

SIXTEEN

I t was clear that Ada was in terrible pain, so halfway to Pilgrim's Progress I made a U-turn and headed back to town. I felt guilty knocking on Calvin Williams' door without at least calling. That, and for the past few years I'd been going to the *Happy Tooth Center* which had an office in Pilgrim's Progress.

The graying dentist, who was six years my junior, came to the door dressed in jeans and a flannel work shirt, his hands covered with dark smudges. 'Lillian Campbell, you're a sight for sore eyes. You look great.'

'Thanks Calvin,' I said, not wanting to divulge that I'd changed dentists.

He looked at Ada, who was holding her hand to her right cheek. 'Not a social visit, I see,' he said, and his smile faltered.

'No, she pulled off a cap.'

'Taffy?' he asked, leading us down the walkway of his Main Street colonial, which had been in his family for many generations, toward the addition that held his dental offices.

Ada lisped, 'Caramel.'

'Terrible stuff,' he commented, and turned back. He gave me an odd look, and shook his head slightly. 'It's the strangest thing Lil, I look at you and I can still see the fourteen-year-old girl who used to take care of me. Let me grab my keys, and I'll be right with you.'

'Nice man,' Ada commented.

'Very,' I agreed. 'I used to babysit for him.'

'I think he's got a crush on you,' she commented.

'Unlikely,' I said, wondering at her comment, and praying she didn't know just how wrong that statement was. It wasn't Calvin, who'd been like a little brother to me, who had the crush; it was me. And everything about that was wrong.

He reappeared wiping his hands with a blue-checked dishtowel. 'Let's take a look.'

We trailed behind as he unlocked and let us in. Things looked much the way I remembered, the orange and red chairs in the waiting room, the piles of magazines and the chest of toys for children. But something was different, and at first I couldn't place it.

'Times sure change,' he commented wistfully as he led us to the treatment rooms.

'How so?' I asked.

'I rarely come back here anymore.'

And that's when I remembered, and felt even guiltier about our surprise visit. 'You closed your practice?' I could have kicked myself; I'd forgotten the mailers that he'd sent following the death of his mother. 'I must be getting Alzheimer's. I totally blanked out that you closed the practice.' The moment I said that, I could have shot myself, remembering that his mother had Alzheimer's, and how he'd taken care of her for many years.

'No harm, and it's not like I'm retired; too young and too poor for that. I do a concierge business to a number of the local nursing homes and to Nillewaug Village. It's just me and a hygienist making the rounds. The overhead is minimal and I don't have to deal with the billing and the insurance; it's so much easier.' He turned on the gooseneck lamp and shone it inside Ada's mouth. He flicked down his magnifying glasses. 'Hmm, the stub looks OK. Are you in much pain?' he asked, stuffing her cheek with cotton.

'A little,' she mumbled. 'A lot if I touch it.'

'Then don't touch it,' he joked. 'That's the nerve. We don't have to drill, just epoxy it back.'

'Oh good.'

'So how's life in Pilgrim's Progress?' he asked, while mixing adhesive.

'Different,' I said.

'I sometimes think about going there myself in a few years, but the thought of moving completely overwhelms me.'

'Your family's been in this house a long time,' I added.

'Eleven generations, and I'm the last.'

'No kids?' Ada mumbled.

'Nope, never went that route. When I go, the historical society can have the house; if they want it. Bite down,' he instructed, 'and hold for sixty seconds.'

I had such déjà vu, sitting next to him. Like all those times I'd fill in for Bradley's nurse and assisted with patients. Even the mention of billing and insurance, the paperwork nightmare that drove Bradley to close his practice. How many times did I have to fight with some faceless reviewer to get approval for a needed procedure or medication for one of his patients? Often spending whole afternoons faxing and phoning to finally be told, 'No, we don't cover that.' Or else them insisting Bradley talk to their physician reviewer to plead his patient's case for a critical, but expensive, medication. Each time they'd said 'no' I could see his rage, his frustration.

'Open.' He placed a small piece of gauze between her upper and lower teeth. 'Now rub gently back and forth. How does that feel?'

'Like it's in place.'

'Good.'

'I can't thank you enough Doctor Williams,' Ada gushed.

'Don't mention it, and the name is Calvin.'

'I thought I was going to be stuck with a throbbing tooth and I can't stand painkillers,' she added, reaching for her purse.

He held out his hand and shook his head. 'This one's on the house.'

'I have to pay you,' Ada argued.

'No,' he said. 'Lil and I go way back.' He would have said more, but a phone rang in the outer office. 'I'll be right back.'

Ada looked at me. 'What a lovely man. And didn't they stop making that particular model? We should invite him to dinner.'

I started tearing up, and couldn't quite figure out why.

'What is it, Lil?' Ada asked.

'I'm not sure. No, that's not true.' I looked around at Calvin's treatment room. It was clear that it had fallen behind the times, but something about it was familiar and wonderful, like Bradley's examination room. 'It's all going, everything that I took for granted is all slipping away.' But there was more, and I was too frightened to give voice. Like yes, I should invite Calvin to dinner, but why would she suggest that, and why would she think he's interested in me? That was not the relationship I wanted.

'Things change,' she remarked. 'They have to.'

Calvin reappeared in the doorway. 'The old town just ain't what it used to be,' he commented wryly.

'What?' I asked.

'That Simpson boy has gotten to be a real pain.'

'Kevin?'

'Yeah, he's after me to dig out some ancient dental records.'

'On whom?' Ada asked.

'Philip Conroy.'

'Why?' I asked. 'I thought they only did that if they didn't know the identity.'

'I guess the body was in pretty bad shape and they want something additional,' he replied. 'All I know is that it's going to take forever. My last assistant was alphabetically handicapped. Unfortunately, I didn't discover it until after the damage was done.'

'Maybe Lil could help you straighten them out; she certainly knows her way around a doctor's office,' Ada offered.

'Could you?' he asked, meeting my gaze.

'Of course,' I said, not knowing what else to say, and wishing that Ada hadn't made the offer.

'You know, I might take you up on that.'

SEVENTEEN

Mattie Perez, wearing purple nitrile gloves stared at the neatly bagged and tagged evidence spread across Hank Morgan's desk. Kevin Simpson looked on from the door, being told by Mattie – not for the first time – to touch nothing. Even so, she'd made him put on gloves.

She softened her gaze and let her mind roam. Her conversation yesterday with the two local women, Lil and Ada, had sparked new possibilities and new concerns.

'It's a real mystery,' Kevin offered. 'Hank says that's rare, that most of the time it's pretty obvious who killed who.'

Please shut up, she thought, wishing she were alone. But she had enough bad cases under her belt to know that it's always best to examine evidence with at least two people in the room. That way if anyone alleges that it's been tampered with you can verify the chain of custody was never compromised. And this was one case where nothing could go wrong. She pictured her boss, Sergeant Ted MacDonald, pot bellied, arrogant and clear on his views about women detectives; he didn't like them. And he would love an excuse – like a high-profile case gone south – to put her in her place.

'What am I missing?' she muttered. 'These murders are deliberate, planned, careful.' But just when she thought the road was clear, some new twist emerged. The jewelry was a case in point; where was the rest of it?

'Hank said Carl had been "gutted like a fish",' Kevin said enthusiastically.

'True,' Mattie said, never taking her eyes off the table of evidence, and saying a silent prayer that the swarms of journalists and news crews now flocking to Grenville would not get wind of the gruesome details of McElroy's murder. Like pieces in a puzzle, bullets removed from victims, McElroy's ledgers and customer databases, photos of the bodies and Conroy's finger, autopsy reports, dental reports, recovered jewelry. 'What am I missing?' Her gaze fell on the blood-smeared auction paddles that had been embedded in McElroy's gut.

'Whoever killed McElroy,' she said, 'wanted us to see his scams. The killer – or killers – wasn't subtle; the falsified ledgers, Carl's files filled with the names of local dealers and attorneys . . . There are connections here, Kevin.' She imagined Lil and Ada might know, or at least help her make connections. 'He was in no hurry.'

'Why couldn't it be a woman?' Kevin asked.

'Sure.' His well-intentioned comments were making it hard to focus. *Mattie, you need him, hold your tongue.* 'But over ninety percent of murders are committed by men. It's "he", until proven otherwise. According to Arvin's autopsy, cause of death was the gunshot wound, all of this other stuff . . . Somebody is making a point.' *Listen Mattie, the killer is trying to talk to you, what's he saying?* She examined the three gruesome wooden auction paddles that had been tipped with razor blades; the killer had used them like box cutters to flay the auctioneer. It was creative, and horrifying, and told her a number of important things. People in general have an aversion to cutting human flesh, clearly the killer did not, and beyond that had some understanding of human anatomy. The last a bit of insight from the ME who'd commented on how some of the cuts had separated layers of muscle from connective tissue; this was no random hack job.

When she'd compared the numbers on the paddles with last

night's bidder list, they had belonged to Pete Jeffries and Salvatore Rinaldo. 'Murder by number,' she muttered, uneasy with the killer's flourishes; too big, too careless. It made her think of past cases, like Malcolm Blade, a serial sex killer who took out crack addicts in the Frog's Hollow section of Hartford. He, too, had left his calling card, in his case elaborate burn marks on the bodies. But what made her uneasy about the connection was Malcolm's desire to be caught, and to be mowed down in a shooting match with the cops. Perps who didn't want to get caught didn't leave these many clues. While she never associated good mental health with murderers, there was something frightfully unbalanced and reckless in these killings.

'Crap,' she exclaimed, her frustration mounting, and with it a sick feeling of being led by the nose. 'The third paddle – number one hundred and eighteen – hadn't been issued last night.' She looked at Kevin. 'I went back through the records; that one always goes to Rudy Caputo.' He was the dealer who hadn't returned Ada's calls. 'How come he gets the same number every week, no one else does?'

'No clue,' Kevin said, edging closer to the table.

'Three dead dealers, all high-end, high-volume traders. Is someone bumping off the competition? There seem to be enough replacements around. So unless someone is planning a bloodbath through Grenville's hundreds of dealers, it's got to be something else.'

'Like what?' Kevin asked.

'The thing I can't ignore,' she said, thinking of the conversation with Lil and Ada, 'is that the three of them, McElroy, Potts and Conroy, were guilty of a variety of scams, or at the very least could be accused of having taken advantage of people who didn't know what their things were worth. What if they'd cheated the wrong person?'

'So payback.'

'Yeah, but there's something more. I can't figure it out and it's driving me up a fucking wall. Like these connections between Pilgrim's Progress, Nillewaug Village and the antique shops. I keep picturing all of these old people being sucked dry of their possessions and their nest eggs by the dealers, lawyers and real estate agents.' She thought of the mostly silver-haired patrons, mostly women, who had filled the dining room of The Greenery.

They were, she knew, the lucky ones. Not like her diabetic mother in a Bridgeport nursing home that smelled of piss. She was dying in stages, losing toes, her eyesight, and finally her mind. It was a modern nightmare, the decision to place her mom was the hardest she'd ever made. But even with a visiting nurse coming twice a day she couldn't manage the constant care, the gaping bedsores that never healed, her mother at the point where she could no longer remember how to handle a fork, or go to the bathroom.

'Wait a minute!' she said.

'What?'

'How could I have missed this?' A moment's clarity.

'What are you thinking? What do you see?' Kevin asked excitedly.

She stared at the paddles and then at McElroy's ledgers. 'Each of these retirees has a cash value; each of them worth hundreds of thousands maybe millions. Way too much money to go unnoticed. What if . . .' She thought back to the conversation with Ada and Lil. *There's a rhythm to all this, like water circling the drain . . . A house in Grenville, then the move to Pilgrim's Progress and finally . . .*

Her gloved fingers flipped through the printout of Carl's consigner database, looking at the addresses and circling names.

'What you doing?' Kevin asked.

And for some reason, she didn't want to say. Maybe it was because Kevin was so comfortable in his community where she felt so outside; he'd given her no cause to distrust him. Still . . . 'Kevin let's get this signed back into the evidence room. I have something I need to do.'

'You want company?'

'Thanks, but no. It's something personal. Keep trying to track down Sal, Pete and Rudy. If you make any contact call me immediately.'

'No prob.'

'Thanks.' As soon as she was alone, she pulled out her cell and made a call to her boss, Sergeant MacDonald. While there was no love lost between the two, Mattie knew that this case was blowing up fast. Keeping her tone neutral and just stating the facts, she laid out her investigation thus far. And then added, 'The three dealers who've not been located, Caputo, Jeffries and Renaldo. The locals are on it, but I've a bad feeling.'

MacDonald's response: 'If you're talking search teams and dogs, I'll need more than a *"feeling"*.'

Not rising to the bait, Mattie briefed her boss on efforts thus far to locate the men, all three of whom lived alone.

'Sketchy. Sounds like they're just on the road, or off on a bender.'

'Then why don't they answer their cells?' she asked, feeling the familiar frustration of trying to reason with Sergeant MacDonald.

'It's too soon.' He was clearly annoyed, but a hint of uncertainty in his tone. 'Tell you what, I'll give you Foster and Daniels. If those three are still missing in twenty-four hours we'll talk again.' And he hung up.

Mattie felt the familiar frustration she got when talking with MacDonald. It wasn't just his dismissiveness and obvious dislike for her, it ran deeper; the man was out to get her. With three murders and three potential victims unaccounted for she had a very bad feeling. And while she hated to think this way, it was impossible not to. If in fact anything had happened to any of those three men, the blame would land fully on her. Realizing this, and hating the necessity for her next passive-aggressive cover-your-ass move, she rapidly typed an email back to Sergeant MacDonald, respectfully disagreeing with his decision not to proceed with a more aggressive search for the missing men. Picturing how pissed off receiving it would make him, she paused, tried to think of a good reason not to send it, and then pressed send.

EIGHTEEN

Less than half an hour later Mattie found herself staring into a lit display of handicrafts; knitted boas with pulled stitches, painted green-ware mugs, and a few blotchy still lifes, made by Nillewaug residents. She turned at the clicking of heels on slate. 'Ms Preston?' she asked, making dozens of rapid observations as the perfectly coiffed green-suited administrator approached.

'How do you do?' Delia said, hand extended, nails manicured almond-shaped and lacquered in burnt orange. 'But please, call me Delia.'

'I'm Detective Perez with the state's Major Crime Squad.'

'Yes, you mentioned you had some questions; we should go to my office.'

'Good,' Mattie said stiffly as she took in Preston's coiffed blonde up-do, and full make up. The detective's silence was deliberate as she contrasted her own navy suit and turtleneck – no make-up – to this administrator's foundation-to-blush war paint. It was like a mask concealing Preston's age, which she guessed at being anywhere between late thirties to mid forties.

Delia Preston prattled to fill the void. 'Most of our residents are in classes right now. We offer a broad array.' She paused for the detective to say something. When she didn't, she resumed the sales-pitch patter. 'We have two full-time activities therapists, an occupational therapist and a staff of social workers. And of course –' she turned to face the detective outside the door of her office – 'we offer a full spectrum of nursing services.'

Mattie half listened as she compared Nillewaug to the nursing home her mother was in. *Worlds apart.* Feeling pangs of guilt and heartsickness as she looked out on sweeping views of well-maintained grounds and gently graded walking paths; all with handrails and dotted with benches. 'It's lovely,' the detective admitted. 'I imagine it's quite expensive.' *Could I ever afford something like this?*

'Quality costs,' the director responded as she ushered Mattie into her lushly appointed fourth floor office.

'How expensive?' Mattie asked, taking in the tufted leather, Berber carpet, and brocade window treatments that framed a stunning view of a man-made pond.

'There's a monthly fee, it starts at three thousand and goes up,' Delia explained, settling behind her gleaming mahogany desk.

'That doesn't seem bad,' Mattie commented, remembering that it had cost far more than that for her mother's nursing home. It had eaten through her Mom's meager savings, and then she'd had to sell the house, and when that was gone, she went on Medicaid.

'The monthly fee is for day-to-day operations, including very good meals. The biggest expense is the buy-in fee.'

'How much does that run?'

'It varies, but somewhere in the neighborhood of two hundred and fifty to five hundred thousand for our deluxe two-bedroom units.'

'It doesn't surprise me,' Mattie said, taking the lower figure, dividing by four and coming up with something close to what the nursing home had charged her mother, and now billed Medicaid, on a yearly basis.

The director beamed. 'A lot of people don't understand that. Many older people get sticker shock when they hear it.'

'How many residents do you have?'

'Over six hundred in independent living, maybe forty of those are couples. We have approximately ten female residents for every male. Then we have an additional fifty in our Safe Harbor Alzheimer's and Dementia unit and fifty skilled and rehab in the Maple Creek building.'

'Skilled?'

'Full care; both of those units are licensed nursing homes, although we shy away from that term.'

'It's something of a gamble, isn't it?' the detective asked, lobbing a deliberately vague question.

'Gamble?'

'Nursing home care is quite expensive, isn't it? If someone were to come to Nillewaug and have a protracted illness, wouldn't that be a drain on your resources?'

'That can happen,' the director commented.

'How can you avoid it?'

'We screen all prospective residents.'

'I assume that's legal,' Mattie commented, 'or you wouldn't be telling me.'

'Perfectly legal. Our admissions criteria clearly state that upon entry to Nillewaug the individual must be able to provide most of their self-care needs. We do of course make exceptions on a case-by-case basis. What happens down the line is harder to predict.'

'So a person with advanced diabetes?' She asked, wondering what would lead Delia to make exceptions. The answer that popped to mind: *money*.

'We don't like to go into the details. But if they couldn't maintain their self-care, probably not.'

'What about Alzheimer's?'

'We try to screen that out.'

'Isn't that hard?'

'Extremely, particularly in the over-eighty group. It's just a fact of the business and why we make a commitment to our residents who do go on to develop Alzheimer's or another dementia. Our

Safe Harbor Pavilion is state of the art.' She made a sweeping motion toward a shelving unit that contained rows of plaques and awards. 'We've been written up extensively as a best-practice model, and three years in a row have been voted top skilled nursing facility in New England.'

'Impressive,' Mattie replied, having the strange sense that Delia was feeling her out, as though she were a prospective buyer. 'What happens when you run out of beds?'

'That's never happened.'

'What if it did?'

'Obviously, we would have to make some sort of arrangement. But we're well prepared for most contingencies.'

'Such as?'

'Maybe move someone to a less restrictive setting with an increase in supervision.'

'Like an aide?'

'Exactly. Expensive, but when we have to do it, we can and do.'

'So where do most of your residents come from?' Mattie shifted to what she hoped would be a richer vein.

'All over the country.'

'And locally?'

'Of course. The majority of our residents come from the tri-state area.'

'What about Pilgrim's Progress?' Mattie asked, not leaving Preston time between questions.

'Some.'

'How many?'

The director hesitated before answering, 'Forty percent.'

'Why so high?'

'Location. It's less disruptive to move somewhere that's close.'

'It must be nice to have such a large built-in referral source. Which came first,' Mattie asked, 'Pilgrim's Progress or Nillewaug Village?'

'Pilgrim's Progress is much older. Nillewaug is only in its tenth year.'

'Really? Any relation to Pilgrim's Progress? I mean other than the proximity and that half of your residents come from there?'

'Forty percent,' the director corrected. She paused. 'You have to remember that we're very different.'

'I can see that, but that's not what I asked. Are there connections . . . business connections . . . between the two?'

'No.'

Mattie sensed Preston holding back. 'Really?'

'Almost not worth mentioning.'

'Try me.'

The director leaned back in her leather chair and folded her manicured fingers together. 'I think some of the Nillewaug investors also put money into Pilgrim's Progress. But as corporate entities they're entirely separate.'

'What about the respective boards of directors? Any members sit on both?'

'I don't know for certain,' Preston said. 'It's possible. I have nothing to do with Pilgrim's Progress, so I really wouldn't know.'

Mattie noted how Preston seemed uncomfortable with this line of inquiry, and made a mental note to pull the charters and annual corporate filings for both Pilgrim's Progress and Nillewaug. 'You're not on the board at Nillewaug?' she asked.

'No, I report to the CEO; it's a very small executive team and because we're a for-profit they also serve as the board.'

'And who is the CEO?'

Preston winced. 'If I tell you, I assume you're going to want to speak with him.'

'Correct.'

'Is there any way that could be avoided?'

'Probably not, but why should that matter?'

The director picked up a black-and-gold Montblanc pen and fidgeted with the cap. She looked across at the detective. 'I know you have your job to do, but so do I, and a lot of what I'm supposed to do is take care of problems. By and large my boss doesn't want to be involved in the day-to-day situations that arise. He leaves that to me.'

'In other words, it won't look good.'

'Yes. I'm not certain what you're trying to find, or how talking to my employer would help you.'

Mattie did not want to admit that she wasn't at all certain where this would lead. Still, the connections opened up a number of possibilities, and 'when in doubt', her first mentor in the department had told her, 'follow the money'. 'His name?'

'You're putting me in a difficult situation.'

'Murder investigations do that.'

'I don't see what Nillewaug has to do with the murders. Let me talk to him first,' she said. 'If you call him out of the blue it will look like I wasn't doing my job.'

'Which is to run interference? Look, Ms Preston, I don't have a lot of time and even less patience. If you want to call him, do it now.'

'I see. Would you at least leave the room while I call?'

'I'll be outside.' Mattie got to her feet. 'Don't keep me waiting.'

As Mattie stood in the hallway looking out the picture window, she strained to hear Delia's conversation.

'Excuse me.' An elfin nonagenarian, in a powder-blue sweater suit, tapped Mattie's arm. 'Is this my street?' the woman asked, tugging at her sleeve.

'What street are you looking for?' Mattie asked, wondering if 'street' was a Nillewaug euphemism for hall or floor.

'Oh you know.' The woman's face broke into a broad, chip-toothed smile and she began to sing as she moved down the hall, 'On the rocky road to Dublin. I met my true love. His name was Tommy. He was my true love . . .'

As the woman ambled away, Mattie's gaze fell upon an electronic bracelet around her ankle. It reminded her of a convict on homebound. Increasingly, she realized that Grenville's chief industry wasn't antiques; it was old people. The seven hundred-plus residents of this facility alone represented hundreds of millions of dollars; it was simple math. Each one of them a cash cow at the end of their lives ready to be milked, bilked . . . and possibly worse. But something didn't quite jibe with the story Preston had just told her. *What's someone who's clearly demented doing in this building? Shouldn't she be in that Alzheimer's Unit?*

Delia's door opened. 'I hope this makes you happy,' Preston said, thrusting a business card at the detective. Her cheeks were flushed beneath her foundation. 'He'll be expecting your call. And if you don't need anything further . . .'

'That should be all . . . for now,' said Mattie, looking down the hall to where the old woman had disappeared from sight. 'Thank you.' And before she could formulate a question about the woman with the ankle bracelet, a visibly shaken Delia Preston had shut her door.

NINETEEN

L ike pulling teeth, Mattie thought as she sat outside Nillewaug
in her state-issue unmarked and aging Crown Victoria and
studied the card Preston had given her. No reason for things
to be this hard. It made her deeply suspicious, but what if this was
a dead end? With the body count escalating, time – that most
precious of commodities – couldn't be wasted. *But this could be
completely unrelated.* 'Something stinks,' she said out loud, and
she pulled for facts to back up her gut. There was something
complicit between Nillewaug and Pilgrim's Progress and whatever
games the local antique dealers were playing. She pulled out her
cell phone and dialed. 'Hank, it's Mattie Perez.'

His voice was cheerful. 'How's it going?'

'Not bad. I've been following some leads at Nillewaug Village.
Did you know forty percent of the residents here came from
Pilgrim's Progress? And another third from Grenville?'

Moments ticked. 'That and a bunch of other stuff. What's the
point?'

'I'm not certain,' she said, her resolve wavering. 'But the
murders keep sending me back to Pilgrim and Nillewaug. At times
I think the murderer does too.'

'The jewelry bit?'

'Yes. The night McElroy was murdered he had just auctioned
off the estate of a Nillewaug resident, did you know that? Or that
a good portion of Mildred Potts' inventory came from Pilgrim and
Nillewaug?'

'You could be clutching. So what was it you wanted to ask?'

'Hank, there's a connection, but I have to be able to look around.
That seems hard to do.'

'What are you getting at?'

Mattie related her session with Delia Preston.

'So she gave you Jim Warren's name?'

'You know him?'

'Of course.'

'Then why the hush hush?'

'Probably what the woman said. Preston's a single mom with a son in college; she doesn't want you bothering the man who signs her paycheck.'

'What do you think?' she asked, realizing she might have misjudged Delia, and knowing first hand what it's like to be the sole support of a family.

'Jim Warren's sharp. He's the most expensive lawyer in town. You won't get much from him.'

'You think this is a dead end.'

He paused. 'I don't know if it's where I'd put a lot of effort.'

'Why?' suddenly annoyed, realizing at the end of the day Hank's loyalties fell in step with his town.

'Mattie, in Grenville, you got to watch whose toes you step on. It's not Hartford or New Haven; it's a small town where everybody knows everybody's business.'

'You telling me to pull back?'

'Nah, you got to go where your gut tells you. Just be careful.'

'Of toes?'

'Yeah.' He chuckled. 'People around here got lots of 'em.'

'You want to come with me when I talk to Mr Warren?'

'What about Kevin? He's got toes too. He kind of figures you've been leaving him in the dust.'

'It's just . . .'

'I know, but people like him, and frankly, you could use the social lubricant.'

'You want me to take him?'

'Couldn't hurt. Anything else come up?'

'Not yet,' she said, feeling like a rookie who's just been chastised. 'I'm waiting for forensics. They told me there was talc residue on the paddles so it seems like the killer was wearing disposable gloves. Of course, around here every other store is a pharmacy or medical supply shop, so it's not the most robust lead.'

'Welcome to Grenville,' he commented dryly. 'Old folks and antiques.'

'Although,' she said, using Hank as a sounding board, 'there could be something with the gloves. We all had to change from latex to these funky purple ones a few years back, because some people had allergic reactions.'

'Same here. What's the point?'

'It could be nothing, but the new ones don't have talc. Do me a favor and see if they're still selling latex with talc, if not our killer is using old gloves.'

'I'll make a couple calls, you're right it could be something . . .' His voice trailed. 'Not a big something.'

'I know, but at this point I'll take anything.'

After they hung up she dialed another number.

'Mrs Strauss?'

'Yes.'

'This is Mattie Perez.'

'Well hello, Mattie,' Ada said, sounding pleased.

'I had a couple questions about things you and Mrs Campbell had said at lunch yesterday.'

'Fire away, dear. Oops, could you hold on one minute while I get my tea?'

'No problem.'

Mattie cradled the phone and heard the whistling teakettle. There was something comfortable in the clatter of crockery and the hollow whoosh of a cookie tin opening.

'Sorry about that,' Ada said. 'You had some questions?'

'Right, they have to do with the woman's estate you're liquidating.'

'Evie's, Evie Henderson.'

'You said that Mildred Potts had given you an estimate and also Tolliver Jacobs.'

'That's right and I got a third from Mr Caputo.'

Mattie felt her breath catch. 'You mentioned him at lunch.'

'Yes, although he hasn't returned my calls.'

Mattie again got that sick feeling about Rudy Caputo, as well as the other two men whose auction paddles had been used to flay open McElroy's gut. Hunting them down had been the sole task she'd handed off to her grudgingly provided reinforcements. 'How did you get the names for the dealers you picked?'

'Some I got from the Grenville Antique Association website, others I got from Evie's attorney.'

'Mr Warren?'

'You've been doing your homework, which I suspect my grandson who's sneaking out the door as we speak, has not. Excuse me.'

Mattie eavesdropped as Ada interrogated her grandson.

'Aaron, where are you going?'

'To the mall.'

'Homework done?'

'Mostly.'

'You know that if your schoolwork goes down, there's no way your mom and dad will let you stay here.'

'I'll do it; I promise. I made plans to meet a couple friends at the mall.'

'I suppose . . . Just be back for dinner.'

'Is Lil coming?' he asked.

'She should.'

'Can we have Chinese?'

'You're getting too used to this, but yes, and yes I'll order the moo shoo.' Ada turned back to the detective. 'I just don't know what I'm doing,' she admitted.

'He sounds like a nice kid,' Mattie offered.

'He's a gem,' Ada boasted. 'I just think it's hard for kids these days. Or harder in a different way from when I grew up. Back then you kind of knew what was expected of you. Now it's all so confusing.'

'Do you mind if I ask you something personal?'

'Not at all.'

'Why isn't he with his parents?'

'My son-in-law and he aren't on speaking terms, it seems.'

'Big fight?'

'A whopper, which reminds me that I should give my daughter a call. I'm still not certain what's going on.'

'In my experience,' Mattie offered, 'and before homicide I worked domestic violence, there are only a few reasons why kids leave home . . . or get pushed out. You want to hear them?'

'Please.'

'Let's get rid of the ugly ones first,' the detective began. 'Sexual and physical abuse are two of the major causes for runaways.'

'No,' Ada said. 'Although . . .'

'Although?'

'As much as I might not care for my son-in-law, I can't believe he's responsible for Aaron's black eye, and Aaron adamantly denies that his father hit him.'

'You know what they say about denial?' Mattie commented.

'Yes, it's a big river in Egypt.'

'As long as you know that. Then comes drugs. Any sense that

he's stoned or high? Any clues like red-rimmed eyes, slurred speech, grades taking a nosedive or tickets for driving under the influence?'

'No, that's not it; at least I haven't seen anything, and Susan – that's my daughter – hasn't mentioned it.'

'Well, that leaves the third one which has to do with sex. Any chance he got somebody pregnant?'

'No.'

'Is he gay?'

Ada paused. 'Bingo.'

'And you're OK with that?'

'He's my grandson. I'd love him if he were an axe murderer. God, that's so politically incorrect going from gay to axe murderer. I don't know if he is gay, and I don't think it makes a difference, although . . .'

'What?'

'I sometimes think Aaron's more than just a grandson. After Susan had him she went back to school; I'd take care of him and his sister in the afternoons. This is probably more information than you want from a relative stranger, and you'll think I'm a nut case, but I believe that there's a purpose why he's in my life and I'm in his. If he's gay, or dealing with something else, I don't think it's going to be his parents – certainly not his father – who are going to be there for him.'

'He's lucky to have you.'

'That's kind of you, but I still feel out of my element.' There was more Ada wanted to add, but realized Mattie was truly a stranger.

'I don't think you need to do much. Just listen and set a few limits. It sounds like he may not have been getting a whole lot of support at home.'

'My son-in-law is a piece of work,' Ada blurted angrily, remembering how hurt and furious she'd been as Jack had essentially banished her from their home, not liking her politics, or that unlike her daughter, Ada would not hold her tongue. He'd made it clear that he felt she was corrupting his children, and it was only his views that were welcome around the table.

'That puts you in a weird position.'

'Mattie,' Ada asked, 'I know you're probably very busy but would you like to join us for dinner?'

She hesitated, having been at this boundary many times over the course of her career. She remembered something her first partner, the now retired Dan Malvoy had told her: '*It's OK to get friendly but not be friends, because today's informant can be tomorrow's perp . . . or corpse.*' Still this town was hard to crack and Lil Campbell in particular had the inside track. With her thoughts zipping fast she realized it was unlikely that either of these women were responsible for the murders, which left the other half of Dan's truism. 'Love to,' she said. Part of her was simply eager for a meal away from her too-cute hotel room at the Grenville Inn, but she also realized that she'd get more information over dinner than in a taped interview at the local police department.

'Let me give you directions. I hope you like Chinese, as with few exceptions I'm a famously bad cook.'

The detective laughed. 'I love Chinese.'

TWENTY

'I got a job,' I told Ada, unable to contain my enthusiasm, and a bit apprehensive, as well.

'What? Lil, I had no idea you were looking,' Ada responded while putting out napkins and her good sterling flatware.

'I wasn't,' I admitted, glad for these moments alone with her. There was so much I wanted to say, and wasn't sure how it would come out. 'I just thought that if you were serious about maybe going back to New York, I needed to find something for myself.' There was this pressure building, and before I could stop myself, 'I don't want you to leave. I know it's selfish. I know family has to come first, but I don't want you to go.'

'I didn't realize.' She looked up, and our eyes connected.

It felt like time was suspended. I desperately wanted to go to her, to hold her . . . kiss her. But fear held me to the spot.

The silence was broken by her: 'Do you think anyone would mind if I left the food in the cardboard containers?'

'No,' I said, realizing that what I felt must never be voiced, that to do so would be to lose the best friend I'd ever had. 'It's fine, less to wash.'

'So tell me about this job. Are you planning to take up Calvin on his offer?'

'No.' I was annoyed that she'd even bring that up. 'You know the new multi-dealer shop that opened at the end of Town Plot?'

'Of course.'

'I'm going to work there four half-days a week.'

Her response was not what I wanted or expected. 'Have you lost your *mind*? Doing what?'

'I'm not entirely certain.' Noting real alarm in her eyes as she stared slack jawed. 'And yes, I'm aware the antique industry in Grenville may not be the safest at the moment. But this job has nothing to do with any of that. It's a lot of showing people things inside the cases, ringing up sales. It sounds easy, and not the kind of thing to get me killed.' I knew I wasn't being honest, but how to admit that part of this move came from morbid curiosity. But deeper, and hard to articulate. Grenville was my town, and someone was messing with it. I needed to understand why and who.

'Lil, I'll say it again. Are you out of your mind?'

'You don't sound exactly thrilled for me.'

'No, really, I think it's great.' Her tone was sarcastic. 'But do you think with all these murders that a job in an antique shop is safe? If anything happened to you . . .'

'Oh please, you know as well as I do that they're not killing the lowly shop girl.'

'That's the job title?'

'Yes,' I said, feeling an ache in my chest as the doorbell rang, and wishing she didn't look so worried. 'Lillian Campbell,' I continued, keeping my tone light, 'shop girl. It has a certain . . .'

'Yes, I'm sure it does. Can you carry a gun?' she retorted.

'You're over-reacting. Let me get the door?' And I let in Mattie Perez who stood holding a bottle of wine, dressed in a navy suit over a gray turtle neck. Her tightly curled hair reminding me of the very first Barbie dolls, but the analogy going no further with the compact woman with her intense eyes and thick brows.

'Someone trained you well,' I remarked, relieving her of the Zinfandel.

Ada yelled in the background, 'Aaron, supper.'

'It smells great,' Mattie commented as I showed her into the dining room. 'Your home is lovely,' she said to Ada, taking in the gleaming mahogany and her array of iridescent backlit art glass.

'Thank you.'

'Tiffany?' the detective asked as she examined a shelf of free-form vases and bowls.

'Good eye,' Ada commented. 'Grenville's starting to wear off.'

'And these?' she asked moving to a display of delicate glass covered with a meshwork of filigree.

'Loetz,' Ada instructed. 'They're from Bohemia. Used to be cheap. I don't think I ever paid more than forty dollars when I bought them.'

'Ada,' I interrupted, 'that was in the seventies.'

'Time flies.' She shook her head at me, clearly not over my revelation about the new job.

'Is it rude to ask what they're worth?'

'Of course not.' Ada turned back to Mattie. 'That's the fun. The small pieces probably run around a thousand each and they go up from there.'

'Based on size?' the detective asked.

I couldn't stop myself. 'Yes, with glass and ceramics size does matter.'

'Lillian, don't be crude,' Ada scolded. 'They don't like that in lowly shop girls. She got a job,' Ada added by way of explanation. 'And where is my grandson? Aaron Michael. Supper! Now!'

'You got a job?' Mattie asked, still perusing the glittering art glass.

'Nothing earth shattering,' I admitted, wishing Ada would just let this drop, and feeling a resistance to telling this detective about it. 'It's more to keep me busy than anything else.'

'Shop girl?'

'Ada's making fun. I'm going to be a floor person at the Grenville Antique Center.'

'The big shop on the green?' The detective gave me a searching look. 'Kind of an odd choice, isn't it?'

'Thank you,' Ada said. 'Why on earth someone would deliberately take a job where—'

'Enough,' I said, feeling the color rise in my cheeks. 'It's a multi-dealer setup and they're forever advertising for help.'

'Multi-dealer? How does that work?' Mattie asked, her tone making me realize that her visit was more than social. She was here for information and details she thought only Grenville insiders would have.

'It's simple. Dealers rent booths or cases, fill it with merchandise and then we try to sell it. They also post and sell over the Internet.'

'So the dealers aren't actually there?'

'Not unless they want to be.'

'It sounds convenient for the dealers.'

'That's the point,' I said. 'I had actually thought about doing that myself. I've accumulated so much stuff and some of it's too good for a tag sale.'

'But if the store makes its money off the rentals, what's the incentive to move the merchandise?'

'They take five percent of all sales, half for commission and half to the shop.'

'That makes sense. Are they making money?'

'I suspect so. These multi-dealer megastores seem to be the wave of the future, that and the Internet.'

'I wonder what the dealers with shops think about them?'

'Hard to say. On one hand it's good for business, on the other; it could be overkill.'

'How so?'

'The antique business is different from most in that you don't want to be the only shop in town. With antiques it's always been "the more the merrier". People go out of their way to come to Grenville because they know they'll eventually find what they're looking for; there are over a hundred shops. If there were only one or two, who'd bother to come?'

'If that's true, why would the local dealers not want the multi-dealer shop? Seems like it would be a selling point.'

'I'm not sure,' Ada said as she reappeared from the kitchen with a blue-willow platter laden with open cartons of Chinese. 'I spent decades in retail, and I think the dealers in the Antique Center have an advantage. Their overhead is minimal; they pay the monthly rent and that's it. Shop owners have to deal with staffing, utilities, all the hidden costs and insurance. That's what drives up prices.'

'That's the other thing,' I added, helping Ada unload supper. 'Prices in the Antique Center are lower than in the shops.'

Aaron, guided by smells of dinner, made his entrance. He grunted a hello to Mattie, sat down and proceeded to heap his plate.

I could see that Ada wanted to comment on his manners, and his choice of an oversized tee with a graphic of a skeleton writing graffiti with a spray can and jeans, but after a moment's hesitation she shrugged and said, 'I guess we should start.'

It was our usual smorgasbord from the Happy Moon Restaurant. The only addition was the fine sterling that Ada had placed as an afterthought into the white cardboard containers.

Ada looked across at Mattie. 'How goes the investigation?'

'It's moving.'

'You sound discouraged,' Ada commented.

'A little. I'm really aware of being the outsider.'

'Don't you get that a lot?' I asked. 'I mean, going into a strange community. It seems like that alone would be an obstacle.'

'At times,' she admitted. 'Small towns are the hardest.'

'That makes sense,' I said. 'We tend to take care of our own.'

'Scary, isn't it?' Ada said. 'But I'm not so certain that's all there is.' She looked at me. 'I know this is your town, Lil, but I've been here over eight years and I still feel like an outsider.'

'You're right,' I admitted, but her words hurt. 'We're a snobbish lot.'

'Do you mind if I ask a couple more questions about what we discussed at lunch?' Mattie asked between bites of beef and broccoli.

'Fire away,' Ada replied.

'Did Mr Caputo *ever* get back to you? Even leave a message?'

'No. I've pretty much given up on him. Why?'

'Just trying to pull together loose ends.'

'Do you think he's still alive?' I asked, horrified at the possibility that he might not be.

'I don't know,' she admitted. 'I have no reason to think that he isn't. Apparently it's pretty common for him to disappear for extended periods.'

'You've got a weird job,' Aaron commented having already devoured his first plate of food. 'Do you get to look at dead people and all that?'

'Sometimes.'

'That's pretty cool.' He reloaded his plate with egg foo young, moo shoo pork and steamed dumplings. 'You have three dead people, maybe more, this seems big time, like *CSI*. On those shows there's always this intense pressure to arrest someone.'

'You got it,' she said, looking at the teen and thinking of her own son, Oscar, now a sophomore at UConn. 'Although here, it's strange; typically there's a real push at the local level to make an arrest. Sometimes it can get so bad it interferes with the investigation. If you move too quick there's a chance that something will be missed or that evidence or a suspect might not be handled right. It gets complicated because even if you catch the perpetrator, it just takes one procedural slipup to lose the case. I'd hate to tell you how often people get off on technicalities.'

'Like PD Martin?' he asked, referring to the high-publicity murder involving a sports celebrity who murdered his wife.

She laughed. 'I can't even begin to discuss that.'

'Why is that?' Ada remarked.

'It makes me furious. I spent five years working domestic abuse cases. Whatever anyone says, the PD Martin case was about spousal abuse. Through that whole circus I kept thinking about all the battered women I've worked with and how the story fit the pattern.'

'Is it a crime if there's abuse but no one gets hit?' Aaron asked.

'There needs to be some infringement on another person's rights for it to be illegal, like stalking or assault,' Mattie explained. 'Now *reportable* is another story. For that all you need is a reasonable suspicion. That's the more common scenario. Most abusive relationships don't progress to legally punishable acts.'

'So what happens in those cases?' he asked.

'Nothing, and people stay in awful and degrading situations, a lot of times women stay because they're terrified of what will happen if they leave; and they're right. Abusive men up the ante when they fear they're losing control.'

'Control has a lot to do with it,' Aaron stated, pushing his food around his plate.

'That must be hard work,' Ada commented, her gaze fixed on Aaron.

'It's frustrating,' Mattie said. 'When this position on the Major Crime Squad opened, I grabbed it. You have no idea what it was like seeing all these women who knew they had to get out or they'd wind up dead, but they just couldn't leave. And it was always the same story: "I can't." "I don't have any money." "I have to stay because of the kids." "Maybe if I tried harder." "Maybe it's my fault." I'd get sick worrying about cases and then the call would come and the woman would be in the hospital . . . or the morgue. This probably isn't the best dinner conversation. I'm sorry.'

'Don't be,' I said. 'It's not like we don't see it in Grenville.'

'I'm sure of that,' Mattie agreed. 'That's the whole point of the PD Martin case; it can happen to anyone, and the stories are the same, rich or poor. You hear women talking about "choosing their battles" with their husbands, women who let power-sick men drain them of all their self-assurance until they're so riddled with doubt and anxiety that they can't see a way out. They're like a bunch of scared rabbits.'

Ada and Aaron shot looks across the table. He spoke up. 'It's something my mother says.'

We grew silent. Ada nodded her head imperceptibly.

I looked at her closely and could see her jaw clench and moisture glittered in the corners of her eyes.

He looked at the detective. 'Ever since I was little my mom has "picked her battles" with my dad. And you want to know the truth?' The words choked in his throat and he fought hard to not let the tears come. 'She never wins.'

Mattie met his gaze with a look of understanding. His black eye – now a faded patchwork of yellow and brown – had not gone unnoticed. 'Is that what happened Aaron? Did your father hit you?'

'No.' He stared down at his plate. 'But I wish he had.'

TWENTY-ONE

'Lil, it's not hard,' Belle Evans said, from beneath her shoulder-length blonde wig. She handed me the bulky set of keys. 'All you have to do is keep an eye on things. If someone asks for something specific, like an Art Nouveau table lighter and you don't know if we have one or not, just get Fred or me. After a while, you get to know what's in the shop. Other than that, keep an eye out for shoplifters; some of the smaller pieces that aren't in locked cases have been disappearing. I keep telling the dealers to use the cases, but most of them are too cheap. I'll hold off on showing you the cash register.' She shuddered. 'It's a beastly thing. Other than that, any questions?'

'No,' I said, wishing I had stuck to flats. Instead, I had unburied a pair of pumps from the deepest recesses of my closet. What was I thinking? My ankles and calves burned, and it was only ten.

I thought back to my breakfast conversation with Ada that morning. 'Why are you doing this?' she'd asked, weirdly upset. 'You don't need the money.'

'True, I just want something different.'

I could tell she was going to push further, but at that moment, Aaron had breezed past on his way to school.

'Strange, isn't it?' she had commented. 'You're going to work and I've got a teenager at home.'

'It hasn't hurt you any.'

'I've missed Aaron, and I like the company,' she'd admitted. 'I hadn't realized how lonely I could get. If it wasn't for you, Lil . . .'

'I know.' I fought the impulse to hug her. I had wanted to say more, to bring up the inconsistency of her feeling lonely and then proposing to go care for her mother in Manhattan. But I'd held my tongue.

On one point she was right: this was strange. I had always expected to go to work, just not when I was coming up on sixty. As a young woman I had wanted a career. Almost finished with my Bachelor of Arts from Smith, I had fantasized about a career in journalism, possibly working for a newspaper, or even one of the glossy magazines. I had been editor of the school paper my last two years, and one of my professors had told me she could get me an internship at *Newsweek*. But then, Christmas of my senior year, I met Bradley. I had gone home for the holidays, and was caught up in the seasonal whirlwind of baking and social visits. It was a glorious time, with fresh snow frosting the antique homes and icicles glistening like ornaments. Mother and I, bundled in fur-lined coats, and armed with rum-soaked fruitcakes, and tins of chocolaty bourbon balls, went calling on the neighbors. At every house we'd stop and chat. And then, and I've often wondered if mother hadn't intended this all the time, we'd stopped at Bradley's house, to pay a visit to the new unmarried young doctor in town. The intent was to leave him with one of Mother's scandalous batches of bourbon balls.

Bradley and I would always say that it was love at first sight; I'm not sure that's true. It was more a knowing that after half an hour's visit, we fit together.

Now, as I patrolled the rows of precisely laid-out booths, I realized that was ancient history. It was a slow morning here in the Antique Center and I was free to browse. My eye caught on a pair of Imari platters; one of my particular passions, I carefully examined them. Something about the almost deliberate too-even wear on the bottoms made me suspicious. The prices were reasonable, but I opted to give them a pass, at least for now.

At the front desk Belle and her rail-thin assistant, a retired engineer called Fred, were focused on the computerized cash register. 'This thing gets me so flustered.' Belle's pudgy hands angrily attempted to thread the paper into the printer. Her approach was too rough and the roll crimped and jammed.

'Let me try,' said Fred.

Gratefully, she stepped back. 'Lil, do you know anything about computers?'

'Some,' I admitted.

'They are the devil's own,' she shot back. 'Why can't they just let us have a regular cash register? You know, the type with keys you push?'

'No paradise like a paradise lost,' Fred remarked, having managed to get the paper on to the roller. He turned on the machine and stared at the small readout box. 'What do they mean by "feed line jam"?'

'Now what?' Belle looked at Fred. 'Can't we just use paper and pencil today?'

'You're the boss . . . Wait a minute.' The machine clicked and whirred. 'Here we go.'

'It's working?'

I left them to their struggles and wandered to the front windows that looked out on High Street. Across from the center stood three of the older antique shops, including the one where Mildred Potts had been murdered. They were all open for business. Apparently Mildred's daughter wouldn't, or couldn't, afford to go on hiatus.

In the windows of her shop were carefully arranged displays of primitive early country furniture. Not my taste, but the sort of thing that sells. I've never understood the charm of overpriced, rickety and worm-eaten ladder-back chairs. It reminded me of Evie's painted cupboard and how that was the one thing that Mildred had really wanted.

Staring out, I didn't notice Fred as he came up behind me. 'Penny for your thoughts?' he asked.

I looked at him and smiled. He was a bit older than me, tall with a full head of salt-and-pepper hair and dark-framed glasses. He reminded me of a college professor or scientist. In fact he'd been a social worker at the local hospital for years. Several months back he'd been laid off; working here was a huge pay cut, but at least it was a job. 'You really want to know?'

'Sure.'

'I was thinking about Mildred,' I admitted.

'Right, there's been a lot of commotion over there. It's ghoulish to say, but we've had a front row seat.'

'Really?'

'Sure. We watched the police, all the different folks from the state. It's interesting. If you think about it, we have over a hundred dealers set up in this shop. People talk.'

'What do they say?'

'Everyone has a theory.' He looked across the green. 'It's a weird sort of crime though, killing antique dealers. What's the motive?'

'And your theory?' I asked, feeling both creeped out and interested.

'It's not very good; but the only thing that connects the victims, other than they were all dealers, is they were all *high-volume* dealers.'

'How's that a motive?'

'There are a lot of dealers in town, probably hundreds, but how many of them can cough up six or seven figures to go after large estates? Maybe half a dozen. Most dealers – and pretty much everyone in this shop – are small potatoes. Even the ones that make their livings at it don't have cash reserves. To buy out a decent-sized estate you need at least a couple hundred grand in ready cash. Or at least have a credit line that big, and right now the banks just aren't fronting that kind of cash.'

'I'd not thought about it quite that way.' And I wondered if Mattie had.

'Sure . . . Conroy, Mildred, Carl McElroy, they all had bucks. Maybe, someone wants to get rid of the competition. Of course the other big theory is revenge.' He lowered his voice. 'Everyone knew McElroy was a crook, and Mildred was so damn cheap. Conroy I don't know about.'

'The part I struggle with,' I said, looking at the display in

Mildred's windows, 'and maybe this is a good thing, I can't quite fathom what would be important enough to kill over.'

Fred grew serious. 'All people in the right – or maybe it's the wrong – circumstance can kill. It's just in Grenville, it seems unlikely. Think about war. I was in 'Nam; we all went and did what we were told.'

'That's true,' I said, feeling I'd intruded. 'It's the Grenville piece. I've lived here my whole life. These things don't happen here.'

'Not true,' he said. 'Over two hundred years ago soldiers came down High Street with muskets. Some of these houses witnessed battles with neighbors and British soldiers dying in their front yards.'

'You're right.' He was referring to the 'Skirmish on Town Plot', an episode in local history that had been indelibly drilled into me as a schoolgirl, where we'd take field trips to the local cemetery and do charcoal rubbings off the tombstones of the fallen.

'Think about it this way.' He stared at Mildred's shop. 'For whatever reason, two hundred years later someone else has come to Grenville to wage war.'

TWENTY-TWO

Mattie Perez braced herself for a second look at the half-dissolved human remains spilled across the stainless autopsy table. Spending the morning in the morgue with Arvin Storrs, the bald, portly and slightly pervy Medical Examiner was one of her least favorite activities. The smell was overpowering, a fetid mix of sulfur and rotting meat. Even dabbing mentholated Vicks beneath her nostrils couldn't cover it.

The body, found in a vat of corrosive fluid outside the Grenville dump, was unrecognizable. Although both she and Hank Morgan had a good guess as to the identity of victim number four. Even now, Hank was hunting down dental records. 'It shouldn't be too hard,' he'd said. 'Everyone went to Doc Williams. Give me a couple hours.'

He'd been eager to get away, she thought as Arvin probed the oily lumps of human remains. *Don't puke*. She swallowed hard. *Focus, focus*.

'Some sort of acid,' Arvin commented as he peered at Mattie through bifocals smudged with human fat. 'Probably sulfuric, from the smell. Too strong for muriatic. Did a good job of getting rid of most of the meat. Even the bones are porous; much longer and there wouldn't have been anything. And this stuff over here –' and he swirled a surgical probe into a bucket of scum skimmed from the. top of the barrel where the body had been found – 'this floating stuff is dissolved adipose, you know, fat, just like the scum on the top when you make a pot of stew. Hard to tell how heavy this guy was. Now he's soap.'

Mattie took small careful breaths through her nostrils. She knew from experience that it was critical to be at the autopsy. But Arvin took too much pleasure in his work, and at some point he'd make a lewd proposition, which she'd laugh off. *I'm too old for this*, she thought. 'Will there be enough for a dental match?'

'Should be, most of the fillings have hung in, and there's a gold bridge that it didn't touch. That alone should give you the match. If the killer really wanted to hide the identity he would have removed anything traceable, at least chopped off the head.'

'Any ideas on where someone would get the acid?'

'It ain't hard. I use muriatic or sulfuric acid every year when I hose down my pool. Of course, whoever did this was buying in bulk. You ever seen my pool? It's great, got a hot tub attached . . . That thing's seen some action.'

She ignored his question. 'So pool supply stores . . . Where else?'

'Hardware stores, chemical supply houses, schools, anywhere there's a lab. If it is sulfuric it's a common reagent. You should see my pool, come for a swim, even now I keep it at eighty-five,' he offered hopefully.

'Cause of death?'

'You're no fun. Here,' he said, and he pointed to the fragile cranium. 'There's your exit wound, and my guess is where there used to be a face was the entry wound.' He worked a stainless-steel probe into the bullet hole. 'It's probably a twenty-two; didn't find the slug, though. But, I'd be willing to bet it's the same as the others.'

'It's small.'

'Yeah, dainty. If the bone weren't so eroded we could get a better identification. But unless you got two maniacs running around in butt-floss Connecticut, I'd say it's the same gun.'

'Lady's gun?'

'Not necessarily, but guys go for bigger. Of course –' he smiled lewdly – 'it's not size that counts.'

'Give it a rest, Arvin. Why acid?' she persisted.

'Dispose of the remains, hide the identity, fertilize the garden, who knows?'

'They certainly weren't trying to hide anything. It was right in the open.'

'Good thing, too,' Arvin said. 'Much longer, and all that would have remained is some yellow fat. And of course the gold bridge.'

'But if someone was trying to obliterate the identity, why leave the teeth?' Mattie pondered.

'Couldn't tell you.'

'What can you tell me?'

'Just the basics.' Arvin tapped the Dictaphone controls with his disposable bootie covered foot and started his dictation. 'The victim is male, judging by bone, approximately fifty-five to sixty-five years of age. The overall condition of the body is extremely poor and has been subjected to a highly corrosive substance. A strong smell of sulfur is noted, making me suspect –' he winked at Mattie – 'sulfuric acid. Accurate assessments of organ weight cannot be obtained.' He tapped the control to pause the recorder. He poked into the rib cage, peeling back what fragile flesh remained. 'Nah –' he stepped back – 'not much left.' He tapped the play button. 'On assessment of the cranium there appears to be a small exit wound on the medial aspect of the right parietal bone, approximately two centimeters above the lambdoid suture. Judging by the walls of the wound, the trajectory was at a slight upward angle, making it likely that the entry wound was in the area of the medial aspect of the right infra-orbital foramen.' He tapped pause. 'There going to be any family coming down to view the body? Hank Morgan seemed pretty sure you'd come up with a match.'

'Don't know yet,' she admitted, thinking about another of her least favorite tasks: notifying family.

'Hmmm, did I mention my pool is heated?'

'Great, Arvin. You know I got a kid in college?' Mattie said in a tone that let him know there was no way in hell she'd be stopping by his pool.

'So? You're just no fun.' And he proceeded with the autopsy.

Mattie held her breath for the last few steps as she exited the morgue. Outside, she gulped the sweet morning air. The stars were still faintly visible and the first lazy fingers of dawn had crept up the eastern sky.

She tried to shake off the sights and smells of the last few hours. She'd be getting a call from headquarters in less than an hour, and, with four connected murders, she needed something. Someone was playing games; all four of them shot, but after the fact, Philip's finger, Mildred's jewelry, Carl's paddle-riddled body, and now, if the records matched, Rudy Caputo's acid-eaten corpse. And still no word about McElroy's missing cronies, Rinaldo and Jeffries. *At least now*, she thought, *MacDonald will have to authorize search teams.* Already formulating the email she'd send that would make it impossible for him to refuse.

In the distance, she watched a Grenville patrol car turn down the street. What she needed was a little luck and, hopefully, Hank was bringing it.

Kevin Simpson was first out of the cruiser, a manila folder with the dental records in his hand.

'You found them?' she asked.

'Got 'em.' Hank pointed toward the Medical Examiner's door. 'Arvin finished yet?'

'Yeah, slid him back in the drawer a few minutes ago.'

'Never did have a stomach for those things,' Hank admitted. 'So what did he find?'

'Same as the others, small-caliber bullet, single shot.'

'In the face?' Kevin asked.

'You got it.'

'Damn, that's cold. So he saw it coming.'

'Right,' said Mattie, slightly peeved that the small-town constable had caught a point that she had missed. All the victims had been shot in the face. She knew that, but Kevin's implication was an important one. The killer wanted them to see it coming, to know that they were going to die. To face their killer.

'What are you thinking?' Hank asked, eyes narrowing.

'Payback. It's increasingly obvious, but there's a sense of something moral with these murders. The killer's making a point.'

'What's the message?'

'I'm not sure, but before I go spinning any theories let's see if we've got a match.'

'Yeah.' Hank turned toward the morgue door. 'How bad is it?'

Mattie handed him her jar of Vicks. 'Put it this way . . .' She took the envelope from Kevin and headed toward the door. 'How long can you hold your breath?'

TWENTY-THREE

I t was Wednesday. I wasn't scheduled to work and Ada had asked me to help out at Evie's. It felt odd, and sad, as Tolliver Jacobs and his crew of red-shirted movers from Grenville Antiques dismantled our friend's home.

Tolliver seemed drained, his face drawn; he'd lost weight. He pitched in with the packing and the moving, but his polo shirt was wrinkled, his hair uncombed; he seemed distracted and the skin on his face seemed loose, as though he'd lost a considerable amount of weight in the span of a week.

'Careful with the gesso,' he cautioned as one of the packers measured the frame of the Hassam painting.

'Anyone for tea?' Ada asked as she buzzed around Evie's condo with pen and paper, and then entered every item into a spreadsheet on her laptop on the dining room table. She'd popped over late last night, nearly in tears. 'He accused me of stealing from his mother!' she had said, following an angry phone call with Evie's eldest. 'I told him,' she'd continued, 'that if he wanted to be present for the entire liquidation process, I'd have no problems with that. What a little *pisher*. It would be one thing if he had helped his mother while she was alive but now, the whole bunch of them . . . vultures!'

We had talked for over an hour and by the end she had calmed down, but today, dressed in denim overalls and turquoise Keds, like some adorable farmer, she was spinning at a furious pace. 'Maybe I should have gotten another quote,' she said, her voice low so Tolliver couldn't hear. 'Mr Caputo never did get back to me and now he's dead. At least I have Mildred's quote, if anyone tries to say anything. I did my due diligence, and it's not like I'm making anything off this.'

'You did more than most,' I reassured her. 'And I've known Tolliver forever; I think he's honest. Plus,' I went on, my tone low to match hers, 'there aren't a lot of dealers who can cut a check for this kind of money . . . especially now.'

She stopped and smiled, and then impulsively reached up and kissed me on the cheek.

'What?' I could feel myself blush as I registered how soft and warm her lips felt on my skin.

'I love you Lil, this would be just awful if you weren't here.'

And then she was off, trying to see what the man who'd just measured the painting was up to.

Confused and light-headed, I sank into one of the dining room chairs where I had often played bridge. I watched as Evie's personal things were boxed and taken out. Her clothes were bagged for distribution to local charities and the family pictures were stacked on the counter alongside the bubble-wrapped china. My anxiety spiked. Too much was running through my head. *The kiss was just a friendly gesture, Lil, don't over-read it.* But that was just the tip of things as I compared Evie's condo with my own and Ada's. Someday, someone would be doing the same in our homes. A life reduced to boxes and bags, our better things carted off to auction, or distributed among family. From there, my mind twitched to this morning's hang-up call. I was getting at least two a day. The one last night – after I was already in bed – had made it impossible to fall back asleep. *And why aren't you telling anyone about them? Because they're just hang-ups,* I told myself. *You're on some stupid marketing list and that's why they're calling. Then why don't they try to sell you something?*

'Don't you think the family will want those?' Ada asked, breaking into my funk as she flipped through a box of photos and albums.

'I asked each of the sons,' Tolliver said, overhearing her. 'None of them wanted them.' He joined us at the dining-room table that gave us unobstructed views of the living room and kitchen. 'That's the saddest thing, when boxes of photographs come up at auction. Unless they're true antiques, or of somebody famous, no one wants them. I wouldn't say anything if you just kept them aside. There might be someone in the family, down the line, who'd like them. Maybe a grandchild.'

'You think I should?' Ada asked.

'Your call,' Tolliver said, 'but I can tell you that if I take them and they don't sell; they'll wind up in the dumpster.'

'Oh.'

'Some people,' he continued as he sat, 'just leave them in the boxes for years.' He seemed lost as he looked out over the living room that was rapidly being dismantled.

'Are you OK?' I asked, noting the circles under his eyes.

'Been better. As long as I keep moving, things will eventually quiet down. At least, that's my theory.'

Without looking at him, and in a voice that only the three of us could hear, Ada spoke. 'You have to mourn. *That* can't be boxed up and put away.'

He looked at her. 'Funny you should say that.'

'It's true.'

'I agree. But the bit about boxing it up; you don't know how true that can be. People sometimes try to do just that, box it up and put it away.'

'Excuse me,' I said, keeping my voice near a whisper, 'are we talking literally?'

'I do a lot of estates,' he continued. 'It's common to find boxes from other estates that have never been opened. Usually, it's like those pictures over there, or letters. Personal things that the heirs never got around to open.'

'Sounds like unfinished business,' Ada remarked. 'How can you get on with things if you never take care of the present?'

'That's what I used to tell him,' Tolliver said.

'You're talking about Philip,' I commented, picturing Tolliver's handsome, blond-haired partner.

'Yes, he was bad about unfinished business.'

'It's hard,' Ada said, 'losing someone who's so much a part of your daily life. It's not just that it's someone you love; it's like losing a limb you didn't know you had. When Harry got sick, and when he died, there were so many things I missed that I hadn't expected. Some of them make me feel pretty shabby, but they matter.' She shot Tolliver a crooked smile. 'He drove and I never learned how. He knew how to talk to my son-in-law and that I've never figured out. But the worst thing, and the thing I still miss, is at night. I miss him in the bedroom and I'm not talking sex.'

'I couldn't go near the bed for a year after Bradley died,' I added, my heart pounding. 'Of course, I think a lot of that was just . . .' I could feel my throat close; the tears not far away.

Ada explained: 'Lillian woke up to find Bradley . . . dead.'

'I'm so sorry,' he said. 'I mean, I knew that when he died it had been sudden. How awful for you.'

I let the feelings pass, as they did, leaving me with a pit in my stomach.

'I miss Philip,' he said simply. 'No matter how busy I am, I can't help but think about what happened to him. I can't focus on anything else. Why would someone do that to him? How could anyone hate him so much?'

'With Bradley, I can't help but think that if I'd woken up, I'd have been able to save him, or get help.'

'That's it,' he said, 'I can't sleep. I have to force myself to eat. Part of me would just like to pack it up and go away. It doesn't matter where. But then who would run the business? We have forty-two employees; it's not like I can just up and leave. It's such a mess right now.'

'It gets better,' I said.

'Yes,' Ada agreed, taking Tolliver's hand. 'Over time, it eases. It's just getting through today, forcing yourself to take care of business. You can't run from these things, they catch up with you.'

'I'm not so certain about that,' he said. 'I think the last few months of Philip's life were pretty miserable because of that.'

'Dear,' said Ada, 'can I ask what you mean by that?'

'You're the second person who's asked me that.'

'Who was the first?' I wondered.

'That detective working on the murders.'

'What did you tell her?'

'I had my lawyer step in to hold her off.'

'Was that a good idea?' Ada whispered.

'Probably not,' he admitted. 'I just wasn't ready to go into certain things.'

'And now?' Ada gently prodded.

'I could do it, but I don't see how it would help. And there's no way I can do it without becoming worked up. The thought of breaking down in front of Kevin Simpson and that woman doesn't really motivate me.'

Ada squeezed his hand. 'This is none of my business, but it might help to tell someone. To get through the worst of it, like a rehearsal before meeting with the detective, I'd be happy to listen . . . and I know how to keep a secret.'

'My lawyer would have a cow.'

I chuckled. 'Yes, but that's lawyers. I agree with Ada, if you want someone to talk to . . .'

'I appreciate that,' he said, 'but I'm not so certain it's that big a thing. For the last three months of Philip's life he was depressed. And it all stemmed from those damn boxes.'

'Boxes?' Ada prompted.

'From his sister.'

Suddenly, I accessed a chunk of information that Ada wouldn't know; small-town stuff. It had been years since I'd thought about Wendy Conroy, Philip's younger sister, and a patient of my husband's. For good, bad or indifferent, Bradley would occasionally talk about patients and Wendy was one who he had spent sleepless nights worrying about. 'She died a long time ago,' I said, feeding Ada some basic facts.

'Ten years ago,' Tolliver went on, staring straight ahead. 'She killed herself.'

'How terrible,' Ada said.

'It was. It tore Philip apart. He loved his sister and was probably the only one who could talk to her at that point.'

'You lost me,' Ada said. 'There was something wrong with her?'

'Wendy had a lot of problems. For the last few years of her life she lived in a mental hospital. We had tried having her come live with us, but every so often something would set her off and she'd go missing. Once, I was showing an armoire to customers and when I opened the door she was inside, curled up in a ball and sucking her thumb. That stuff didn't bother us so much, but when she'd go wandering and be missing for days, Philip would go crazy. Either we'd find her by some stream or she'd come back covered with dirt and bruises. We couldn't take care of her. We'd find her medicine hidden all over the shop and the house. She'd either refuse to take it or else spit it out when Philip wasn't looking. We had to send her back. It was a horrible scene. She screamed at Philip and me and called us "Nazis".'

'It must have been awful,' I said. 'I remember Wendy; she was a beautiful girl.'

'She was. I often wondered if that didn't make her problems worse. We'd go for meetings at the mental hospital and the psychiatrists and the psychologists were always asking Philip about childhood trauma. Had she been abused? Molested? That kind of stuff.'

'What about her parents?' Ada asked. 'It sounds like you and Philip pretty much took care of her.'

'That's a whole other story. Philip's parents decided that having one child who was gay and another who was crazy were reasons enough to get out of town. It's tragic if you think about it; both of their children are dead and they're still alive living in Boca.'

I held my tongue, as I had known the Conroys. Ellen Conroy would bring Wendy in to see Bradley on almost a weekly basis. It wasn't long before Bradley understood that the girl's problem was psychiatric and he had referred her to a specialist. But Ellen Conroy could not accept that assessment and kept bringing Wendy back, hoping that there was something else that Bradley could find that might account for the girl's mood swings and strange behaviors. Wendy was fourteen or fifteen when the problems had begun. I remembered her vividly, the beautiful girl with straight blonde hair, dark lashes and blue-green eyes, like her brother's.

'I must be missing something,' Ada said. 'Didn't you say that Wendy died ten years ago?'

'That's right.'

'Then why was Philip more depressed about it now? It seems like after all those years, things might have gotten better.'

'They had. But it's just what you said, that if you put something away and don't think about it; it's just putting off the inevitable.'

She looked at him. 'Philip put something away?'

'Literally. Wendy was a writer. She was always scribbling and drawing in journals. We had assumed it was part of her therapy, but after time, it was the only thing that would ground her. If she started to go off, or would wake up screaming, Philip would have her write in her notebook. Occasionally, she'd show us a poem; she even published a few. Once, right before we had to send her back to the hospital, I caught a look at a couple pages of her journal. The sheets were covered with tiny letters, and over and over she had written the same thing.'

'What did it say?'

'It was gibberish, completely insane. She hadn't slept or eaten for days and was having religious fantasies, like she was a saint. I think the pages were some sort of incantation. Anyway, about a month after Wendy's suicide, we got four boxes delivered from the hospital. Three of them were filled with journals, dozens of them. At the time, I wanted Philip to throw them out; he couldn't. So we stuck them in one of the upstairs rooms and that was that.'

'Did he read them?' Ada asked

'Not then. But a few months back we decided to work on the upstairs of the main house, and he found the boxes. Suddenly, going through them became some sort of mission. At first, I thought it was healthy, finally give him a chance to put Wendy's ghost to rest. But the more he read, the worse it got. He became obsessed. He'd sit up at night, reading page after page of that nonsense. It changed him.'

While we'd been talking, careful to keep our voices low, Evie's condo had been stripped bare.

'Mr Jacobs.' The foreman came over to us. 'Do you want these chairs to go?'

'Everything,' he said, getting to his feet. 'Ada, Lil, thanks.' And he walked back to where the Hassam painting had been tidily crated into a custom plywood box. He examined the joinery and gently rocked it from side to side. 'Good, this goes in my car.'

TWENTY-FOUR

How did this happen? I wondered as I approached the two cardboard cartons that had been delivered to my doorstep. What was Ada thinking?

'I can't do it, Lil,' Tolliver had said over the phone after we'd finished Evie's cleanout. Ada and I had been having tea in my kitchen, reminiscing about our friend, and, of course, speculating about the murders. Not to leave her out, I'd put the phone on speaker. 'I can't look at them. I know I have to do something with them,' he'd explained. 'But if I gave them to the police without knowing what was in them, it might just be a horrible waste of their time. What am I supposed to tell them? My husband read these and got depressed, and maybe that has something to do with why he was murdered. They'll think I'm nuts. They already think I did it. I keep waiting for them to come and lock me up.' He'd sighed. 'I feel trapped. I can't just throw them out. Someone has to go through them.' Before he asked, I could feel it coming. 'Would you do it for me?'

And before I could stop her, Ada had agreed. Of course, now she was conveniently out of the house with Aaron on some shopping expedition just as the boxes arrived and I was getting out of the shower. In the spirit of fairness, I threw on a wrap-around dress, and, still in slippers, let myself into her condo and had the delivery guy from Tolliver's shop leave one of the three cartons in her foyer.

The boxes were heavy and crisscrossed with clear packing tape and silver duct tape that had been used and peeled back. I got a serrated knife from the kitchen and sawed through the layers.

'Oh my.' So many spiral-bound notebooks, like the ones I'd buy for my daughters each year before the start of school; different sizes and colors, the work of a lifetime. Where to start? It was overwhelming. And not that I believed in ghosts, but there was something eerie about this stack of writings from a girl who had gone insane and committed suicide. The scent of death lingered. I know it was just my imagination, but sitting there, I had a foreboding, that maybe I should have called Mattie or Hank and had them taken away. 'You promised,' I reminded myself. More accurately, Ada had promised. Still . . .

I pulled out two of the books and settled back in my blue-and-white upholstered wing chair. I switched on the lamp and flipped open a red notebook. On the inside cover, she had written her name and what I took to be a room number. The first entry was dated June 15, 1998.

Fresh book, fresh life. Nice . . . sweet. I should be nice and sweet. The road to freedom is nice and sweet. Wendy, a nice and sweet name, pity the girl can't follow. Like follow the leader. Maybe if I let my name lead, and I followed all would be well. In a world without pills, in a world without doctors. Come for your medicine, nice, sweet girl. Take your pills in a world without thrills. Come Wendy Wendy Wendy. Come Wendy Wendy Wendy.

Roar my faithful nurse. 'Med time. Med time.' Meet her at the station, it's in my contract. Show more enthusiasm, swallow pills, become sweet and nice, nice and sweet, like good and plenty, I'd be good to eat.

Well, fresh book, new book, sweet book. I must take my meds. Good meds sweet meds, sugar-coated pills, yummy yummy yummy. Screaming in my tummy.

I calculated her age in 1998, somewhere in her mid twenties. Within two years she would be dead. I wondered if there was significance to this being on the top. Was this one that Philip had read? I turned the pages.

June 30, 1998

They gave me privileges in my prison without crime. When can I leave, Dr Kluft, Dr Kluft? He smiles; I'm doing better, better every day. Now that I take my pills, I have privileges and wander grounds, beneath watchful eyes. I feel their eyes, heavy through my back as I sit and write. Eyes that search me out and strip me naked. I face the shallow pond, with its fake waterfall that fools the frogs. How deep is the pond, enough for Ophelia to float away? I think not. My privileges do not extend that far. The eyes would pull me back and tie me down. Strap me to the bed. Tie me down, tie me down.

My tongue like dust. It's the pills. It's the pills. Haven't shit in four days. It's the pills. It's the pills. I squint to see the frogs. It's the pills. It's the pills. But without them, they won't let me feel the grass or see the frogs, or, dare I hope, leave.

Come Philip, sweet brother. I will be good this time. I will be good. I promise. I will sit in my room, that overlooks the Nillewaug. I will not move. I will not worry you or Tolliver. I will do as I am told, I will take my pills and never shit again. I will squint at the frogs and do as I am told. I will not be sweet Ophelia Plath floating in the pond; it's probably too shallow anyway.

I wondered if anyone had read these while she was alive. Had they been part of some therapy? Had she read them to her doctor? In the end, she did drown, perhaps at the very pond she'd sat beside.

I turned pages, focusing on the small careful writing that even in its symmetry betrayed a fine drug-induced tremor, like someone with Parkinson's. She wrote daily, many of the entries an accounting of the groups and the therapies that she had attended. Some like poems and many spoke of death; her death. Occasionally, she dropped little hints of what had happened in her family, but vague and off-center.

July 22, 1998

I find a tree and I sit down.
I follow ants as they merry round.
I speak to the man with gray threaded beard
I call to brother, bent and weird.
I call to mother with tears in her voice
I touch father who left no choice.

I sit with ants as they merry round
I dream of Freedom dug deep in the ground.
I wonder if dirt will tickle my toes, stick in my hair?
Clog my nose?
Will it take the pills that swirl in my blood?
Will it fly me to heaven when the doctor is done?

The phone rang, and I was startled. I checked the caller ID, and picked up.

'Ada?'

'Lil? I've found something. At least I think I have.' Her voice was tentative.

'You're looking at the journals?' I asked.

'Yes.'

'I didn't hear you come home.'

'We got back an hour ago. The poor girl.'

'I know,' I agreed. 'I just started. What did you find?'

'Come over, or better yet, why don't I bring it there.'

'I'll put on water.'

'Lovely. And, Lil . . .'
'Yes.'
'Brace yourself.'

TWENTY-FIVE

stared at the torn and dirt-spattered page. It felt as if someone had punched me; the room swam and my heart pounded. I couldn't breathe.

'Lil, I'm sorry.' Ada's voice sounded disconnected. She stood behind me and tried to give some perspective. 'We shouldn't take it literally. The girl wasn't in her right mind. It was some fantasy or wish she had.'

Her words made sense, but they were no antidote for the venom that had leapt off the page. How could someone say these things? They couldn't be true. I forced myself to focus on the crumpled paper. The notebook it had come from was mangled and dirt smeared. It stood out from the rest that were all carefully arranged and stacked.

'It was on the top,' she had said.

Like the mushrooms in *Alice In Wonderland* it had demanded attention – *read me read me*. And, like the mushrooms, it changed everything.

The page was dated May 14, 2000. Very close to her death. The writing was wild and angular, much different from the careful printing in the book I'd looked at earlier. I forced myself to reread the hateful prose.

> *Take me to my lover, mother*
> *Drive me in your car.*
> *Curl my hair, shine my shoes*
> *Twinkle twinkle little star.*
> *He'll touch and probe*
> *Explore my wonders*
> *As above the heaven thunders.*
> *No, you mustn't*
> *Don't touch me there*
> *Your nurse will wonder*

Is she your wife?
She'll see my blush
My virgin's blood.
She'll know you've touched
I've come undone.

Take me to my lover, mother
In the Main Street manse just down the road.
A pretty girl in a big white house.
My bicycle won't carry
I shouldn't go that far.
He'll touch me in my privates
His tongue will search me out
He'll poke and prod
My wonders, lady
Then hide away the dribble bits
With cotton from his cubby
He'll sponge me gently.
Then send me to my Mummy.
When he's done.
He's had enough.
He's taken all.
I've come undone.

There had been more to her verse, but the page was torn, as though she had reread her poem and found it too offensive . . . or someone else had.

I couldn't move. I couldn't think. I felt Ada beside me. I knew what she must be thinking; how could she not?

'It wasn't Bradley,' I said. 'It's completely ridiculous.' She was insane after all; this was some sort of delusion. Didn't her mother go into the examination room with him? I tried to remember; it was typical for parents to go in with their children. But wasn't Wendy Conroy older when she came to visit? When the problems had started, she had been a teenager. With teens, he usually left the parents outside in the waiting room. Outside with me, his nurse . . . *or is she his wife?*

What was it Bradley had said? I pictured his face, his pale blue eyes that crinkled with his smile. '*When they get to a certain age, they won't tell me what the problem is if their mother's in the room.*

*Usually around eleven or twelve, I ask Mom to stay outside. You'd
be amazed at what some of the kids ask me, but it's perfectly
normal. They all want to know about sex.'*

We had laughed about that, how fifty percent of what he did was
closer to being a psychiatrist than a general practitioner. People were
forever stopping him in the street, asking for advice. It didn't seem
to matter if it was related to their belly pain or their in-law problems.
It had always filled me with a quiet pride that my husband, my
Bradley, was someone that people came to with their problems.

And now this, from the mind of a tortured young woman came
obscene accusations. I wanted to burn it.

'Could she have been talking about someone else?' Ada asked.

'I don't know. Bradley was her doctor for years. He was everyone's doctor. No one has ever said something like this, or hinted.
This is outrageous. And he can't defend himself.'

'Lil.' She sat beside me. 'We can't jump to conclusions. Wendy
Conroy was psychotic. There's no way of knowing the truth.
They're poems; maybe it's a metaphor? She saw a lot of doctors;
maybe it had nothing to do with Bradley. She could have been
talking about one of her psychiatrists, or some other kind of doctor.'

I tried to listen, my mind raced; she was talking about Bradley.
The white house, me filling out appointment slips in the waiting
room, 'cotton from the cubby'. I pictured his tidy office, with the
glass-fronted cabinets stocked with everything needed, whether to
handle an emergency delivery or to set a fracture. Maybe he had
given her a gynecologic exam and it had become twisted into one
of her delusions. That could happen, couldn't it? A young girl on
the brink of madness, what would she think of the stirrups and
the speculum? Although, he always had me or Gladys, his nurse,
assist him with gynecologic exams. He never did them without a
chaperone in the room . . . but is that true?

I couldn't even entertain that what she alleged had actually
occurred. Bradley was not a pedophile.

'It was right on top,' Ada had said. 'It may have been her last
journal, I've been flipping through the others, and they're all older.
Some from when she was a teenager.'

'Why would she write that?' I put the book down, resisting an
impulse to tear it up, to burn it.

'Tolliver said she was very sick. It's probably a delusion. I'm
sure it has nothing to do with Bradley.'

I felt numb. 'He was the only doctor in town, certainly the only one on Main Street. He was the only one she ever saw. At least until her problems started. Then there were a lot of doctors. A lot of psychiatrists, neurologists . . .'

'Maybe it was one of them?' she offered.

'I can't do this,' I said. 'I know we promised Tolliver, but it's too much.' My stomach churned; how could she say things like this? And there was no way to answer back. She and Bradley were dead; what possible use could this serve? And what other accusations lurked inside those college-ruled pads? 'Ada, I need to take a walk.'

'I'll go with you.'

'No, I need to think . . . I have to think.'

'Lil, are you sure?'

I headed for the door, and looked back at her. My thoughts were swimming, everything turned upside down, including my feelings for Ada. 'I need to think,' I stammered, barely able to find words, and before she could object I walked out.

A crisp leaf-whipped October wind buffeted my cheek as I headed down my walk toward the road.

It was too much. Two years after burying my husband, this girl, although she was a woman when she wrote that entry, accused him of molesting her over a decade before. It was obscene. It was not my Bradley . . . It couldn't be.

Without thought to direction, I headed toward the walking path that circled the ten-acre lake in the center of Pilgrim's Progress. Geese squawked as I passed, and a pair of swans headed toward me, anticipating I'd come to throw breadcrumbs. I stared at the crushed gravel and thought about Bradley and the year of our courtship. He was older than I was, twelve years, but I was no child. I was twenty-one. And didn't pedophiles like them young; wouldn't that argue against his guilt? Our sex life had been good. Although, I didn't have much to compare against. I'd been a virgin on our wedding night. Ours had been a quiet sort of lovemaking. Not the romance novel, bodice-ripping kind of thing. For lack of a better word, it was normal and gentle; and, over time, less frequent. But he'd hold me at night, before we went to sleep. We kissed every night and every morning. I could still feel his Saturday morning stubble against my cheek.

I remembered the late-night emergency calls, his black bag

always ready by the front door. Sometimes our bell would ring at two or three in the morning and I'd get up with him, throw on my robe and slippers and go down to meet whatever emergency had come knocking. How many children with croup or broken bones had there been? How many drunken men who had fallen, and rather than stumble home bruised to their wives, had come to Bradley to get patched up and to practice their excuses. He was the keeper of secrets and I was his partner. He took to the grave the knowledge of which men had cheated on their wives and visa versa. There were things he would never write in his patients' charts. 'We'll just keep this between the two of us,' he'd say, after administering a shot of penicillin to a local alderman who had contracted gonorrhea in New York City. He knew all the little-town lies and truths that if they ever leaked could destroy families and careers. He knew of the abortions and even mercy killings; he never judged. 'It's hard enough,' he'd say about a family struggling with a terminally ill parent. 'You have to give them choices, help them through.' On more than one occasion, I know he hastened death with the gentle kiss of morphine. He was there at the birth of his patients and we always attended the funerals. Not once was he sued. And while our move to Pilgrim's Progress was supposed to presage his retirement, he practiced medicine until the day he died.

He'd loved Grenville, even though he'd been born outside of Boston. We would joke about how you couldn't really be accepted in Grenville until you'd lived here at least three generations. But he had been accepted, and respected, and loved.

I veered from the footpath edged with clumps of purple and rust mums, and headed toward the road. Everything here in Pilgrim's Progress was too tidy. I needed to see something older, something real. I thought about going back for the car but I needed to walk. I moved quickly toward the gated entrance to the community and turned right on to Cedar Swamp Road.

As I passed Miller's farm and the riding stables, I thought of Wendy's poem. There were a couple other doctors in town, none of them in white houses, none of them GPs. And most of them weren't even around when Bradley was in practice. For years he was the only physician in Grenville. More importantly, he had been *her* physician.

I cleared the end of the road and turned left on to Main Street.

I took in the shops and houses that had watched Town Plot for the past two centuries. The few Victorian mansions, with their multi-hued paint and busy gingerbread trim, were the most recent additions to the stoic colonial and federal homes. Even the office buildings dated back to the 1840s. Familiar, like the back of my hand, yet it all looked different, as though someone had taken Grenville and turned it into a movie set. I had always taken pride in how well we cared for the town; the yearly tree plantings, the near-fascistic historical society which mandated the size and style of every sign, door knocker or mullion placed on the antique homes. I loved the symmetry of Town Plot with its absence of graffiti, litter or other urban blight. As I walked past the one-room schoolhouse, now the headquarters for the historical society, I overheard a pair of tourists.

'It's so perfect,' said a woman in Hawaiian print culottes and a blue cardigan as she read the bronze plaque.

'Too quaint,' her friend agreed as she focused her camera on the bell-topped school.

I didn't slow. *Quaint?* A lovely town where people are murdered and young girls go mad and kill themselves. Yes, I know people are flawed, my life as the GP's wife took care of any illusions. I'd sit in church with people I knew were cheating on their wives, or were addicted to pain pills. I knew who was alcoholic, who suffered with depression, and who – despite being wealthy – never paid their bills. 'It's just human nature,' Bradley would say as he'd write off thousands of dollars in unpaid fees.

What would he say to this? Could he write off the murders and the accusations? Sure it's human nature, but that doesn't make it OK.

I now stood in front of our house. It was still white, and the climbing pink roses and pale-blue hydrangea I had planted over thirty years ago were at their exuberant best; the last gasp of color before the first frost. The current residents had done little to change the exterior, and, secretly, I was grateful. The only notable differences were a new screened-in porch off the back and the gravel driveway was now asphalt.

I didn't really know the new family – the Jensens – a young doctor and his wife. I had met them at the closing and once or twice after that. I occasionally saw her in the grocery store and we would exchange hellos. I didn't like to think of them in our house. But there again, Bradley had been pragmatic. *'They're almost rented, these old homes. Think of all the families that have come before us and those still to come.'* We had collected the records, our home's genealogy back to before the Revolution. I gave it to the Jensens at the closing.

And then I passed the eyebrow colonial where I had been born. For the past twenty years it had been an antique store. Occasionally, I would go in to pick up the scents of my childhood. Unfortunately, the current owners were prone to potpourri and I would find myself fleeing the noxious fumes. Now, in the front window – what used to be the living room – was a display of wrought-iron fireplace tools and rustic salt-glazed stoneware filled with dried leaves and flowers. I stared up at the tiny half window of my childhood bedroom. So small, like a doll's house carefully polished and preserved.

It's all a facade, I thought as I turned and counted the antique shops, one after another. These had been homes. I could still remember the names of the families; many were still in town, just not in their original houses.

Then, out of the corner of my eye I caught someone crossing the street. I turned and saw Mattie Perez, coming toward me. I tried to work the corners of my face into a smile; it didn't work.

'Lil, are you OK?' she asked as she hurried toward me. Her expression showed more concern than was warranted by my mid-afternoon walk.

'I'm fine, why?'

She looked at me, trying to decide whether or not to say what was on her mind.

'Just go ahead,' I said. 'I'm a big girl.'

'Well, for starters,' she said, looking down at my feet, 'there's that.'

I followed her gaze and realized I had just walked three and a half miles in my pink bedroom slippers.

TWENTY-SIX

Bacon sizzled in the Brown Bear Diner, filling the air with a smoky tang as late-afternoon diners, most of them older, sat around bottomless cups of coffee and talked about the weather, the news, and of course the murders.

I looked up as the pretty young waitress, possibly a high-school student, filled our mugs.

'It's good to see you, Mrs Campbell,' she said as she turned over the cups.

'Thank you,' I said, searching for a name. 'Joanie, isn't it?'

'You remembered.'

'Yes, but it gets harder and harder.'

She laughed politely and headed back to the kitchen of the Brown Bear.

'It must be nice,' Mattie said, 'living where you know pretty much everyone.'

'You'd think so,' I offered as I watched the waitress.

'What is it, Lil?'

'What do you mean?' I tried to focus on Mattie, but my thoughts ran in a dozen directions. For instance, the waitress was about the same age as Wendy, at least the age I remembered. She had the same blonde-haired blue-eyed features.

'Lil,' Mattie interrupted. 'Are you OK?'

'You asked me that before.'

'Yes, and you didn't answer.'

'I got some news today . . . I'm just distracted.' Noticing a local reporter at the table across from the pass-through kitchen interviewing an antique dealer over coffee and pecan pie. And two tables down from them were three men and a beautiful dark-skinned woman who I recognized from the Channel Eight news.

'About Ada?'

'No.'

'Could you tell me what it is? I might be able to help.'

'Thanks . . . but I don't think so.' I stared at my knife and fork, trying to focus on the paper placemat with its advertisements for local merchants: the well digger, two realtors with old Grenville names, the travel agent, the health food store, the blacksmith; *and how many towns still have one of those?*

'Is it something physical?' she persisted.

'No, and please . . . no twenty questions.' My voice sounded harsher than I had intended. 'I'm sorry; I didn't mean to be rude. It's just . . . someone I care about has had very disturbing accusations made about him.'

'Accusations?'

You idiot, Lil! What a stupid thing to say to a detective. Oh well, in for a penny . . . 'Child abuse.'

'That is serious. What sort of abuse?'

'Sexual.'

'And he's denying it?'

'He doesn't have to. I know he's innocent.'

'That can happen,' she offered, her words carefully chosen. 'And when it does, the damage from the accusation can be as bad as if it were true.'

'Exactly,' I agreed. 'Once the thought is planted in people's minds, that so-and-so is a pedophile, it doesn't matter if it's true. Your reputation is ruined.'

'How do you know he's innocent?'

'I know him too well. If that had been going on I would have known.'

'OK, let me play devil's advocate. I've been involved in a lot of child-abuse cases, and the last person to know, or to suspect, is the person closest to the perpetrator. Often the wife or mother . . .'

I met her dark-eyed gaze. She so reminded me of my oldest, Barbara, a tough-as-nails casting agent, brutally direct and honest. She'd say it was part of the job, I think it went the other way, it was part of her and the job fit like a glove.

'Was this something recent?' she continued. 'Or in the past?'

'Past.'

'And now someone's made an accusation?'

'Yes.'

'Have they filed a complaint?'

'No, and they won't.'

'Why not?' Gently prodding.

'Mattie, I really would like to confide in you, but I haven't thought this through and it's not like you're a disinterested party.'

'Lil, if a crime has been committed, and a child has been hurt, someone needs to know about it. Because the thing about child abuse is if the accusations are true, perpetrators repeat. So you may not be talking about one child, but many.'

I watched as the waitress returned with our sandwiches. She had been one of Bradley's patients when she'd been a little girl; they all had. I'm sure she'd played with the toys and read the picture books we had always kept in the kiddies' corner of the waiting room.

'Tell me about that,' I said. 'If someone were molesting children, how do you know? I mean, if you don't catch someone . . . where's the evidence? You have the child's word, but children can lie. And now you have all these people saying they were molested as children, but didn't remember it for years. Can that really happen?'

'Repressed memories. It's controversial. A few years back people took repressed memories at face value; now there's a lot more skepticism. Basically, you need some form of corroborative evidence to make a charge stick.'

'But if something took place fifteen or twenty years ago, that seems hard.'

'Almost impossible, unless evidence was taken, in which case you can run DNA and either confirm or rule out . . . Someone has made an accusation against your husband?'

I couldn't look at her. I had been deliberately dropping hints. She had picked them up and made the logical connections. 'Yes.'

'Have they asked for money?'

'No,' I said, surprised at the question. 'Why?'

'Just thinking through the options. If they haven't gone to the police and they haven't asked for money . . . Do they have a therapist putting them up to it?'

'No.' I'd gone too far to not tell her the whole thing. Granted we had promised Tolliver to keep the journals to ourselves, but this hit too close and my allegiance to my husband and my family took precedence. 'The person is dead,' I said. 'She was a local girl who killed herself many years back.'

'So who made the accusation?'

'She kept diaries.'

'Who had the diaries?'

I paused, knowing that I had hit the point of no return.

She waited out my silence.

I stabbed my fork into a small hill of coleslaw. What business did I have going through Wendy Conroy's journals anyway? 'I'm torn,' I admitted. 'I was reading them as a favor, and now . . .'

'I can be discreet, Lil. But if there's a chance that they have some bearing on these cases, you have to tell me.'

'The diaries are Wendy Conroy's.'

She let the name sink in. 'Philip Conroy's sister?'

'Yes.'

'Why would he have given them to you?'

'He didn't. It was Tolliver.'

'OK,' she said. 'Why would Tolliver want you to see them?'

'He said that he couldn't bear to look at them. Apparently, Philip had read them and become depressed. Tolliver didn't think he could handle whatever was in them.'

'So that's what it was,' she said, coming to some conclusion that I couldn't follow. 'I'm going to need to get them, Lil.'

'I figured. Let me talk to Tolliver before you take them.' I didn't relish the thought of telling Tolliver that I had broken his confidence. Or worse, I was so frightened of having the journals scrutinized in the light of day. 'Mattie, there are things in those notebooks that could ruin my husband's reputation. There's no way he can defend himself.'

'I'll do what I can,' she said. 'But things come out in murder investigations that no one wants to see.'

I pushed my untouched sandwich to the edge of the table. I had no appetite, and there was a weight in my chest that made it hard to breathe. 'What am I going to tell my daughters?'

'Nothing,' she said. 'Not yet. Trust me. I'll be as careful as I can.'

I wanted to believe her, to believe that the life I had lived for more than thirty years with Bradley had not been a lie. The room felt warm and close. 'I need air,' I said, getting to my feet. My head felt too light. I should have eaten something. The tightness in my chest worsening, like someone pressing in.

'Lil?' Mattie got up and put her hand on my shoulder. 'What's happening?'

'Nothing,' I muttered, loosening the collar of my dress. My skin felt hot, my tongue thick; I was sweating. 'It's so warm.'

'Sit down,' she said.

I tried to oblige, but – 'Oh my' – like a fist squeezing my ribs. The pain . . . I grabbed on to her but my balance was off and my slippers lost their grip on the waxed linoleum.

Mattie caught me and eased me to the floor. A crowd gathered.

'Someone dial nine one one,' Mattie barked, further loosening my dress.

I stared up into the waitress' cornflower blue eyes – only, they weren't hers, they were Wendy's. And as I lost consciousness, she smiled.

TWENTY-SEVEN

I lay in Cardiac Care, watching the glittery drip of the intravenous. To my left, hidden by a privacy curtain and partial darkness, my roommate snored. Occasionally, her monitor chirped as she shifted, but other than that, it was quiet.

I desperately wanted to get up, but had been cautioned with all manner of life-threatening complications that if I moved, disaster could follow. My groin throbbed where they had snaked the catheter into my femoral artery up through my aorta and finally into the blood vessels that surrounded my heart.

'You were lucky, Mrs Campbell,' Dr Green, my doom-and-gloom cardiologist had said as he'd showed me the images of the clogged vessel. 'It looks like it's been building up plaque for a while and then it had a spasm.'

I wondered what Bradley would have said. These advances in medicine were the things that had excited and renewed him. I pictured him beside me, explaining the tiny balloon that had been inflated to clear an opening in the clogged artery. He'd tell me what everything was for; the fluid that dripped into my arm, the glowing red numbers on the monitor above my head.

An aide in pink floral scrubs appeared in the lit door. She smiled and squeaked in on rubber-soled shoes. 'Trouble sleeping?'

'It's OK,' I whispered, not wanting to wake the woman by the window.

'I could have the nurse bring you a pill,' she offered as she checked the bandage on the inside of my leg, as she and her earlier counterpart had done every half hour since the procedure and the removal of the catheter afterwards.

'No, that's fine. I'm just thinking.'

'Well, if you need anything,' she said, rearranging my covers, 'just ring.'

I thanked her, and stared up at the darkened ceiling. That I could have died wasn't my major concern. There were too many other things. Obviously, the conversation with Mattie lay heavy on my mind, or, more accurately, my heart. My doctors would probably disagree, but I think the plaque would have been fine and dandy if I hadn't been so . . . heartbroken. While I never knew Philip Conroy, other than by sight, I understood why his sister's journals had depressed him. They'd almost killed me.

I wondered if Mattie had retrieved them yet. She had stayed with me up until I went into the cardiac catheterization lab. Ada had greeted me in the recovery suite, putting on a good face, but clearly distraught. She'd stayed until they'd kicked her out at the end of visiting hours. She'd argued that she was family, but they'd adamantly refused to let her stay.

'You're going to be OK, Lil,' she had told me. 'The doctor said it was a little one. You're going to be fine.'

I wished I could have put her mind at ease. She'd been next to me when my girls had called, first Christina and then Barbara. They'd both insisted on flying out; they'd be here in the morning. And while I loved my daughters, there was something about their coming that made me jumpy. Perhaps it was Christina's 'We can talk about things' that had me worrying. What sort of things needed to be discussed? I'd had a minor heart attack and according to the doctor there was no appreciable damage to the muscle.

I could imagine my children's conversation, certain that they would have been discussing things behind my back: *'What will we do about mother?'*

For God's sake, I'm only fifty-nine! I don't want them to see me like this.

'It's nothing serious,' I had told them. 'Really no reason to fly out. I'm fine.'

To which Barbara had shot back, 'The nurse said you had a heart attack.'

'It's nothing,' I'd repeated, miffed that she had gone behind my back; wasn't that a breach of confidentiality?

'I'll be there in the morning.'

My concern wasn't for me alone; I was afraid of what they would find when they came. I looked at the phone and then at the clock; two a.m. Clearly too early to call Ada, but I needed to know the journals were out of my house. I didn't want my daughters knowing about the murders or the accusation against their father. I wanted them to continue with twice a year visits and once a week phone calls. The status quo was fine, and people were messing with it. I felt the fabric of my existence being shredded. People in Grenville – my town – weren't supposed to get murdered or accuse my husband of being a pedophile. *And you, Lil.* I stared at the tiny dots in the ceiling tiles and thought of Ada. *You're in love with your best friend, and you must never let her know.* There were too many things happening at once and something had to give; apparently, I was it.

'OK,' I whispered into the darkened room. 'Pull yourself together.' The sound of my voice – strong and clear – like a balm on my worried spirits. 'You can't do anything this very minute, but in the morning . . .' I closed my eyes, nothing to be done, go to sleep. And amidst the drip-drip of my intravenous and the ding-ding of my neighbor's pump, I drifted.

I dreamed. It started in a wooded glade. A shaft of light pierced the forest canopy, dappled reflections skittered across a bubbling brook. In the water, my reflection, but there was too much movement and my face lost form. Birdsong surrounded me and I felt a need to follow the stream. *It leads somewhere. There's something you need to see, Lil, follow the water.*

The earth grew soft underfoot. I looked down as my shoes sank into oozing mud. *Why did I wear pumps?* The slimy wetness ruining the hand-stitched Italian soles. *Done is done*, I thought, and I followed the stream as it gathered volume and speed.

Sinking deeper with each step, my ankles slick with the strange mud. I thought about turning back, but thick storm clouds were gathering over the once idyllic glade. And again: *there's something you need to see. Follow the stream.*

The water swelled, and a wind whipped whitecaps. *Is this going to town? Where is this?* Something so familiar. *The road leads you to town. You don't know where the water goes.* I looked around as my feet sank deeper. I wondered if it was quicksand and, with a great sucking noise, I pulled myself out; but lost my shoes.

A crack of lightening lit the sky. For an instant I saw clearly, and realized that the mud, which covered my legs, was a dark viscous red, like clotted blood.

I held my breath and counted the seconds, waiting for the thunder. *Why am I here?* I wanted to be home.

The stream widened, threatening to break over its banks. In horror, I watched as it rose, its dark surface bubbled. I edged back into the shadowy woods, bare feet on the slick forest floor. Behind me, I heard the heavy fluid as it crested over the bank crushing twig and leaf as it advanced. I tried to outrun it. I plunged into the forest; my eyes struggled against the dark.

Finally, blocked by brambles, I turned to face the oncoming flood.

Like a tsunami, the dark fluid crested, and then, as though held by the hand of God, it hung suspended in front of me. As I stared at it, I saw pieces of jewelry floating in its depths, and it smelled like garbage cans left in the sun. 'You have to go into it, Lil,' I told myself. 'You can't run.' And I walked into the wall of blood.

There was a sensation of weightlessness. *Am I drowning?* But my lungs were full of air and before long I bobbed to the surface. My eyes blinked on to the familiar surroundings of the Pilgrim's Progress golf course. I wasn't lost; I was in the eleventh hole water trap. I swam toward the shore and got out. I smoothed down my clothes and smiled at the strollers on the walking path. No one seemed to think it odd that I'd gone fully dressed into the pond, or that I was covered in blood.

In the distance, Ada was holding a ringing phone. 'It's for you,' she called out. 'I told them you'd be right there.'

'Pick it up,' I yelled back, wondering why she hadn't answered it. The ring grew louder, more insistent.

I woke. The phone rang again. I pulled myself up by the railing on the side of the bed, the pain in my groin less sharp. My eyes struggled to focus in the darkened room. It must be morning, catching the filtered light as it seeped past my roommate's privacy curtain. Contorting my wrist back and trying not to upset the intravenous, I picked up.

'Hello?' I said, and listened to the silence that stretched over the line. 'Hello?' I heard the faintest trace of breath. 'Who is this?' It must be a wrong number, I thought, and was about to hang up, when a muffled male voice spoke.

'You're next,' he said, and it clicked dead.

TWENTY-EIGHT

Mattie Perez stared at a copy of the crumpled page of Wendy Conroy's journal. Seated behind a battered wood desk in a windowless office Hank had commandeered for her, she now had some idea as to why Tolliver Jacobs had been so cagey. '*We were having problems,*' he had said, before calling his attorney. This was not what she'd expected.

She reread Wendy's poem. Poor Lil, she thought, her earlier conversation with Ada Strauss at the hospital having filled her in on the details.

'Lil's convinced Wendy was talking about her husband,' Ada had said.

'Aren't there other doctors in town?' Mattie had asked.

'Lil said there weren't, at least not then. And . . . he was Wendy Conroy's doctor.'

'Did you know Bradley?'

'Yes, the kind of man who'd drop whatever he was doing to help. A very kind person, and completely ethical. This makes no sense. And I told her that. The girl was clearly out of her mind. If she was talking about Bradley it had to be a fantasy, not something that actually happened.'

Mattie studied the poem; it had been torn off along its bottom edge. There had been more to it, almost as if someone had gotten to a particularly offensive part and ripped it out. *And why was this one on top of the stack and in such poor condition?*

In the next room she heard Kevin Simpson at the copier, going through the other journals, making duplicates and bagging the originals as evidence. At least she had found something he could do without getting in her way. Granted, he had to be reminded to wear gloves and he had no idea how to correctly process and label the evidence. It wasn't her job to show him, but if the evidence got screwed up, it would be her neck on the chopping block. Sergeant Ted MacDonald was already furious with her, screaming at her on the phone – '*I don't have these kind of resources! You think this is the only case in Connecticut?*' – when she'd insisted he authorize search teams and dogs to go after the still missing Sal Rinaldo and Pete Jeffries. The final straw, and what she knew she'd end up paying for, was the email she'd sent clearly stating what she needed and copying his immediate supervisor and both the commanders of field and administrative operations. His response – also copied – had been a curt two-line answer finally authorizing a single search team.

She looked across her desk at the bulletin board she'd assembled. On index cards she had placed the names of the victims and beneath each of these were rows of yellow post-it notes with potential motives and leads.

Wendy's poem added a twist, one that might have nothing to do with the murders. Still, the timing of its discovery with Philip's murder made it too hot. And the torn edge needed explanation. Where was the missing piece? Who took it? Philip? Tolliver?

Tolliver was hiding things; she could feel it. Ada had said that he had wanted her and Lil to take the journals and read them. But what if he had already looked through them and taken out a bit here and there?

Nothing added up and she kept coming back to the poem. She stared at a picture of the dead girl, perched on a rock and smiling at the camera. Next to that was the news clipping from the local paper.

Local Woman Found Dead at Silver Glen Hospital

The body of Wendy Conroy (28) was discovered early yesterday morning on the grounds of Silver Glen Hospital. The young woman had apparently drowned in an ornamental pond. Miss Conroy had been a resident at Silver Glen, a private psychiatric facility, for five years.

Doctor Gerard Helmut, the medical director for Silver Glen, stated, 'This is a great tragedy. Miss Conroy has been a vital member of our community and she will be greatly missed.' Doctor Helmut offered his condolences to the family and stated that a memorial service would be held at Silver Glen for staff and residents.

Miss Conroy is survived by her parents, Ellen and James Conroy, and her brother, Philip Conroy. The funeral is to be private, and donations will be accepted in her name by the Grenville Arts Council.

Mattie reread the clipping. What was she missing? Or was this just a time-swallowing blind alley?

She listened to the steady hum and click of Kevin at the copy machine.

She thought about Lil and Ada, how they had been more helpful than either Kevin or Hank. Lil in particular had a good sense of the players in town and how they worked. What must she be going through? She thought back to the diner; Lil stood to lose so much. To find out that after more than thirty years of marriage, your husband wasn't who you thought he was. Or worse, that he'd committed the most heinous of acts. It didn't fit. Lil was too savvy for that. Although, it wasn't rare for a woman to discover that the kind and attentive man she thought she'd married was a fiction. How many of them had she sat with? '*He's never done it before,*' they'd say, while cradling their broken ribs. She'd encourage them to fill out a report and to have photos taken of their bruises. Few of them followed through. For the first-timers it was: '*He promised not to do it again.*' And for those who'd been through repeated bouts, where the violence came harder and faster: '*It'll just make it worse. What good would a restraining order do?*' They would leave her office after being given referrals to the proper agencies and a pep talk to 'stop the cycle of abuse'. Armed with numbers for the local women's shelter and the hot line, they would walk bruised and battered back into the arms of their men.

This was different, though. The pieces didn't fit, unless Lil was being less than frank. Most pedophiles had difficulty with adult relationships. If what Lil had said about their marriage was accurate, Bradley didn't fit the profile.

Kevin popped his head into her office. 'What you up to?'

'Thinking,' she said, wishing he'd finish his copying and leave her in peace.

He followed her gaze to the corkboard where she'd pinned her notes. 'She connects with at least two of them,' he offered.

'Who?'

'Wendy. She connects with at least two of the murder victims.'

'You knew her?'

'Sure, we went to school together.'

'Same class?'

'Some of them. She was in my homeroom in junior high. Then

I think she got pulled out of school either in her sophomore or junior year.'

'What was she like?'

'Pretty, real quiet. Kind of the artsy type. She was editor of the school paper. These poems and stuff don't surprise me. Kind of weird though, especially that one about Dr Campbell.'

'You knew him too.'

'Everyone did. I don't think there was another doc for twenty miles, unless of course you went to Danbury.'

'Ever heard any rumors about him?'

'The Doc? Nah. He was a cool. Even made house calls.'

'So there was never any talk or scandal?'

'Not that I knew.'

'Tell me more about Wendy. Who did she hang out with?'

'That's a tough one. I was more into sports. She was someone who was there, but you didn't really notice her a lot.'

'So there was nothing at all unusual?' Mattie asked, feeling like she was pulling teeth. Here Kevin might actually have some useful information, and he was holding back.

'Well –' scratching the back of his head – 'now that you mention it, there was some strange stuff in high school. People thought she was weird and then before too long she just went away.'

'Weird how?'

'To me, everyone acts flaky in high school. So I didn't think much about it. But she started getting into all this punk rock stuff, wearing a lot of silver jewelry and black clothes.'

'You said she was connected with two of the victims. Philip was her brother; who else?'

'Mildred Potts was her aunt or something. I remember seeing her around the shop. She'd, like, change the windows and stuff.'

'What about Rudy Caputo and Carl McElroy? Did she have anything to do with either of them?'

'I don't think so, but it's a small place. People know each other and know each other's business.'

'Right. I'm going to head over to Silver Glen. You feel like tagging along?'

'Yeah. What do you want to do there?'

'I'm not sure, see if anything pops up. How far is it?' she asked.

'Bout half an hour.'

'Good, let me call ahead and see what sort of roadblocks they'll put up. If we want to look at her records we'll probably need a subpoena.'

'Maybe not.' He picked up the phone.

'What are you doing?'

'Watch.' He dialed the operator and scribbled down the number. Without stopping he punched in the digits. 'This is Kevin Simpson for Wayland Green. Sure, I'll hold.' Kevin's head bobbed amiably with the music that spilled out of the receiver. 'REM,' he said to Mattie, by way of explanation. 'Hey, Wayland, how's it hanging . . . Not bad. Saw your new car; sharp. Is it a two thousand and twelve? . . . Sweet. Six cylinders? No kidding . . . Kids are good? Great . . . So when's the baby coming? You stopping at three? You're an animal.'

Mattie listened in bemusement, wondering when he'd get to the point. And grudgingly, she had to admit that his banter might be useful.

'So, Wayland, you remember Wendy Conroy? Right, exactly . . . Yeah, I know she was up there; that's why I'm calling. I'm working on the murders and something came up. We're going to need to take a look at her records . . . Maybe fifteen years ago . . . How hard will that be? So if we left in like half an hour, you think you could get them? You're a stand-up guy . . . Hey, I wouldn't know about that, but it is your third kid . . . Thanks, man.' He hung up, and like a child wanting his mother's approval, he looked at Mattie.

'So?' she asked.

'He said her records were either in the warehouse or on microfilm, but he'd track them down.'

'Strong work,' she acknowledged. 'So who's Wayland?'

'Wayland Green, he's a Grenvillian.'

'Helpful.'

'Nice guy,' he said, missing Mattie's point entirely. 'We went to school together. He's the director up there. I figured it would just be easier to call him than have to bother the judge for a subpoena.'

'Let me think about this,' she said. 'You have to be careful with anything that might become admissible.'

'What do you mean?'

'You need to be careful in how you acquire and handle evidence. I can't tell you how many good cases fall apart because of short cuts with the evidence.'

'You think we should get a subpoena, anyway?' he asked.

'I do,' she said. 'And it really puts a crimp in doing this today.'

'Not necessarily.' He grinned and picked up the phone. 'Yeah, Marge, you want to get me Judge Blasely . . . Try his cell; he's probably playing golf . . . Thanks.' He made a quick note under the number for Silver Glen, and then dialed. 'Hey, Ken, it's Kevin Simpson . . . Look, I'm working on the murders and I need a favor . . .'

TWENTY-NINE

'**M**other, stop it.' Barbara scolded. 'The doctor said you should stay for at least another twenty-four hours.'

'It's not his life, is it?' I shot back as I hunted for my belongings.

'You're behaving like a child,' she scolded. 'What would Daddy say?'

'Don't bring your father into this. All they want to do is keep me for observation, and frankly, I'm feeling better and I want to get home.' The last thing I needed was for Barbara to get on her high horse. *Why couldn't her plane have been delayed?*

'Fine, but if you drop dead . . .'

I looked at the concern on my daughter's face as she hovered. I stopped and sat on the bed. 'I'm going to be fine, dear. The doctor said the damage was minimal. And besides, your father always said the hospital was the worst place to stay once you were feeling better, that you could pick up all sorts of bacteria that would make you sicker than anything you came in with.'

'Maybe you shouldn't have taken that job at the Antique Center,' she offered. 'Maybe it was too stressful.'

'Maybe I should take up knitting and plant myself in a rocking chair?'

'That's not what I meant.'

'Dear, we seem to have gotten off to a bad start. Why don't we get out of here and go for a sit-down somewhere.'

'I wish you'd stay.'

'I know.' Satisfied that I had my few possessions, I went into the fluorescent-lit bathroom to check my appearance. I daubed on a quick swipe of coral-pink lipstick that Ada had brought and tried to pinch some color into my cheeks. I could see why Barbara was concerned. The hospital was no beauty cure. I looked a sight, my hair hopelessly flattened by the hours in bed, and my face – *God, I look old* – like I'd aged ten years in the past twenty-four hours. When I walked, a deep throbbing pain reminded me of where the catheter had gone up my inner thigh.

I tried not to think about the hang-up caller. Even though that that was part of why I had to get out of here. Someone was trying to frighten me, and they were doing a damn good job. I tried to tell myself it was just a prank caller, someone trying to rile me up . . . a lady who'd just had a heart attack; maybe they wanted to frighten her into another . . . into her grave.

In the mirror, I watched Barbara pace in front of the bed. She had Bradley's chin, my pale blue eyes and a tall, thin frame that she maintained with daily jogs and Pilates. Her short, beautifully styled chestnut hair was not entirely natural, and I wondered if she'd started to go gray. I subtracted backwards and realized she was thirty-six; Christina was two years younger. *My children are middle aged*, I thought. Despite all these magazine articles insisting that thirty was the new twenty and sixty the new forty. At that moment I felt far from forty and looked about a hundred. Maybe being in the hospital made that more explicit, that we were all getting older. I remembered a not-funny joke Bradley used to make: '*In every day and in every way we're just that much closer to death.*'

As I came out of the bathroom, a stocky nurse entered armed with her clipboard. She quickly assessed the situation. 'What's going on?'

'Finally,' Barbara said, 'someone to talk some sense into her.'

The nurse looked at me expectantly.

'I was telling my daughter that I felt fine and was ready to leave. Doctor Green even said I was just here for observation.'

'You're not scheduled to be discharged until tomorrow.' As she spoke my roommate's intravenous pump began to ding. The nurse went to adjust the clogged tubing. 'Let me give the doctor a call and see what we can do,' she said over her shoulder as she reset the machine.

'I can recuperate much quicker at home. Please, tell him that.' And then added, 'And both of my daughters have come into town to take care of their ailing mother.'

Barbara shot me a look.

'Well,' I said, perching on the bed, my purse in my lap, 'apparently we have to wait for the good doctor.' I patted the mattress next to me. 'Sit.'

Grudgingly, Barbara obliged.

'Don't be that way,' I chided. 'If I was having any symptoms I'd stay.'

'I suppose you know what you're doing.'

'Thank you. I'm not completely senile.'

She looked at me. 'You're smudged,' she said, pulling a tissue out of the bedside box. I let her minister to my uneven lip line, enjoying the moment of calm.

'So when does Chris get in?' I asked.

'Soon. She was going to your condo first.'

'Good.' *Please God let those journals be out of there!* 'Then we'll meet her there.'

'You know you scared us to death,' she said, rubbing rouge into my cheeks.

'Not my intent.'

'Were you having pains before?'

'No, this came out of nowhere. They'll probably never let me back into The Brown Bear Diner. I'm sure having patrons drop on their floor can't be good for business.'

'So glad you can joke about it.'

'I don't want to make it bigger than it was.'

'I wish I could have been here sooner,' she said, looking out the doorway into the busy corridor.

'What for?'

'I just feel bad that you're out here all by yourself.'

'Yes,' I admitted, 'it is hard being the last living person in Connecticut.'

'That's not what I meant.'

'I know, dear, but I'm not alone.'

'You don't have family.'

'I do. I have you and Chris.' But I was thinking about Ada, and wishing she were here to help bolster my case. But I'd told her not to come this morning, knowing that Aaron was with friends and she'd have to call a cab.

'On the other side of the country.'

'I'm not complaining.'

'I didn't say you were. I just think that it might be easier if we all lived closer.'

'I don't want to move,' I said. 'Do you?'

At that point the nurse returned with Dr Green. He looked first at me, dressed with purse in lap. Then he looked at Barbara.

'The nurse tells me your mother wants to sign out.'

'Yes, she's pretty insistent.'

'Let me take a look,' he said, flipping through my clipboard. 'Mrs Campbell, would you mind laying back on the bed?'

I obliged, not enjoying the odds of three of them against one of me. 'Really, I feel fine.'

With a finger to his lips he motioned for me to be quiet while he insinuated the bell of his stethoscope beneath my dress.

It was such an intimate gesture. How many times I had seen Bradley do the same. Of course, he always warmed the metal with his hands first.

Dr Green's fingers sought out the pulse in my wrist. I waited, listening to the silence and catching glimpses of my daughter. Despite the fact she was annoying me no end, I had a moment's pride noting how well she looked with her quietly chic navy suit and perfectly styled hair.

But how dare she blow in from out of town, albeit with the best of intentions, and attempt to ride roughshod over my life? I can't imagine what her response would be if I told her about the journals, the murders, or my mystery caller. Right then, I determined to tell her nothing.

The cardiologist withdrew from his perch beneath my bra and, with a clicking sound between his lips, he removed the stethoscope.

He looked at me and then turned to Barbara. 'Will anyone be at home with her?' he asked.

'Both me and my sister.'

'Hmmm,' he responded, weighing the options. He looked at me again, I thought he might even speak to me, but he turned back to Barbara. 'I'm going to want a home nurse to visit. I'll have the social worker make the referral.'

'Excuse me,' I said, having had enough of being referred to in the third-person invisible. 'I don't want some stranger in my home.'

The doctor looked at me and in the tone one takes with a young – and not terribly swift – child said, 'Mrs Campbell, you just had a heart attack. You're going to need to have someone check in on you.'

'For what? I can't see what some stranger coming into my home is going to do for me. If you want me to see my internist, or go for rehab, I'd be happy to do that.'

'Mother,' Barbara broke in, 'would you please listen to the doctor?'

'Fine, then at least have the courtesy to speak directly to me. I'm not a child.'

'I just find,' he said, sounding annoyed, 'that it is sometimes easier to communicate instructions to family members. You've been through a lot.'

'Yes, I have, and fortunately it didn't rob me of my ability to think. I'd like to leave . . .' I tried to regain my composure, while rewrapping the top of my dress. 'OK,' I said, 'I'll go along with the nurse for one visit. After that I'm not making any promises.'

'It's your life,' he said.

'Exactly.'

'You'll need to come in for some tests over the next few weeks.' He was about to turn back to Barbara and then stopped himself. 'I'll have my office give you a call.'

'That would be fine,' I said, already thinking that the first thing I would do when I got home was give my internist a call and have him refer me to another cardiologist.

'That's it then,' he said, rising from the bed.

'You're going to let her go?' Barbara asked, clearly alarmed.

'It's not like I'm a serial killer,' I reminded her, 'just your mother.'

'Are you sure she's ready?' she persisted, tagging after the doctor as he headed toward the door.

'Like I said earlier, I thought another day for observation was warranted, but clearly she doesn't wish to stay and as far as any imminent danger, she should be past that. It'll be important for her to rest for the next few days, take the medicine and follow up in the office next week. Then we'll get her started in rehab.' He flashed her, what I'm sure he considered, a reassuring smile. 'She should be fine. Just keep an eye on her.'

Wonderful, now she's been given doctor's orders to boss me around. This is not what I needed. What I needed was time to think. There was too much already and the cavalry-like arrival of my children wasn't helping. I thought back to my dream as snippets of the dark wood and the river of blood flashed to mind. A few years back, Ada and I had gone to a series of lectures on dream interpretation. For a while, both she and I had been caught up in a daily ritual of sharing our dreams and then trying to decipher them. I had no doubt that my subconscious wanted to tell me something. *But what?*

Barbara followed the doctor into the corridor. I overheard whispered traces of their conversation. It did little to calm me. The theme appeared to be: *what should I do with mother?*

I thought about my own mother and how Bradley and I had taken care of her in those last hard years, when everything seemed to give out: her eyes, her ears, and finally her memory. We never once thought about a nursing home and up until those last few months, I looked after her in her own home. When things had deteriorated to where she could no longer remember to turn off the stove, we had it disconnected and she joined us for all our meals, or else I'd go over and fix her breakfast. When she couldn't make the stairs, we moved her bedroom into the back parlor and put a safety gate across the stairwell. We put support bars in the bathroom and installed a separate shower where I'd bathe her. I remembered the intimacy of that, of helping my mother dress in the morning, of carefully powdering her after her bath so that she wouldn't develop rashes or pressure sores.

The day she no longer recognized Bradley was the day we moved her into our house. In retrospect, I'm not certain it was the right thing to do. A month after she had moved into our spare bedroom, which we had arranged to mimic her own, she developed pneumonia, and within a week had died.

The end had been awful. Every day I had to hover over her, lest she bolt out the door and head back to her house. At least in Grenville people knew who she was and on those couple occasions where I didn't catch her fast enough, Hank Morgan or one of the neighbors would spot her and bring her home.

I then thought of Ada and what she was facing with Rose. Of course, someone has to look after Mom, and for her that meant either returning to New York or figuring some way to get Rose into Nillewaug or something similar. If I were truly her friend, I would have seen this.

Barbara returned without the doctor. 'Here –' she reached for my blue plastic *Patient's Belongings* bag – 'let me help you.'

In the doorway an orderly appeared with a wheelchair. It was an archaic ritual, which Bradley never explained to my satisfaction, but I allowed myself to be helped into the chair for my ride to the front door. The whole thing begged the question: *if you still need a wheelchair maybe you shouldn't be leaving?* Then again I was thrilled to be on my way and wasn't going to make waves.

As I was rolled out, I spotted Doctor Green, surrounded by a bevy of young doctors and medical students. He looked briefly in my direction, shook his head, and then returned to his disciples. My cheeks burned as I imagined his comments.

Perhaps he was right and I should have stayed longer. Still, I felt relief that I would be out in the light of day heading toward my own home and my own bed.

Unfortunately, as we neared the lobby I saw an increasing number of dripping umbrellas.

'Well, at least here you don't get mudslides,' said Barbara as she fished a portable umbrella from her briefcase-sized pocketbook.

'We do need the rain,' the orderly commented as he wheeled me toward the glass-domed portico. 'If you want, I can have the valet get your car.'

'Will that take long?' I asked, just wanting to be away from there. I had this uneasy sense, that one wrong look and they'd whisk me back to my monitored bed.

'Couple minutes.'

'It's OK,' Barbara said, 'a little rain never hurt anyone.' And with that, she bolted into the driving torrent.

'What time is it?' I asked the orderly.

'Getting on eleven,' he replied. 'If you make it out the door before eleven, they don't charge you for the day.'

'Check-out time?' I offered.

He chuckled. 'Yeah, but no mint on your pillow.'

We lapsed into silence.

My thoughts drifted, lulled by the rhythm of the rain. Water, water everywhere. Throughout my dream there had been water that turned to blood. Like Wendy, who drowned. Perhaps that's what the dream was about. My surfacing in the golf pond, the juxtaposition of the familiar and the hidden. That was it. Grenville . . . How many times had I said that I knew my town like the back of my hand? It wasn't true, at least not now, and if Wendy's horrible accusation wasn't a lie or a delusion, perhaps I didn't even know my husband . . . or myself.

The beeping of a horn interrupted my thoughts. A shiny white rental sedan pulled into the carport. Inside, Barbara motioned for me to get in.

'Looks like you're going to make it,' the orderly said.

I didn't know if he was referring to the eleven o'clock checkout time or my fear that I wouldn't be allowed to leave.

He wheeled me out under the sheltered parkway and opened the door.

'Wait a minute,' he said, adjusting the brakes on the wheelchair. 'OK, you're all set.'

With shaky hands I gripped the sides of the chair and felt the pavement beneath my slipper-clad feet. My knees wobbled and I knew that three days lying in bed had destroyed my muscle tone. As soon as I can – I told myself – it's back to yoga class.

'You OK?' Barbara asked as I gripped the doorframe.

'I'm fine,' I said, wishing I felt steadier. I settled into the car and caught the warm musty smell of wet clothes as they mixed with the car's heating system. It was a comfortable cocoon-like feel, the hum of the motor and the patter of the rain. I looked across at Barbara, her profile more relaxed now that we were away from the harsh light of the hospital. 'It's good to see you,' I offered.

She smiled. 'You too, but I still think you should have followed doctor's orders.'

'Just ornery, and judging by what went on in there, I seem to have passed that on.'

On impulse she reached across and gave me an awkward hug and kiss. I could see that she had been crying; a tear clung to her cheek like a raindrop on the windshield.

'I was really scared,' she admitted, settling back into the driver's seat and adjusting the safety belt. 'When Mrs Strauss called and said you'd had a heart attack, I kept thinking about Daddy. It's like he was fine one day and then he was gone.'

'I'm going to be OK,' I reassured her. 'Trust me, I know lots of people who've had more serious heart attacks and they go on for years and years.'

'Thanks,' she said. 'I'm just not ready to lose you.' She was crying, and trying not to show it. She looked straight ahead, and pulled out into the driving rain.

'I'm not going to die Barbara, not yet. I really do feel fine. I've just had a lot on my mind and I think things caught up with me.'

'Like what?' she asked. 'What's going on, Mom?'

'Different things, nothing to be worried about.' As I said that, I thought back to the phone call. A pit in my stomach. It had to have been a wrong number.

'Could you be more vague?' she responded.

'Let me think . . . How are the kids?'

'Nice transition,' she commented wryly. 'They're fine.'

'Now who's being vague?'

'OK, let me see. Josh wants to marry his second grade teacher, a lovely woman with a nose piercing and, I suspect, a multitude of tattoos she keeps covered around the kids.'

'How exciting.'

'Exactly, and Heather lives for soccer, and absolutely refuses to play in the all-girls league.'

'Good for her.'

'I guess it's raised some eyebrows, and as she gets older it could be a problem. At this point, it's kind of wait and see. But she is good, and I think she takes a thrill in giving as good as she gets with the boys.'

'Fights?' I asked, thinking of my nine-year-old granddaughter, whose Christmas list invariably involves a trip to the sporting goods store.

'Oh, yeah. Got a mean hook on her. And with all this Ralph is making noises about having a third. Frankly, with work and all, I can't see it. Plus, I'm thirty-six, I'd be close to your age by the time that one got through college. I think two is enough. So, enough of me, and your transparent attempt to change the topic. Your friend Ada told me that things have been pretty exciting in the old town.'

'Really?' I dreaded what might come next. 'What did she tell you?'

'That there'd been a string of murders. I mean, really, Grenville?'

'It's true.'

'Why is it happening?'

'Lots of hypotheses, but no one really knows. They've all been antique dealers.'

'Like *Who's Killing the Great Chefs of Europe*?'

'What's that?' I asked.

'An old film, where someone went around killing famous chefs.'

'What was the motive?'

'You know, I can't remember. It was a black comedy. The sort of thing I'll flip through late at night when I can't sleep.'

'It has that feel around here. Not the comedy part, but this sense of wondering why and who's next?' *If she knew . . . but my caller can't have anything to do with this. Lil, you have to tell someone, just not Barbara.*

'It's scary,' she commented, pulling into the gates of Pilgrim's Progress. 'I knew Mildred Potts. I remember her from growing up. I used to look at the jewelry in her window and drool. Of course, I never could afford anything.'

As she spoke, I realized that she was around the same age as Philip and Wendy. 'I wonder if you didn't know one of the other victims.'

'Who?'

'Philip Conroy?'

'Oh my God! Philip?'

'You knew him?'

'Knew him? He was a few years ahead of me. I had a major crush on him in junior high; he was gorgeous. Why would someone kill him? Oh, God.'

'Welcome to Grenville,' I replied as we pulled up to my condo.

With relief I noted that everything was unchanged. The rain-drenched hydrangeas bent under the weight of their purple-blue blossoms and the leaves of the maple – vivid orange and red – were falling fast. My pulse quickened as I caught sight of Ada in my doorway, cloaked by the curtains of water.

'Ready to get soaked?' Barbara asked.

'Ready.'

We ambled up the steep walk toward the front door. With each step I was painfully aware of how weak I had become.

Once over the threshold, I breathed the smells of home. Like coming back to a piece of myself that had been forgotten.

Ada followed. 'Here let me do that,' she said, helping me off with my coat and pushing me toward the living room and my wing chair. 'Just relax, Lil.' Her fingers brushed my cheek. Our eyes met. 'Don't do that again,' she scolded, holding my gaze. And lowering her voice below what Barbara could hear: 'It's selfish . . . but I don't think I could bear it if something happened to you. Now sit, I'll make tea.'

My cheek tingled from her touch as I scanned my home and saw that the boxes of journals were gone. *Thank God.*

Ada returned with tea and a kitten-soft lavender mohair throw, which she draped across my lap. She stepped back, and there were tears in her eyes.

'I know, I look terrible,' I said. 'But really, I'm going to be fine.'

She shook her head, and glanced back toward Barbara, who was talking on her cell in the kitchen. 'Lil, you're not fine and we both know it, and it has nothing to do with your medical condition, although I think that's what brought it on.'

I was about to argue when the phone rang. Without thinking I reached over and picked up. Silence. My stomach clenched with each passing millisecond and I felt a dangerous twitch in the center of my chest. Then the gravelly male voice.

'You're next.'

THIRTY

'Lil, what is it?' Ada asked.

Still holding the phone, and staring out at the pouring rain through the back sliders, I didn't know what to say; my hand felt disconnected from my body. I tried to make it obey, but it clenched tight to the receiver. My head felt fuzzy. It was no prank call; he'd followed me home.

Still frozen, Ada pried away the phone as Barbara came to my side.

'I'm fine,' I said.

'Mom, you're shaking,' Barbara said, sounding scared and young. 'Are you having any pain?'

'No.'

'Who was that?' Ada asked.

Before I could answer, the doorbell rang.

No one moved.

Ada gripped my hands in her own. I looked down at her slender fingers, so delicate and yet so strong from years of working in her stores.

'Someone should get the phone,' I said.

'The door,' she corrected. 'Who was that on the phone?' Worry on her face.

'You're right,' I said, not wanting to tell her in front of my daughter. I needed to get Barbara out of there. Whatever evil had landed in Grenville was heading toward me; I wanted my children away from here.

'Who was it, Mother?' Barbara asked, smoothing back my still-wet hair and feeling my forehead, such a motherly gesture, one that I had done with her as a child. I imagined her doing it with her kids.

Ada squinted, and nodded slightly. *She knows. Please God, let her keep quiet about it in front of Barbara.*

The doorbell rang a second time and then a third.

'I'll get it.' Barbara rose from the sofa. The touch of her fingers lingered. I wanted to stop her.

'Ask who's there.' I blurted out.

She looked back at me, a queer expression on her face.

Ada whispered, 'No name, no number?'

'I think so,' I said, matching her tone, not wanting my daughter to get involved.

'He called me at the hospital. But he said something, and then hung up. He's followed me here.'

'Who?'

'I don't know.'

'What does he say?'

I couldn't bring myself to say it.

'Tell me,' she persisted.

'Chris!' Barbara's voice came clear from the foyer; my younger daughter had arrived, drenched, but smiling.

'Lil.' Ada squeezed my hands, trying to get my attention.

I looked at her, at the concerned intensity of her dark-blue eyes. 'You're next,' I whispered. 'That's all he says.'

Before she could reply, Barbara returned with Chris. I sat and watched as my children approached. I felt like an actress, trying to portray 'normal', not wanting them to know how frightened I felt. *Just focus on them.*

'Mother,' Chris said, giving me a soggy hug and kiss before settling on the sofa by my wing chair, 'what have you done?'

'Well, I thought,' I said, struggling to keep my fear in check, 'I'd try something new.'

She chuckled and whispered, 'Don't do that again.' She took my hand in hers.

'I won't. I promise.'

'You're awfully warm,' she commented.

I shot a glance at Ada, who was clearly frightened by what I'd told her.

'Would you like me to open a window?' Chris suggested.

'No, I'm fine.' I felt like a parrot, which could only repeat the same phrase. I'm fine I'm fine I'm fine; the words had lost their meaning. I wasn't fine. I wanted them out of there and at the same time it felt so good to see them, to breathe their healthy scents, to witness their strength, their vitality.

'OK,' Barbara said, from behind the couch. 'You have to tell us what's going on. Because clearly you are not fine.'

'I beg your pardon?' I shot back.

'Don't start,' Chris pleaded. 'I'm not in the door thirty seconds and you two are going to start one of your pissing contests.'

'Our what?' I asked.

'You heard me. You two have been doing it since I can remember. *Yes I will. No I won't. Yes I will. No you won't. You can't make me. Yes I can. No you can't.*'

'So this is how professors talk?' I asked.

'On a good day,' she quipped. 'Can we start again? I feel like I just stepped into the middle of something.'

'You know,' Ada said, coming to my rescue, 'the kettle's still hot, anyone want tea?'

'I'll get it,' Barbara said. 'You know, Mother, I don't know why you feel like you have to keep things from Chris and me. We're not children anymore.'

'I realize,' I said. 'I just wish you wouldn't try to boss me around. It's the last thing I need.'

'Barbara,' Chris chided, 'I can't believe that you would try to boss Mom around.'

'I'm not,' she protested.

'Yeah, right,' my youngest commented. She turned to Ada. 'When we were young and would play make-believe, Barbara would get all the neighborhood kids together and tell us what we had to say. It was the most heavily scripted make-believe there ever was. She was a total fascist on the playground.'

'I was not.'

I smiled at the memories, of looking out my kitchen window and seeing a gaggle of children hard at play. Chris was right. Barbara used to direct the others in a variety of convoluted games of make-believe, everything from pirates to Batman to elaborate marriage ceremonies. I could still hear her eight-year-old voice, ordering her playmates, '*OK, you say, "with this ring I thee wed", and then we walk down the aisle. But you stop us and say, "You can't marry her, because I'm the one who loves her", and then you push him out of the way . . .*' It didn't seem to bother the other kids, her total domination. They'd play for hours only to be stopped by the dinner bells, which often sounded in unison at six o'clock. If I concentrated, I could still hear the voices of the neighborhood mothers calling their children to dinner.

'Enough said,' Christina commented. She turned back toward me. 'So what *is* going on?'

I shot Ada a warning glance. 'It's nothing,' I said. But knowing I had to give them something, added, 'I've been getting some hang-up calls. It's just an annoyance, some kid playing a prank.' Although I no longer believed that, but if I wanted to get my daughters safely out of town, I would not be sharing the truth.

'Don't you have caller ID?' Barbara asked.

'I do, but all it says is "no name, no number".'

'You can have that blocked,' Barbara said. 'I have all my phones fixed so only calls that can be identified come through. You wouldn't believe how many people try to fake it past my secretary, wanting to know if something has been cast. "Is there maybe a part for them?" "Have I considered so-and-so?" I screen everything. And if they're trying to block their information, I'm just not interested in hearing from them.'

'Geez, Barbara,' Christina chimed in. 'You've moved from call ID to caller totally paranoid. Although it's not a bad idea.'

'Did she tell you about the murders?' Barbara asked.

'No, haven't heard a word about it. What murders?'

I was about to pipe in with a suitably timed 'it's nothing', but I realized under the circumstances, my credibility would plummet.

'Sleepy little Grenville has woken up,' my eldest commented. 'There've been three murders.'

Christina looked at me. 'You've got to be kidding!'

'It didn't seem pertinent,' I commented.

'It's actually four,' Ada added, unable to keep quiet.

'What! Who?' Chris asked.

'Let's see.' Ada sipped her tea. 'First there was Philip Conroy, or at least we think he was first; they didn't find his body for quite some time. Then came Mildred Potts, Carl McElroy, and finally Rudy Caputo.'

'Jesus, Mother, why didn't you tell me?' Christina said accusingly. 'Wait a minute . . . Did you say Philip Conroy? Not . . . Oh, no.'

'I know,' said Barbara, 'it just doesn't seem real.'

'Why would anyone kill Philip?'

Ada couldn't help herself. 'That's what everyone's wondering. Lots of motives being tossed around . . . All the victims were antique dealers. Everyone in town pretty much knew them, or knew of them.'

'Is someone bumping off the competition?' Barbara wondered.

'Probably,' I said, wanting the conversation to die.

'Maybe,' said Ada, 'but it doesn't add up. Why would someone actually kill? It seems excessive.'

'You're right,' Christina commented. 'If you look through history, money is a great motive, but usually there's more to it; some sort of emotional context. Unless of course we're talking contract murders, in which case the person who pulls the trigger is strictly in it for the money and the motive lies with their employer.'

'What sort of emotional context?' Ada asked, warming to the topic.

'Powerful things, often sexual in nature, even though that may not be what appears on the surface.'

'These weren't sex killings,' I said. 'These were, with the exception of Philip, not attractive people.'

'Doesn't matter,' Chris explained. 'Although the disparity in types clearly eliminates the sexual sadist.'

'How do you know so much about this?' I asked, wondering what my assistant-professor daughter was doing expounding on murder motives.

'Just an interest,' she said. 'I've even been toying with the idea of doing a Shakespearean-review course that would focus on homicide.'

'Like Lady Macbeth?' Ada asked.

'Exactly. Shakespeare's plays contain an encyclopedia of murder and motive.'

'So what do you think the motive is here?' Ada asked.

'Off the top of my head, I'd say it had something to do with small-town secrets.'

A swallow of tea went down the wrong pipe; I choked and coughed.

'Are you OK?' Chris asked, patting me gently on the back.

'What leads you to that conclusion?' Ada persisted, a concerned expression on her face as my coughing continued.

I carefully took a sip of tea, and tried to calm the flutters in my chest. *Why do they have to talk about this?*

Chris explained her reasoning. 'They all knew each other, moved in the same circles, right?'

'Yes?' Ada prompted.

'And if they're antique dealers they probably all buy up estates and go through people's belongings.'

'Also correct,' Ada said. 'In fact I'd gotten quotes from two of them; actually three if you consider that Tolliver is Philip's . . . was Philip's partner.'

Chris looked at Ada. 'That's a strange coincidence.'

'Don't look at her that way,' I said, having got my breathing under control. 'This isn't *Arsenic and Old Lace*; we've not been poisoning the locals with elderberry wine.'

'I loved that play,' Ada remarked.

'I didn't say that,' Chris interjected. 'But you have to admit it's odd.'

'We've thought about that,' Ada said. 'Odd and scary. Anyway, you were saying.'

'Think about it, antique dealers are forever digging through other people's stuff. What if one of them found something they weren't meant to see?'

Ada shot me a look. 'What sort of thing?' she asked.

'Something big.' Chris said.

'Something worth killing over,' Barbara stated, completing her sister's thought.

The phone rang and there was silence. Barbara looked at me and then at her sister. Before I could get out of my chair, Barbara had picked up the receiver.

'Hello?' she said. There was a long pause. 'I'll get her.' She cupped her hand over the receiver. 'It's for you, a Detective Perez?'

'I'll take it in the bedroom,' I said, not wanting them to overhear.

'Secrets, Mother?' Barbara asked.

'No, I want privacy.' As I walked to my bedroom I marveled at how quickly my oldest daughter and I were able to push each other's buttons. I hated to think it, but I was glad that most of the year three thousand miles separated us. I loved her dearly, and she drove me crazy.

I picked up the phone, and yelled back into the other room, 'You can hang up now.' I waited before speaking, listening for the click. 'Mattie?'

'Hello, Lil, how are you feeling?'

'Physically, I'm fine,' I said, settling on to the edge of my bed. I looked across at my reflection in the mirror. It was unsettling, as though I could see my skull beneath the skin. 'My nerves are shot, though.'

'Anything I can help with?'

'Not unless you can drive my daughters to the airport.'

'Car trouble?'

I laughed. 'No, I'm just not used to playing the invalid.'

'Oh. I think I have some news you might want to hear. I've been looking through those diaries; I don't think Wendy Conroy was talking about your husband.'

I let her words wash over me, like a balm on my jangled spirit. I didn't want to say anything lest she change her mind.

'You still there?' she asked.

'Yes, just enjoying the first bit of good news I've had in a while. It sounds like you found something.'

'Maybe. I needed to ask you if you knew who she was seeing as her psychiatrist?'

I racked my memory, trying to remember whom Bradley referred to in those days. 'I can't remember. There was no one in town; it would have to have been someone in New Haven or Danbury. I bet it's in her records.'

'Who has those?'

'Good question. When Bradley passed away I gave all the open charts to Winston Fairbanks. The old records, the ones that had been closed out, are still in boxes. I should probably have done something with them, but I never once saw Bradley destroy a chart.'

'Where are they?' she asked, a sense of urgency in her tone.

I turned toward my walk-in closet, with its abundant rows of built-in shelves. 'I'm looking at them.'

'Can you find her chart for me?'

'They're all in boxes.' And I hated the next words out of my mouth. 'The doctor told me not to do any heavy lifting. I'm going to need someone to help get them down.'

'I'll be right over.'

Before I could mount an objection, or at least ask her to come after my daughters had left, she had hung up. I sat, phone in hand, looking around at the familiar room. The mahogany and tiger maple furniture that had been a wedding present from my parents, the four-poster where I'd slept with Bradley for over thirty years. Some nights as I fell asleep I could still see him, always on his back softly snoring. Across from the bed stood two Chippendale highboys that had descended through my family for over two centuries. Their reddish, intricately grained wood gleamed with the efforts of a thousand polishing rags. Years back an appraiser had told me that some distant relative had refinished them, which had seriously diminished their value. That was fine by me; they would pass to Barbara and then to my granddaughter, Heather.

Muffled voices carried from the other room. I knew that Barbara would be trying to worm information from Ada. I wondered if there was any way that I could get them out of the house before Mattie arrived. As I got up to go back into the living room, the phone rang. I picked it up. 'Hello?'

Again, the silence. I wasn't going to wait for his ominous pronouncement. But as I went to hang up the receiver, I heard Barbara's voice over the earpiece.

'Who is this?' she asked.

I held my breath, hoping that there'd be no reply.

'You're next,' the voice rasped and hung up.

I sat there, holding the receiver. 'Barbara?'

'Yes, Mother,' she said over the line.

'You know it's not polite to listen in on other people's conversations.'

'Yes, Mother.'

'I don't want you to say anything about this to your sister.'

There was silence. 'I can't do that. We need to talk.' She hung up.

I seethed. At what point did my daughter turn into my mother? Who was she to tell me that we needed to talk?

From the other room I heard Chris ask, 'What is it?'

I held my breath.

'Mother's hang-up caller, and in light of what's been going on around here, I don't think we should dismiss it as nothing.'

I hung up. My cheeks flushed. That last comment had been a direct hit. I remembered why I liked having Barbara on the other side of the country. Granted it was her choice, but sometimes absence did make the heart grow fonder. As an adolescent, Barbara and I had struggled over everything. It didn't matter what the topic was. Something as simple as a request to turn down the music would dissolve into screaming and slamming doors. She had no right to intrude this way and I didn't know how to stop her.

A gentle knock at the bedroom door. I looked up and saw Ada.

'Can I come in?' she asked.

'Sure.'

She took a seat in the satin-striped slipper chair next to my mother's hope chest. 'Barbara seems quite upset.'

'Seems so,' I whispered, listening to the steady beat of rain on the roof. 'She has a tendency toward the dramatic.'

'She's worried,' Ada replied, keeping her voice low. 'And so am I. Lil, if anything happened to you . . .'

'I know, it's just something about the way she shows it. I know it sounds paranoid, but ever since she came, I've had the feeling that she wants me in some protective setting. She didn't want me to leave the hospital. I was really worried she'd get them to commit me or something, and now she's trying to butt into things that are none of her business. You have no idea how tense I feel right now. And these calls have me so frightened.'

She moved from the chair and sat beside me on the bed. 'We're going to get through this.'

'Try telling that to my daughter. If someone had given her permission to tie me to that hospital bed, she would have done it.'

Ada leaned against me. 'It's not that bad. At least Chris seems reasonable.'

'She is. I mean, they both are, and I feel guilty talking like this. I know they love me and I know they're worried. It's just not what I need right now.'

'What do you need, Lil?' She took my hand; our eyes locked.

My breath caught, and cutting through my fear and worry like a knife was how much I wanted to kiss her. And then the unthinkable. She leaned in and kissed me on the lips. I was stunned at first as her hand pressed tight in mine. And her lips so soft, unlike any kiss I've ever had. I smelled jasmine and had the sense of falling, of being weightless and of wishing this moment could last forever; it was perfect.

And then the doorbell rang.

Reluctantly, we parted, and it felt like something was being ripped from me. She wore a strange smile, and if I had to name the expression on her face, I couldn't; part impish smile, a whiff of embarrassment, and a heart-stopping image of the young girl she'd once been, and who apparently still existed. 'I've wanted to do that for a very long time,' she said.

I desperately wanted to say something, but I couldn't find the words.

And the door rang again.

What was I supposed to say? My best friend had just kissed me, and not like friends, and I really liked it . . . not like friends. 'That's probably Mattie,' was all I could manage. My mouth was dry as I let go of Ada's hand – *she has the most beautiful eyes* – and got off the bed. 'She wants to look through Wendy Conroy's old records.' *Lil, you idiot, tell her how you feel. Do it now!* But before I could figure what to say, a new voice from the other room.

It was Aaron, not Mattie. 'Is my grandma around?' he asked, coming in from the rain. He spotted us coming out of the bedroom. 'Grandma, Mr Jacobs came over. He needs to talk to you.'

'Hold on.' She headed toward the door, and as she did our moment faded. *Perhaps it never happened*, just some psycho aftershock of my heart attack.

In the doorway I spotted Tolliver's BMW, getting pounded by the relentless storm, and pulling up behind it was Mattie Perez's unmarked black car.

As Aaron waited for his grandmother, Tolliver stepped into the doorway. 'There you are,' he said. 'Lord, when it rains . . .'

'What is it, Tolliver?' Ada asked, her cheeks flushed.

He looked around and saw Barbara and Chris.

'I should probably tell you alone.'

Before he could follow through on that, Mattie slammed her car door and sprinted up the walkway.

My lips tingled, and I couldn't look at either of my daughters. *What would they think?* But I was also deathly curious as to what had gotten Tolliver so worked up. Something was wrong, or, more accurately, something else was wrong.

Mattie, in a yellow police slicker knocked on the open door, and stepped into the foyer.

'Who's that?' Barbara asked.

Ada blurted, 'That's Detective Perez.'

'Thank God.' Barbara brushed by Tolliver and Aaron. 'Detective Perez,' she called loudly, stopping a dripping Mattie in front of the door, 'my mother's been getting death threats. You have to do something.'

THIRTY-ONE

My living room had turned into an Agatha Christie denouement, complete with lightning and the roll of thunder. I watched as Mattie, dressed in a navy slack suit and cream turtleneck, surveyed the assembled: me, Ada, my two daughters, Aaron and Tolliver Jacobs.

She caught my eye. 'Death threats, Lil?'

'At first I thought they were nothing, hang-up calls.' All I could think was that I did not want to be talking about this with my daughters here.

'Mother! I heard,' Barbara shot back and turned toward Mattie. 'You've got to do something.'

'What exactly did the caller say?' she asked, accepting the ubiquitous cup of tea from Ada.

'He's after my mother,' Barbara stated, her voice half an octave higher than usual.

'What did he say?'

I interrupted. '"*You're next.*" That's all he said.' Before Barbara could embroider, I coughed up the details. 'It started yesterday, before that I swear they were just hang ups.'

'While you were in the hospital?' Mattie asked, placing her tea on a coffee table and pulling out a flip pad to take notes.

'Yes, I didn't think about it, other than it made my stay less than pleasant. I figured when I got home, they'd stop.'

'But they didn't.'

'No, I've had another two since I came home.'

'So it's someone who knew when you were discharged.'

Aaron, who had gone largely unnoticed, piped in. 'What if someone saw her come home?'

'A possibility,' Mattie agreed. 'It sounds like they're coming pretty close together.'

'I don't think it's someone watching us,' I said. 'I don't think he wants there to be anyone around but me.'

'But I spoke on the phone,' Barbara said. 'He knows that you're not alone.'

'Maybe not,' said Mattie. 'You two sound remarkably alike.'

'We do not,' I said, trying to keep my tone light, not wanting anyone to know how frightened this had me.

'You do,' said Ada.

'Yeah,' Chris agreed. 'You always have, particularly on the phone.'

'Let me make a couple quick calls,' Mattie said. 'I'm going to want to trace the call.'

'He doesn't stay on the line long,' I said, harking back to numerous television shows where it took minutes to trace a call.

'That doesn't matter any more; it's instantaneous,' she explained. 'And for right now, I don't want anyone to leave. She looked at Tolliver. 'And what are you doing here?'

'I was going to call the station, but I needed to talk to Mrs Strauss first.'

'Why?' Mattie asked.

'What's wrong, Tolliver?' Ada asked.

The dealer took a deep breath. 'The Hassam painting is missing.'

'Missing?' Ada asked. 'As in misplaced? Or missing as in stolen?'

'I'm pretty sure it's the latter.'

'What are we talking about?' the detective asked. 'What is the Hassam painting?'

Tolliver filled in the details. 'Mrs Strauss had commissioned me to liquidate an estate for which she was the executrix.'

'This is a nightmare.' Ada said. 'What am I going to tell her children?'

'It's insured,' Tolliver said. 'But the insurance company is going to launch a full investigation.'

'How valuable a painting?' Mattie asked.

Without pause, Tolliver answered, 'Over two million, maybe as high as three.'

'What?' Ada rose to her feet, spilling tea on her beautiful wool skirt and my Persian rug. 'You said it was worth three hundred thousand! Where did two to three million come from?' she waited for his reply.

He stared at his hands and said nothing.

Ada exploded. 'I am so sick of the lot of you! The way you come traipsing through somebody's home telling them that all of their possessions are worthless and then going out and selling them at a ridiculous markup. I was in retail for forty years and if I had conducted my business the way everyone around here seems to, I wouldn't have lasted a year.'

I'd never seen her like this; she was furious, her face red as she bore down on Tolliver. 'What were you planning to do? Sell the painting and then tell me it went for a fraction of what you got? Don't you think I would check? This whole thing makes me sick. Is it any wonder that someone is going around bumping you all off. I think that's what it is, you cheated one person too many and now it's payback!'

'Ada . . . Mrs Strauss,' Mattie said. 'Let me handle this.'

'I'm so angry.' Ada stormed toward my kitchen. On the threshold she stopped, and glared back at Tolliver. 'What gives you the right? You should be ashamed. I hope the insurance company does a thorough investigation and I will be all too happy to supply them with whatever information they need.'

'Mrs Strauss—' He tried to speak.

She cut him off. 'Save it, tell it to the detective.'

'That's it,' said Mattie. 'No one's leaving till I get some answers.'

'You wanted to use the phone,' I reminded her.

'Thanks.'

'The one in the bedroom is best. If no one listens in,' I said, looking pointedly at Barbara.

After she was out of the room, we all looked at Tolliver. He'd grown pale under Ada's tirade.

'I'm sorry about Philip,' Chris said, giving him some breathing room.

'Thanks. Look, about the painting . . .' He was about to say more, but then stopped himself. 'She's right, you know,' he said after a long silence. 'We all do it, and it becomes so much a part of what we do, that you don't question it, or think it's wrong. I mean, most of the time people are just so grateful to get money for their things that they don't really care.'

'I imagine,' I said, curious as to where this would go, 'that a lot of times people don't know what their things are worth.'

'You have no idea. That's how we make a living. Buy low and sell high. And every year there's less merchandise and more and more dealers. And now everyone's selling on eBay; it's gotten much harder. And you have to believe me, that when I first saw the painting I really didn't know how high he listed. It's a museum piece.'

'But you did look it up,' I said, certain that he had.

'Yes, I should have told her.'

I settled back on the sofa, wondering what would happen next. Sounds of Ada assembling another round of tea emanated from the kitchen. I so wanted to go to her, to hold her and try to calm her. I winced as I heard the rough clang of my Fiesta ware. But something told me she needed time, and several cups of tea, maybe even a slug or two from one of the many unopened bottles of excellent single malt patients were forever giving to Bradley. I had a moment's reverie wondering what it might be like to throw a few back with Ada; maybe some more kissing, maybe loosen my tongue to where I could actually tell her how I felt.

My head swam, too much all at once. Barbara and Chris were conversing in hushed tones by the sliding glass doors that over-looked the woods behind my condo. I was convinced that I was the subject of conversation; a battle brewing between me and Barbara, and I suspected she was trying to recruit Chris. Tolliver sat across from me, occasionally looking up from his hands to give me a weary smile. Aaron sat on the step between the foyer and the living room. He, too, seemed subdued.

After a while, Mattie reappeared in the bedroom doorway. 'Lil, you were going to get me those records?'

'Now?'

'If you could. Kevin is working on tracking the calls with the phone company.'

'Let's see if we can find them,' I said.

'What records is she talking about?' Barbara asked, breaking off with Chris.

'Some of your father's old charts.'

'What? Are you sure you should do that, Mother?'

'Of course,' I answered, 'if they can help with the investigation.'

'Don't you need some sort of warrant for that?' Barbara persisted.

An imperceptible change came over Mattie as she confronted my daughter. 'Your mother offered the records of her own free will. I intend to obtain them in a manner consistent with the law. What that entails is her signing a release form that states she gave me her permission to review the documents and, if need be, to remove them for the duration of the investigation and any subsequent trial.'

'I'm not so sure you should do that, Mother. Shouldn't you at least talk to a lawyer?'

'Why would I do that? Lawyers just slow everything down. If I have something that can be useful to a homicide investigation, it's my duty to help.'

'I don't think you should just let her walk in and rummage through Daddy's medical records. Those are supposed to be confidential. I don't think he would have allowed it.'

'Dear, your father is dead. And right now I intend to go with Detective Perez and help her find what she's looking for.' My heart beat uncomfortably fast inside my chest.

'I don't think you should.' Barbara's nostrils flared.

'I understand that, now would you mind getting out of our way?'

I led Mattie back toward the bedroom.

Barbara shot out, 'I forbid you to do this.'

'What?' I turned to face her. 'That's it. I want you to get back in your car and get out of here.'

'Would you two stop it!' Chris stepped in. 'I can't stand it when you do this. We haven't been together for an hour and look at what's happened.'

'It's just like I told you,' Barbara said, driving her case home. 'She's not in her right mind. She shouldn't be making decisions like this. For God's sake, she signed herself out of the hospital two days after having a heart attack.'

'It was three,' I corrected. 'And it's my life and my decisions. And I really want you to leave.'

'No one's leaving,' the detective said. She turned to Barbara. 'And your mother has full authority to do with her possessions, which include your father's records, what she will. And as for you forbidding her to do so, it borders on coercion. I intend to conduct this investigation to the letter of the law and I assure you that under no circumstances will I jeopardize the confidentiality of any records that are not germane to the current case.' She looked at me. 'Mrs Campbell, are you willingly and of your own free will showing me the medical records of Wendy Conroy?'

'Yes, of course,' I answered. Barbara was apoplectic.

'Do you understand,' Mattie continued, 'that these records may be used in a court of law and entered into evidence?'

'I do,' I said.

'Fine.' Mattie foraged through her valise for a blank form. Balancing the paper against her briefcase, she filled in spaces on the printed page and then handed it to me. 'This is a permission to search,' she explained. 'At the top I've filled in the specifics about what I'm looking for and that you're giving me permission to take it. Why don't you take a couple minutes to read it over.'

'I don't need to,' I said, taking the pen from her hand. 'I'm sure it's fine.'

Barbara fumed as I signed the double-sided document.

'I need someone to witness,' Mattie said, looking around the room.

'I will,' Ada stepped from the kitchen. She shot Barbara an angry look, took the pen and signed below my signature.

I was shaking as I led Mattie back into the bedroom and opened the double doors to my closet.

Without asking permission, my daughters and Ada followed.

'Are you sure you know what you're doing, Mother?' Chris asked.

'Dear,' I said, trying to keep my voice steady, 'I would appreciate it if you and your sister would go back in the other room.'

'And she gets to stay?' Barbara asked, looking at Ada.

'Yes, that's right,' I said. 'Now please get out of my bedroom.'

I waited while Chris half pushed her older sister toward the living room. I heard Barbara mutter something about my mind and that I'd obviously lost it. It had an ominous, almost legal overtone.

Mattie looked at me with the embarrassed expression people get when they find themselves in the middle of someone else's family quarrel. 'I'm sorry,' she said. 'I didn't mean to stir things up.'

'It was already stirred,' I reassured her, while pulling back my winter clothes to reveal a wall of neatly stacked cardboard archival boxes. I started to pull at the top box.

'Lil, stop,' Mattie said. 'I'll do that.'

'Thanks,' I said, finding it hard to think straight. 'They're all alphabetical, but unfortunately I didn't think to label the outside of the boxes with the contents.'

'Not a problem.' She pried the first box free from its perch and slit the packing tape open with her penknife. 'Looks like S through Z,' she commented and reached for the next. The third box contained 'A' through 'Danielson'. She found Wendy Conroy's chart and pried out the two-inch-thick folder. 'Big chart.'

'She came often,' I explained. 'I think it was more for her mother, who was frantic. Not that I could blame her. Her only daughter was having a breakdown and there didn't seem to be anything she could do.'

Mattie fanned the chart.

I looked on as pages of Bradley's quickly scrawled notes passed before her eyes.

'Ouch,' she commented, trying to read one of the entries. 'I hate to say it, but your husband had lousy handwriting.'

'He was a doctor.' Ada tried to lighten the mood. 'They're all that way. They do it intentionally so no one can read what they've written.'

'That's not true,' I said, catching Ada's smile. 'It's just he was always in such a hurry to get the note written. And he had all those strange abbreviations.'

'What's this?' Mattie asked, pointing out a line with a caret over it.

'That's his down arrow,' I explained. 'It meant decreasing, so let's see, the line reads . . . I need my glasses. Hold on.' I retrieved them from the bedside table. 'Let me look.' I sat on the bed and smelled the forgotten scent of an old office chart. 'OK.' Mattie sat on my right and Ada on my left. 'The note reads:

'"August seventeenth, 1986. Vitals stable, afebrile. Fourteen-year-old patient brought by her mother, again exhibiting rapid alterations in mood. Mother reports patient has decreased sleep and appetite with ten-pound weight loss. At times she states her daughter is confused. In the office Wendy's speech is rambling with an odd impressionistic quality.

'"Patient is complaining of dry mouth and light-headedness from the antipsychotic medication. Mother states she thinks there may have been some improvement since increasing the dose, so I will hold at the present level. I again encouraged patient and her mother to follow-up with my referral to a psychiatrist."'

'It doesn't say who the psychiatrist was?' Mattie asked.

'You want me to try another?' I asked.

'Please. Try going back a bit.'

'OK, here's one. "June twelfth, nineteen eighty-five. Vitals stable, afebrile. Thirteen-year-old patient appears calmer and less agitated. However, mother reports there have been extended periods where Wendy has isolated herself in her room, refusing to come down even for meals. Mother is concerned that her daughter may be using illicit drugs. In the office patient is fully alert and oriented. At times she appears to stare excessively, but there is no other evidence of frank psychosis.

'"My continued impression is that in the absence of any notable physical impairment, patient is suffering from the early onset of some nervous disorder.

'"At her mother's request I will pursue urine and blood toxicology. However, I have begun to discuss with patient and her mother the usefulness of referral to a psychiatrist." He doesn't say who, though . . .' I commented. 'You want another?'

'Yes,' said Mattie, looking on as I read. 'Although, I'm beginning to get the hang of his writing.'

'Forward or backwards?' I offered.

'Try that one,' Ada said, pointing to a particularly lengthy entry.

'All right, let's see. "September first, 1987. Slightly tachycardic, afebrile. Fifteen-year-old patient agitated and disheveled. Mother reports she has been this way since first meeting with psychiatrist, P. Gruenwald. On observation client makes poor eye contact and rambles. Mother reports that Dr Gruenwald recommended weekly therapy. At present, both mother and daughter are unwilling to follow through with this recommendation. I will contact Dr Gruenwald, and am strongly encouraging Wendy and her mother to keep the next appointment. I have also discussed the usefulness of tranquilizing medications, and will pursue this further with patient's psychiatrist." Maybe that was it,' I commented.

'What?' Mattie asked.

'It was a long time ago, but I actually think I set up appointments for Wendy with the psychiatrist. Maybe that's what the note in her poem is about. Not that it was Bradley who did . . . whatever she said was done, but that he was somehow involved in sending her to someone who . . .' I heard desperation in my voice.

'It's a possibility,' the detective commented. 'At least we have a name. If I need you to help me decipher the rest of these, would you?'

'Of course.'

As Mattie struggled to restack the boxes in my closet, the doorbell rang.

'Do you want me to get that?' Ada asked.

'No, I'm sure the girls will.'

I heard a man's footsteps and then Kevin Simpson knocked on the outer frame of the bedroom door. He was soaked. 'OK to come in?' he asked, half out of breath.

'Sure,' I said. 'The more the merrier.'

'Mattie,' he started, 'Hank wanted me to find you.'

'What's up?'

He looked at Ada and me. 'It's OK with them here?'

'They're fine. What's happened?'

'The search team found another body,' he blurted. 'Actually . . . two.'

THIRTY-TWO

'Damn,' Mattie muttered as she followed Hank down the treacherously slick and steep leaf-covered ravine. Behind them, a couple dozen men and women in yellow police parkas and mud-soaked boots took a break, drinking coffee from thermos flasks, their focus on Mattie and Hank. One trooper and handler with the canine team held an umbrella over the four-year-old bloodhound that lay against at his feet, contentedly chewing on a rawhide bone.

'We left them the way we found them,' Hank explained, hanging on to a sapling to keep from tumbling forward. 'Give the Medical Examiner a chance to see them as we found 'em.'

'Who discovered them?' she asked, struggling to keep her footing on the slick ground of the steep incline.

'A bloodhound named Daphne and her handler. I guess you were right about the whole thing.'

'Wish I hadn't been. So it is Jeffries and Rinaldo?' she asked, stepping over a half-rotted log.

'Can't say for sure.'

'Not more acid?'

'Nope, just the swamp and lots of critters looking for food. I think the raccoons and maybe some coyotes had a go at them.'

The smell of carrion rose from the gorge. It reminded Mattie of opening the lid on one of her garbage cans after it had sat inside her garage baking in the summer heat. At least in the open, the stench got diluted with the earthy smells of the trees and the swamp. As they neared the bottom their shoes sank in the muck. Her feet made wet sucking noises as she followed Hank to what looked like a cement pipe that stuck straight up out of the ground.

'What's that?' she asked.

'A bad idea,' he answered. 'A while back some fool got the notion of putting drainage pipes in a lot of the wetlands. We forever have to cover them up. Kids love to play in them and then they get stuck. I'm surprised the killer didn't dump the bodies into one of them – would have kept them hidden longer.'

'That's not what he wants.'

'True.'

The smell of rotting meat grew, but aside from the muddy trackings of the cops she couldn't see where the stench originated. Then, not ten feet in front of her, Hank stopped.

'Here's number one,' he said, standing in front of the gristly remains of a man.

It was like one of those children's puzzles, where objects are hidden. The body melded into mud and fallen leaves, and where woodland creatures had torn the flesh, the wounds showed bits of slick bone, yellow fat and red muscle, now oxidized to a sickly gray. The body lay twisted on its side. She walked around it, careful to touch nothing, hating the damage that her hiking shoes did to the surrounding ground. She crouched in front of the body by the place the face should have been. With slow breaths, she tried to identify features from the pictures she'd seen of the two missing dealers. It was useless; but she could see what might have been a small dark entry wound in the middle of the forehead.

'What do you think?' Hank asked.

'Maybe when we get them cleaned up and on the slab. Were there any good footprints?'

'You've got to be kidding. After the last two days of rain we're lucky the bodies weren't completely submerged.'

At the top of the ravine she spotted Kevin, the Medical Examiner and two other detectives as they started their descent. Behind them the sky had grown dark and was filled with heavy gray clouds. A wind kicked up the branches overhead and she could tell that the storm, that had briefly abated, wasn't over.

'So how the hell did they get here?' she asked. 'I can't imagine someone dragging them down here all by themselves.'

'Good point, so they had to come under their own steam.'

'Which leaves . . . Did they come willingly or under duress? So where's the other body?'

'You're practically standing on it.'

She turned and scanned the ground. Her gaze caught on a filth-smeared bit of red-plaid. She traced it back to a mud-caked mound, which, as she stared at it, took on human form. 'Jesus, you can barely tell it's there. Did you get pictures?'

'First thing. Figured this would be a hard scene to protect.'

'So how long do you think they've been here?'

'Few days. Must have been here before the storm. Anything after and they wouldn't be so badly covered.'

'You think that was intentional?'

'The storm?'

'No, to get them down before a big rain. Otherwise there would have been a lot more physical evidence.'

'Could be. We had a couple days' warning.'

Mattie felt a hollow victory and suspected that after the Medical Examiner and the forensic team got through with the bodies her earlier suspicions would be confirmed: that Jeffries and Renaldo had been killed not long after Philip Conroy. Her mistake was in not demanding a search team and dogs sooner. *Two more dead.*

She looked up as Kevin, the Medical Examiner and two other detectives from Major Crime descended. 'We have to put Lillian Campbell under surveillance.'

'What are you talking about?' Hank asked.

'It sounds like our boy . . . or someone pretending to be him . . . has staked her out. She's been getting hang-up calls saying "*you're next*", and I don't think he's talking about the Irish Sweepstakes.'

'Lil Campbell? She doesn't fit the profile.'

'I know, so maybe we've got the profile wrong. There is some common denominator but it may not be what we thought.'

'What are you getting at?'

'I'm not certain . . . You remember a girl named Wendy Conroy?'

'Sure,' he said, after a moment's pause. 'Real tragedy. Killed herself. What's she got to do with this?'

'Near as I can figure, there's old secrets coming out.'

'Like what?' He eyed her closely.

Before she could respond, the winded Medical Examiner called out. 'Couldn't you at least keep your murders someplace dry?' Arvin Storrs struggled through the last few yards, his boots slipping and slurping in the mud. 'So what have we got?' he asked, smiling broadly at Mattie.

Hank pointed. 'Body one and body two.'

'Cause of death?' Arvin asked.

'Thought that was your job,' Hank said. 'My guess is bullet wound at close range, at least for this one here. That one over there I haven't wanted to turn over.'

'Looks like a herd of elephants has been through here,' the examiner commented as he surveyed the pockmarked mud. 'Any chance someone took pictures before they trampled the scene?'

'Done,' Hank assured him.

'Find anything else?' he asked.

'Some garbage, a few old beer cans, some less old than others. I got them bagged, but I think it's less likely from the murderer and more likely some high school kids coming down to party. I even found a used condom.'

'Where?' Mattie asked.

'Just dangling over a branch,' he said, pointing with his stick.

'Looked like it had been there for a while. I took some pictures of it before I bagged it.'

Mattie looked at the mud-crusted bodies that melded into the swamp. 'Any chance it was from one of those two?'

'We shall see,' said Dr Storrs as he snapped on a double layer of gloves. 'You still got your camera, Hank?'

'Yeah.' He slogged his way toward a boulder covered with a variety of sealed plastic evidence bags, and retrieved his high-resolution Nikon.

'Just follow me,' Arvin instructed. 'Let's see what we got.'

Kevin and the pair of detectives joined the group and watched from the sidelines. In the distance two pairs of patrolmen had started the descent carrying a rolled-up stretcher and shiny black PVC body bags. And behind them, members of the search team dotted the crest as they sipped coffee and watched.

'Mattie, you want to give me a hand?' the examiner asked. 'Here, put some gloves on.' He bent by the first body, studied its position, and scraped off a layer of leaves. Then he tilted back the left shoulder to get a clear look at the head and face. 'Terrible,' he commented as several plump white maggots fell to the earth. 'Raccoons have been gnawing at this one. You want to get some shots, Hank?' The examiner made clicking noises with his tongue as he surveyed the body. 'It's going to be hard pinpointing the exact time of death. Judging by the size of those larvae, I'd say a week.' And taking a pair of tweezers he dropped three shiny maggots into a specimen bottle. 'I'll be able to tell when we get him inside. Looks like an entry wound here,' he said tilting up the forehead. 'Oops.' The body shifted and the head tilted back, almost detaching from the neck. 'My goodness,' he commented, scraping mud off the back of the cadaver's neck. 'Something's really been chewing away at this; you'd think this was the Thanksgiving turkey. Mmm mmm mmm. Another few days and there wouldn't have been much. Mattie, give me a hand; let's get him on his back.'

Together, the two pried the half-gnawed body free from the mud and flipped it. The stench of methane and rotting flesh roared over them. Mattie stepped back; her stomach lurched.

Completely unperturbed, Arvin commented, 'Pants are zipped. Other than that, his clothing is pretty shot; I'd bet that all came after the fact. See, look at this?' He poked a twig into a tear in the flannel shirt. 'See how jagged that is, and if you look close you can see dried bits of saliva, that's not human . . . At least I hope not.' He scanned the body. 'Yeah, not a lot more to say. Male, forties, probable cause of death is a bullet, small caliber, to the brain. Was there much in the way of splatter around the body, like a struggle or anything? Any tracks of a dragged body?'

'Not so as you could tell,' Hank replied. 'But you got to remember it's been raining pretty fierce. This is the first real clearing we've had.'

'Lucky us,' Arvin said, glancing up through the trees at the darkening sky, and the small crowd of onlookers lining the crest, including the bloodhound, now straining at her leash. 'Any chance you took some mud samples from around the body?'

'Didn't think to. Why?'

'Maybe get lucky and see if there was some blood mixed in, otherwise we'll never know if there was much movement before death. Shall we take a look at body number two?' He got up with a groan. 'The knees don't work the way they used to. Look at this,' he said, in the tone of a TV-commercial mother who's found muddy footprints on her just-washed floor. 'I tell you –' he surveyed the half-submerged body – 'what a mess.'

A trickle of water ran by the corpse's outstretched hand and meandered toward the stream at the bottom of the ravine. From overhead came the spatter of rain landing on the trees.

'God, he's stuck,' Arvin complained as they struggled to pry the body from its muddy cradle.

'Let me help.' Kevin snapped on gloves and gripped the body around its middle.

'On three,' Arvin instructed. 'One, two, three.'

A wave of brackish water rushed to fill the hole left by the body.

'Hank, grab some pictures, quick,' Arvin ordered as he stared down at the cavity.

'Wow,' Kevin commented, still hanging on to the body's flank. 'It's Pete Jeffries.'

'You're right,' Mattie agreed, getting a clear look at the filth-smeared face, which had been preserved in the mud.

A droplet of water landed on Mattie's neck and the woods rustled with the sound of falling rain and leaves. Thunder rumbled and the wind whipped the trees. A trunk creaked ominously, and in a matter of moments, darkness fell. Mosquitoes, emboldened by the coming storm, swarmed. Arvin squashed one on his forearm in a bloody smear.

'OK to bag?' Hank asked.

'Yeah, let's get out of here,' Arvin agreed. 'Not much to say. Except, this body looks a whole lot better and I'd be willing to bet it hasn't been here as long as the other one.'

'Killed at different times?' Mattie asked.

'I'll let you know for sure once I get them on the slab; but I'd say this Jeffries guy has only been dead a couple days, maggots haven't even hatched. That other one's over a week.'

'So someone got them down here one at a time,' Mattie said. 'Makes sense, it's easier to control one person than two. But why here?'

'Guys –' Arvin stepped back to let the patrolmen pack up the bodies – 'I'd love to stay and chat, but it looks like I'm going to be spending the day in the morgue and frankly, I can't do that on an empty stomach. So, Hank, where can a guy get a decent meal around here?'

A torrent of rain swept the ravine.

'I'll show you,' he replied, gathering his evidence and tucking his camera inside a plastic bag.

Leaving the officers to collect the bodies, and the other detectives to wait for the crime-scene team, Mattie, Kevin, Hank and Arvin started the climb.

All the while, Mattie was thinking what it must have been like for the two men they'd left behind. What, or who, had induced them to come down here in the first place? There were no signs of a struggle. Although, the rain might have washed that away, but still. As she struggled upward, grabbing at saplings and low-hanging branches, she thought about Lil. With a surge of energy she barreled her way up the rest of the incline, overtaking her colleagues. At the crest she shouted back over the driving rain, 'I'm going to check on Lil. I'll call from there. But Hank, I wasn't kidding, get her some protection.'

Hank yelled something in reply, but his words got lost in the storm.

A crack of lightning split the sky and without waiting, Mattie raced to her car, and with a worried feeling gnawing at her gut, she sped back to Pilgrim's Progress.

THIRTY-THREE

Lil, you're overreacting, I chided myself as I stormed out of my condo and toward my garage. But after Mattie had left, the fight with Barbara had deteriorated. I needed to get out of there. I knew that Mattie had wanted us to stay, but Barbara was driving me crazy; if I'd stayed another minute, I would have done or said something regrettable. Even the simple act of taking a ride to clear my head had been a cause for discussion.

'Are you safe to drive?' Barbara had asked as I'd reached for the raincoat on the hooks by the door. I'd worn it home from the hospital, and it was drenched.

'Would you let your mother alone!' Ada had interjected.

'Of course I can drive,' I'd shot back, before Barbara could turn on Ada. 'I had a heart attack, not a stroke.' Abandoning the raincoat, I opened the hall closet and grabbed my hooded green-wool winter coat with the wooden toggle buttons.

'I'll come with you,' Ada had said.

'No,' I'd replied too fast. 'Mattie didn't want any of us to leave. I just need to drive around, clear my head.' I smiled, suddenly aware of the hurt on her face. 'I'm sorry, I'll be right back, promise.'

Before anyone could say more, I was out the door. The rain was blinding, and I wished I'd taken an umbrella as well. I pulled the broad hood over my head and walked quickly down to the garage. My head was pounding and my knees felt weak and rubbery as I slid behind the wheel of the Lincoln. I had no idea of where I wanted to go as I backed out. I half expected Barbara to try and stop me. Even more than the threatening phone calls, or my heart attack, her attitude had made me nuts. This was the kind of stuff my older friends talked about. But Barbara was my own daughter; why was she being like this?

The rain eased and the sky was dark with low-hanging clouds. The air felt thick, and my coat smelled of wet wool and mothballs. I flicked on my low beams and drove toward the gated entrance to Pilgrim's Progress. I turned left and toward town. I had no destination; I just needed to think.

The rain quickened, and I turned the wipers to high. I don't like driving in bad weather, but the familiar feel and smell of my car was like a salve. The steady whish and whir of the wipers and the hum of the engine gave some relief. And why wasn't Chris doing more to defend me? Was my getting behind the wheel more evidence that I was slipping into an early senility? And if that wasn't enough, what would they think about my kissing my best friend? While confusing the hell out of me, that at least felt good; better than good. *And wasn't that a huge problem?*

On impulse, I turned down the side street that led to Nillewaug Village. I passed the trimmed hedges that lined the long drive. It looked nothing like a village and I couldn't tell if the dense greenery was to keep people out, or in. I cruised among the outlying buildings placed like spokes on a wheel, where the hub was the massive faux-Georgian residential complex where Ada and I had met with that awful Ms Preston. Was that where I was destined to end up? Maybe Ada and I together, like a pair of spinsters . . . only, not so spinsterish.

An ambulance was parked beneath one of the outer red-brick structures, its flashing lights were turned off, but some sort of activity was taking place inside. I tried to remember what Preston had said about these buildings, some kind of specialized nursing home units. I pulled over and with the motor idling, I watched as a female medic got in the driver's seat. She put the vehicle into gear and pulled out in front of me. Through the back windows I could see a second attendant filling out forms as he bent over a figure swaddled in sheets. It wasn't until they had moved beyond the front gates that they turned on the lights and siren.

I looked back to where the ambulance had been parked and realized that each building had been designed with a hidden bay for this purpose. They were like factories only instead of smokestacks they had ambulance bays.

I followed the drive to its central cul-de-sac and then back out to Cat Swamp Road. With lights on and going no faster than twenty, my tension slowly eased. I knew that Barbara was upset; my heart attack had hit her hard. I knew that she loved me and was afraid that I was jeopardizing my health. Maybe she was right. Three days after a heart attack, should I be driving? What would Bradley have said? 'Bradley's dead, Lil . . . You're not.'

As I came to the stop at the end of the road, I turned away

from Grenville. There was little traffic and almost no visibility as I headed toward Shiloh and Jefferson, small rural towns to the north.

The windshield was steaming and my defrosters were fighting an uphill battle. I cracked the window and let the cool air try to clear the milky film.

I thought about Barbara and Chris; I didn't really know them. And lately, that seemed true of too many things: my town, my husband, even myself.

Through the driving rain, I passed by fields of Guernsey cows huddled against the storm. The road twisted and climbed around ancient oaks and farms that were falling one by one to developers who filled the fields with million-dollar homes that sprouted – seemingly overnight – like mushrooms in dung.

My thoughts drifted back to my dream, and how it ended with that call. The more I thought about it, the more he'd sounded familiar. It wasn't a prankster teen; it was somebody older, trying to disguise their voice, but definitely not young.

The car lurched violently forward and the steering wheel jumped beneath my fingers. I both felt and heard tearing metal from my back bumper. My adrenaline raced as I struggled to steady the wheel while catching quick glances in the rearview mirror. I could barely make out the darkened outline of a van. A lone figure struggled at the wheel as he bore down. At first I thought he wanted to pass me, but as I tried to find some purchase on the edge of the road, I could see that he was coming straight at me. I hit the gas, but it was too late and he clipped my right rear. *Turn into the spin*, I reminded myself struggling to stay on the road. I clung white-knuckled to the wheel as I skidded, the tires squealing on the asphalt.

I lost all sense of direction as I finally came to a stop. I looked for my pursuer in the window, but the rain was too heavy and I couldn't see him. I peered through the opened crack, my breath having fogged up the windows to the point I couldn't tell where the road ended. I had to get out of there. Gently I applied pressure to the accelerator, having caught a glimpse of the white line outside my window. I felt the road beneath my wheels and prayed that I was headed back in the direction from which I had come. Shiloh and Jefferson were too deserted; I had to get back to Grenville.

As I stepped on the gas, I opened my window further to try and get a better look at the road. As long as I could see the white line I'd be OK. I picked up speed, my heart was racing as I glanced in the rearview mirror. I couldn't see further than a few feet but there were no lurking shadows of the dark-colored van. Leaning forward, I took the side of my sleeve and tried to clear some of the fog from the glass. As I did, a towering shadow sped toward me. There was nothing I could do. I stared into the space where the driver sat, and, as if in slow motion, I watched as his eyes came into focus, meeting mine.

Even before I could clearly see, I knew who it was. I should have known. It all made sense, I thought of a childhood saying: *close only counts in horse shoes and grenades.*

A moment later, impact, and my world went black.

THIRTY-FOUR

'Where is she?' Mattie fumed, while pacing tight circles in Lil's living room.

'I couldn't stop her,' Ada said. 'She was upset. She said she'd be right back.'

Mattie glared at Barbara.

'What? This isn't my fault. Mother has been behaving erratically ever since I arrived. This is just more of the same.'

'I had said no one was to leave.' Mattie tried to control her temper; the anger clouded her thoughts and made it difficult to think. The stench of the bodies still hung in her nostrils. 'Where did she go?' Mattie demanded, already having been told that none of them knew. She looked around. 'Great . . . Any more phone calls?'

Chris shook her head. 'No, the last one was right before she left.'

'What is it, Mattie?' Ada asked. 'Oh no!' A hand to her mouth. 'He had been calling, and now . . . Lil . . .'

Mattie nodded. 'I've got to look for her.' She picked up the phone and dialed Hank's cell. 'Look, Hank, Lil Campbell has bolted in her car and there's a chance she's being followed.'

'What are you talking about?' Hank said.

'She's been getting threatening calls. I don't know why.' She lowered her voice, so none in the room could hear. 'Don't let anyone leave from the search team. Get everyone out looking, call in everyone you can.'

'OK, where should I have them focus?'

'Start at the gates of Pilgrim's Progress and fan out from there. She left about forty-five minutes ago.'

'What if she just went for a drive?'

'I pray to God she did. But until she drives up under her own steam, I wouldn't assume anything.' She hung up, and looked around. 'So, did anyone see anything?'

Her question was met with silence.

'I'm going to look for Mother,' Barbara said.

Mattie was going to tell her to stay put, but between the driving rain and the shortage of manpower, she changed her mind. 'Do you have a cell?'

'Yes,' Barbara said, fumbling through her purse.

'OK, if you find her and she's alone, great. If she's with anyone else, I want you to call for help. Even if it's the most trusted member of the community. You got that? If she's with anyone.'

'Got it.'

'Ada, any idea which way she would have headed?' Mattie asked.

'If I had to guess, I'd say she headed toward Grenville. Although . . .'

'What?' Mattie prompted, itching to start looking.

'Sometimes, when we just go driving, we'll go up north through the country.'

'That's what she and Dad would do whenever they had a fight,' Chris said. 'She told me they didn't want us to hear them argue. So they'd get in the car and go up to Jefferson, hash out whatever they needed to discuss and then stop for ice cream before coming home.'

'Ada,' Mattie said, 'I need you to stay here. If Lil calls or shows up, phone the dispatcher.' She wrote down the number and headed back into the rain.

Still inside, Barbara seemed stricken. 'What have I done?'

'How far away is your car?' Chris asked her sister.

'Close. You ready?' Barbara asked.

'Yeah, let's just find her.'

*   *   *

Ada and Aaron – left behind – looked at each other. A heavy silence settled in the room. 'You think she's OK?' Aaron asked.

'She has to be,' Ada replied. 'I wish that creep would call again.'

''Cause then you'd know he wasn't after her?'

'Right.' She looked at her grandson. 'I should be doing something.'

'Mattie said to stay here in case Mrs Campbell called.'

'That's right, but even so . . .' She walked over to the table where Mattie had left Wendy Conroy's chart. She fanned through the pages and went to an entry that Mattie had tabbed with a yellow post-it. 'Aaron, find me a pen and something to write on. There should be something in the kitchen.'

'Sure,' he said, not certain what his grandmother was up to.

As soon as he had left, Ada picked up the phone. Balancing the open chart with one hand, she crooked the receiver between shoulder and cheek and dialed information. 'I'm looking for a Doctor P. Gruenwald,' Ada said. 'I'm not sure what town, possibly New Haven, maybe Hamden or Cheshire but somewhere in that general vicinity . . . No, I don't know his first name.'

Aaron returned and placed a small note pad and pencil next to the phone.

'Oh, I see,' said Ada. 'Nothing at all . . . Do you have a listing for a Doctor Adams? Also a psychiatrist . . . No, Danbury I think . . . Great. Thank you.' She scribbled the number, and redialed. 'This is Ada Strauss for Dr Adams . . . Yes, it's urgent . . . I'll hold.' Ada fidgeted with the pencil while Muzak filtered through the earpiece. The line clicked. 'Doctor Adams?' Ada asked, expectantly.

'Yes?' a man's deep voice answered.

'I'm sorry to bother you, but some time ago you spoke at one of our seminars at Pilgrim's Progress, and I didn't know any other psychiatrists . . .'

'What seems to be the problem?'

'I'm trying to track down another psychiatrist, a Doctor Gruenwald.'

'That's going to be hard,' he replied. 'Peter Gruenwald passed away . . . Must be three or four years now.'

'Oh.' She sounded crushed.

'Is there something that I could help you with?'

'No, it's for a friend of mine. I was trying to . . .' She stopped herself. 'Let me ask you this: what sort of reputation did Dr Gruenwald have?'

'Fine, as far as I know. He was a little before my time, but his patients were quite devoted.'

'I see.' Disappointed, she sank down on to Lil's needlepoint-upholstered wing chair.

'Anything else?' he asked.

'No, thank you.' Ada held on to the receiver, listening for the click on the other end.

'No luck, huh?' Aaron asked.

'No,' she agreed, letting the cordless rest in its cradle.

'What were you looking for?' he asked.

'It's a long story.'

'I have time,' he said.

She tried to smile, but was so frightened, *I should never have kissed her, that's why she ran out and didn't want me with her.* 'Aaron? What doctors do you see?'

'Huh? I don't see any. Every couple years before school starts I have to get a physical, but that's about it. Unless you consider the ophthalmologist for my contacts and the dentist.'

'What? Say that again.'

'Eyes and teeth. Don't you consider them doctors?'

'I hadn't,' she admitted, reaching for the phone. 'But maybe I should.'

THIRTY-FIVE

Holding her umbrella against the driving wind and rain, Mattie surveyed the wreckage of Lil's Lincoln. The hood had taken the worst, crumpling like an accordion. The airbags hung limp and empty. The driver's door wide open and Lil was gone, her pocketbook unmolested on the passenger-side floor.

Scrapes of dark paint bore witness to the other vehicle that had rammed her head on. Even more disturbing were the scrape marks on the rear bumper. This hadn't been a simple collision. Lil had been forced off the road.

Mattie felt sick, knowing she needed to act fast, but not having clear direction. There had to be something here, but the raging Nor'easter was rapidly erasing traces of what had happened. Puddles flowed into roadside streams, washing away evidence. Traces of blood on the driver's door grew faint and would soon be gone.

On either side of the road cattails, wild roses, bramble, sumac and poison ivy formed an impenetrable wall. There were no signs of broken branches or fresh footprints. Either dead or alive, someone had taken Lil.

Flashing lights from more than a dozen cruisers and unmarked cars clouded her thoughts. Lillian Campbell, a respected doctor's widow, had been taken, but where? By whom? And most importantly, why?

She examined the tire marks beneath the sheets of water. She placed her foot against the skid marks, using it to measure; the wheel had to be at least a fifteen-inch tire; a small truck or van.

What worried her most was that it had been a head-on collision. How could the killer have been certain that he would walk away? It stank of desperation. The mounting pace, the persistent phone calls; he was out of control.

Hank, in galoshes and yellow slicker, approached; he followed Mattie's gaze to the blood-tinged puddles. 'Why would he go after her?' he asked.

'It has do with Wendy Conroy. Those diaries . . . I had the dispatcher trace down her psychiatrist but that's another dead end . . . literally. The guy died four years ago. We're missing something.' She looked at the local chief as he stood in the rain with the flashers reflecting off of his slicker. She was about to say more when her cell rang.

'Here, let me.' Hank held her umbrella, while she answered.

'Detective Perez, here.'

It was the dispatcher. 'I have an Ada Strauss, said it's very important.'

'Put her through.' She waited, praying that Lil had come home.

'Mattie?' Ada sounded winded.

'What is it, Ada?'

'It wasn't the psychiatrist Wendy was talking about.'

'I know,' Mattie said.

'It was her dentist.'

'What?'

'That's who the other doctor was. She was having all sorts of dental work. It's in her chart. I've been going through it.'

Mattie stood holding the phone. How could she have missed that? She looked at Hank. 'Who was Wendy Conroy's dentist?'

'Same as everyone: Doc Williams.'

'On High Street?' she asked.

'Yeah, doesn't practice out of his home anymore, but the family's been there forever.'

'Ada, I've got to go.'

'You haven't found her, have you?' Ada's voice betrayed her fear.

Mattie surveyed the wreckage, while moving fast toward her car. 'No, but we will.'

THIRTY-SIX

Ada paced, then stopped. 'Aaron, get me the yellow pages; it's in Lil's bottom-right kitchen drawer.'

'Sure.'

As soon as he left the room, she grabbed the phone and dialed the Pilgrim's Progress taxi service. 'This is Ada Strauss. I need a cab right away. If you get here in the next couple minutes it's a fifty dollar tip.' She gave them the address and hung up.

'It wasn't there,' he said, holding the local yellow pages. 'It was in the drawer next to the sink.'

'She must have moved it. Let me see.' She flipped it open, found Calvin Williams and ripped out his number and address. As she stuffed it into her cardigan pocket a horn beeped twice.

'Who's that?' Aaron asked.

'I called a cab,' Ada told him. 'I have to take care of a couple errands. I won't be long.'

'I thought we were supposed to stay here.'

'You will. If Lil calls, you'll need to phone the dispatcher at the police station, let them know where she is. Then call me on my cell.'

He eyed her suspiciously. 'Where are you really going?'

'Don't question your grandmother.'

'I won't stop you,' he said. 'But at least tell me where you are in case I need you.'

'I'm going to the dentist's.'

'You think he may have done something to Mrs Campbell?'

'I don't know; but I can't stay here doing nothing.'

'Grandma! That's for the cops. What are you doing?'

'I called them. They'll be there.' The cab tooted again. She dumped her pocketbook on Lil's couch and grabbed several items, rapidly stuffing them into her jacket pockets. 'Good, money and keys.'

'Is that mace?' he asked as a small silver cylinder vanished into a pocket.

'Pepper spray, dear.' She kissed Aaron's forehead, snatched an umbrella from Lil's hall tree and bolted down the slick path.

Ada thanked the cabbie for being so prompt, and gave him the address.

Recognizing Ada as one of his regulars, he started to chat. 'Nothing worse than having to wait on a rainy day. Tooth problems?'

'Something like that . . . Please hurry.'

'I thought Doc Williams closed his office,' he commented while pulling out.

'Not entirely,' she replied. 'You know him?'

'Not so much, but you know around here, everyone's business is everyone's business. I just thought after his mother passed away, he closed things up.'

As they drove down High Street, the pulse of red and blue police lights glittered on the rain-spattered windshield. 'That's odd,' he commented as they drove up. 'Something's going on.'

Ada peered through her window as they approached. 'Pull up close,' she instructed.

'Sure.' He eased in behind a cruiser that had blocked the dentist's driveway. There were easily twenty vehicles, equally split between the local black-and-whites and an assortment of unmarked cars and SUVs.

Through the rain, Ada counted more than a dozen officers in yellow parkas as they swarmed the eighteenth-century house, some carrying large black rifles. On the back of several were large fluorescent letters: SWAT.

'How much?' Ada asked, opening her door.

'You're going in?' the driver sounded incredulous.

'Yes, I need to see what's happening.'

'Want me to wait?'

'Could you?'

'Sure, I'll just keep the meter running.'

'Thanks.'

She opened her door, feeling the cold rain against her cheeks. She pulled her jacket tight. The wind swirled down and then changed direction; it grabbed her umbrella, ripping it inside out. She dropped it, and struggled up the sloped drive. Thankful for her rubber-soled shoes, she inched toward the house.

'Mrs Strauss,' Kevin Simpson called out, and offered her his arm. 'What are you doing here? Go back!'

'I had to see if I could help.'

'That's real kind, but you shouldn't be here.'

'She's my best friend,' Ada pleaded. 'I couldn't stay at home. Have you found her?'

'No. Not yet.'

Ada felt tears. What if she was wrong? What if she'd pushed all of this in the wrong direction?

In front of them, an excited voice called from the garage. 'There's a van in here . . . It's been in an accident.'

Kevin seemed torn between being polite to Ada and checking out the discovery.

Ada had no such qualms and, grabbing his arm, said, 'Come on.'

Mattie Perez was the only one without a parka. Her dark hair plastered to her head, she ran to the garage. 'Open it,' she ordered.

Three officers strained to raise the door, while two others stood back with guns raised. 'It's not budging,' one of them panted.

From the side came the sound of breaking glass as the officer who had spotted the van wrapped his hand inside his coat and smashed the window. Mattie, her service-revolver in one hand, ran around and shone a flashlight into the darkened space with the other. She spotted streaks of white paint on the crumpled front bumper. 'Probable cause enough,' she muttered. 'Hank!' she yelled.

'Right here,' he said, following the trail of her beam. She shone it quickly around the interior of the space; dirt floor, no upstairs.

'You,' she barked, to the officer that had smashed the window, 'check out the garage. We're going into the house. You –' motioning to a trooper with the SWAT team – 'we're going in the back door.'

'No problem.' Half a dozen rifle-armed troopers joined him.

Using a metal truncheon, he smashed the side of the door and the hinges splintered off the ancient frame. Two helmeted troopers entered, securing the entry as others swarmed behind.

Without waiting for an invitation, Ada let go of Kevin and, staying close to Mattie and Hank, followed them inside. Someone found the switch and flooded the room with a rose-colored light filtered through a cranberry-glass shade. It was only the kitchen, but Ada couldn't help but notice how carefully it had been decorated, and how incongruous it was with the drawn semi-automatics, carbines and pistols. As booted and muddy feet stormed the house, she couldn't help but notice the exquisite cabinetry and millwork that appeared original to the house. An oversized step-back cupboard rose majestically against the far wall, its shelves filled with early flow-blue china. There was a massive fireplace on one wall, surrounded by a staggering collection of hand-forged cooking tools and, across from it, a beehive oven. Everywhere she looked were fine antiques and dust and cobwebs.

'Hold up,' Mattie said, noting a single set of half-dried footprints, different from those of the booted troopers, that tracked across the floor. They disappeared inside the pantry. Cautiously, Mattie approached, her revolver drawn. She pulled back the door while one of the officers flooded the space with his flashlight.

Mattie shone her beam on a pair of muddy boots that lay on a plastic mat.

'Bag those,' she said as she scanned the shelves.

'Look at this stuff,' Ada commented as they confronted row after row of pre-colonial pewter: teapots, chargers and porringers that crowded the pantry from floor to ceiling, like some overstocked two-hundred-year-old department store.

'What about it?' Mattie asked, needing to get on with the search, but wanting to make some sense of the crammed pantry that held no food.

Ada grabbed the closest teapot, freeing it from its mooring of spider webs and dust. It bore no signs of machine manufacture and the hallmarks were eighteenth century. 'This stuff is worth a fortune. It's all over two hundred years' old.'

'Jesus,' Mattie muttered as she surveyed the vast collection. 'Just in the closet.'

'It doesn't make sense,' Ada agreed as they stepped out of the pantry. 'It's museum quality. This whole place is like a museum.'

'You shouldn't be here,' Mattie said to Ada.

'Please,' Ada said, determined to not leave, unless forcibly removed.

Mattie realized having a civilian was a dangerous breach of protocol, but then again . . . 'If anyone asks, you're a consultant. And stick with me.'

Ada nodded, and followed Mattie from the kitchen to the dining room. Ada could not remember ever having been so afraid, her thoughts on Lil: *please be OK. But this house.* 'Are you kidding?' The words blurted out as she stared at the mahogany furniture.

'What now?' Mattie asked.

'The dining set – it's Chippendale – not repros.'

'What's it worth?'

Ada quickly tipped a chair and stared at the underside. 'It's real American Chippendale . . . either Philadelphia or Newport. The chairs alone are six figures. And that's one hell of a table; maybe a couple hundred grand.'

The living room, now with armed troopers at every door, held more of the same: priceless antiques covered in dust, but no trace of Lil.

They passed through a small parlor with a side door that led to Williams' dental suite. Even here, there was a sense of having stepped back in time. Careful rows of stainless-steel drill bits and grinding wheels that seemed archaic and cruel. Plaster molds of teeth lay toppled in large bins, with their owners' names scribbled in pencil across the bottom.

As they searched, Mattie tapped walls with her knuckles and listened for the reverberation of her foot on the solid floors. There were three examination rooms, a small area for a receptionist and a waiting room. Mattie took a cursory glance through the appointment book; even that was covered with dust.

'He closed his office,' Ada commented. 'He works in nursing homes now.'

'You know him?' Mattie asked.

'Not really. I lost a cap last Sunday after you left. Lil brought me here.'

'What was he like?'

'Nice . . . Accommodating. He didn't bat an eye when we showed up. Although, he looked like he'd been working on something and maybe we'd interrupted.'

'Working on what?'

'No idea; he had smudges on his hands and arms.'

'What else do you remember?' Mattie asked as she retraced back to the main house and toward the front-hall stairs.

Ada followed. 'Not much. Kevin Simpson called while we were there, looking for dental records.'

'How was he with Lil?'

'Like old friends. I kidded her, because she'd been his babysitter, and I kind of thought he might have a crush on her, or at least did at one point.'

The upstairs was typical colonial; four small bedrooms and a single bath that had been added at a later date. In each of the bedrooms, the floors tracked with mud from the troopers, Mattie did a quick but thorough survey of potential hiding places.

Back in the hall, she located the pull-down stairs to the attic. She yanked on the rope. 'You stay here,' she cautioned Ada as she disappeared up.

With her flashlight in one hand and her revolver in the other, Mattie moved cautiously. She noted the thick undisturbed dust that coated the wide floorboards. She stood on the top rung and let the beam traverse the sharply pitched space. It was like looking in the warehouse of an antique store. Jumbled floor to ceiling were chests, chairs, bookcases and trunks. Carefully labeled boxes were stacked in towers, their contents hidden from view. 'What's three-mold glass?' she yelled back, reading the label on one of the cartons.

'Early-American glass,' Ada replied. 'Three-mold is how they made it.'

'Expensive?' the detective asked.

'Can be.'

'What about historical flasks?' she asked letting her flashlight play over the labeled boxes.

'Big money,' Ada replied. 'They're old whiskey flasks. I don't know why, but those go for thousands of dollars each.'

Mattie holstered her revolver and came back down. 'Where the hell is he?'

They went down the small back stairwell that ended in the kitchen. Hank was coming up from the basement, two of the heavily armed troopers at his back. 'Nothing,' he said. 'Not a trace.'

Kevin came in, water puddling at his feet. 'Anything?' he asked.

'No,' Mattie replied.

'The engine's still warm,' he informed them. 'And it's white paint on the bumper . . . freshly scraped.'

'So where is he?' Mattie asked, walking back to the pantry, and looking at the puddles that had been left by the boots. 'He can't just have vanished.'

Ada followed; as she did, her eye caught on a tiny swatch of rain-soaked dark green wool that had gotten snagged and shredded on the cast-iron lock plate. 'That's Lil's,' she stated, holding up the material to the light.

'What?' Mattie turned to see what she was talking about.

'There,' Ada said. 'I couldn't tell at first because it's so wet. But it's Lil's coat; She grabbed it as she was leaving.'

'You're sure?' Mattie said, feeling a rush of emotion; relief that this wasn't a goose chase and a mounting fear as the seconds ticked.

'I'm positive.'

'What about secret passages?' Kevin asked.

Mattie glared at him.

'I'm serious. A lot of High Street houses have hidden tunnels. They date back to the Revolution and the War of 1812.'

'He's right,' Hank agreed. 'Whenever we do street repair, or a new septic system gets dug, it's not uncommon to break into the remains of a tunnel or false cellar.'

'Great,' Mattie replied. 'So where do we start?'

Ada stared at the torn fabric. 'She's trying to leave a trail.' Ada reached for the lock plate, remembering a detail from a lecture she and Lil had attended at the historical society.

'What are you doing?' Mattie asked.

Ada twisted and pulled back on the plate. As she did, a dull click was heard behind the far wall of the pantry.

'There you have it,' Hank replied as he stepped into the pantry and pushed back the wall of priceless pewter.

THIRTY-SEVEN

il, I thought as my teeth chattered uncontrollably, *he's going to kill you.* A single lantern illuminated Calvin Williams' face as he paced the narrow confines of the dirt-floor cellar. Shadows flickered against the ceiling and the walls. My wrists throbbed from the sharp metal of hand-forged cuffs and I felt blood, thick and warm, oozing down my forehead. I'd been injured in the accident, and soaked by the driving rain, but other than the ache in my wrists, I couldn't register pain; just fear and a chill that ran deep. *He's going to kill you.*

I listened to Calvin's heavy breathing and the sound of his boots. I thought about the little boy I had babysat, and the man who'd been my dentist. He stopped and stared at me. 'Get up,' he ordered.

I struggled to oblige, the weight of my soaked winter coat making it particularly hard.

'It's time. I have to show you something. Move!'

It seemed he'd forgotten that I was handcuffed, or that he was carrying a loaded handgun as he led me down a tight passage that ended in a partially excavated cave. I wondered if this was where he had killed the others. I searched the shadows for traces of blood. All I saw were the rough-hewn walls, spider webs and the smooth floor walked flat and level over the centuries.

'Stand back.' He motioned me against the wall.

Keeping his eye on me, he placed the small handgun into the pocket of his camouflage hunting jacket and reached overhead. His hand disappeared behind a rock; I heard a snap and flinched. I wondered if the gun had discharged, but it was too soft for that, more like a branch breaking.

He backed up, and the wall fell away behind him.

'Incredible.' I heard the word leave my mouth. *This is impossible, but what is that smell?*

'It is, isn't it?' He motioned for me to follow. 'I thought you'd appreciate it. Wait.' He led me into a darkened space. The panel closed behind us. I watched as he moved around the room lighting kerosene lamps. As their glass shades smoked to life, I tried to make sense of the scene. The air was thick with the oily fuel. It was an arsenal, only all the weapons had been made centuries ago. Along one wall stood rows of ancient muskets, their barrels pointed at the ceiling as though waiting for some long-forgotten militia. Above those hung in neat rows was an exquisite collection of pewter-and-brass powder flasks, and beneath them barrels of iron ramrods.

'It's like a museum,' I commented as he illuminated his exhibits.

'My great-grandfather collected the muskets and the flintlocks. I managed to get most of them back,' he explained. 'Now, sit.'

'Back from where?' The words coming out choppy as I shivered. *Just keep him talking*, I told myself as I eased myself to the floor.

'My mother did very foolish things.'

'She sold them?' I asked, finally coming to rest. I felt so helpless, off my feet, my hands shackled. *Remind him of your history together.*

'It wasn't her fault; none of it. She got Alzheimer's. Although, I didn't know that for years. And one by one she let the vultures into the house. They all told her how sad it was to have invested in "reproductions" and "inferior quality antiques". Of course, they would be willing to help her get rid of them, but really, they couldn't offer much.' His voice dripped with sarcasm.

'Couldn't you stop her?' I asked, watching his every move. I knew he was six years younger than I was. He was clearly fit, judging by the ease with which he'd carried me around like a sack of mulch. He had always been considered an attractive man and it was a source of curiosity as to why he had never married. The commonly held belief was that in caring for his mother, he'd opted not to have a family.

'I didn't know until it was too late. By the end, she was so far gone she didn't even cash their checks, just hid them in her jewelry box, which that Potts woman was only too happy to empty out for her. All of the heirlooms that had been in my family, even the cross that came over on the *Mayflower*, all sold to that evil woman for two thousand dollars. Imagine how I felt when I passed her store and saw my great-grandmother's gold pocket watch on display. Then, when I went inside, all of my family's treasures tagged and priced for the tourists.'

'Couldn't you buy them back?'

'I did. It took all of my savings. But that was just the tip of it. What I discovered was that while I was working away inside the mouths of Grenville's solid citizens, Mother was selling my inheritance. When I found out, it was too late. I didn't have enough to buy things back.' He paused and looked around the cellar space. 'I hid what I could, anything I thought she could carry. That should have been the end of it.'

'It wasn't?' I asked, wanting to keep him talking.

'She invited them in. Can you imagine what it was like, my poor demented mother showing the local sharks untouched pieces of American Chippendale?'

'They took advantage,' I offered, wanting to sound sympathetic.

'They robbed me blind.'

'Couldn't you go to the police?' As soon as the words left my mouth, I knew I'd said the wrong thing.

His mouth contorted. 'Are you making fun of me?'

'No, I just thought . . .'

'You thought that our kind and goodly Chief of Police would right this egregious wrong? Perhaps for you and your precious Bradley he might have. Hank Morgan and I don't exactly see eye to eye.'

'Why not?'

'So much history,' he answered. 'Does it bother you getting older, Lil? All those years back when you'd look after me; did you know I loved you? I even thought that we'd get married when I grew up. Then later, I'd watch you and Bradley, so well liked and respected. Everyone always deferred to Doctor Campbell. "Should we put in sewers? Dr Campbell, what about town water? Do we need a new school?" For God's sake, the man was a GP.'

Ada had been right, and I'd never suspected; he did have a crush on me. 'It must have been hard,' I said, struggling to keep him talking. In the flickering lanterns I could see him again as the little buzzed-headed blond boy I'd babysat for. He'd tell me he loved me, and that he wanted to marry me; who knew that a seven-year-old's crush for a thirteen-year-old girl could turn to murder?

'I'm a doctor too. You think anyone remembers that? Well, this is one dentist people won't forget.'

'What were you saying about Hank Morgan?'

'Nice stall. It doesn't matter. Everything's all set.' From his pocket he retrieved a box of blue-tipped matches.

I glanced around the flickering space, the ancient weaponry and the acrid odor of kerosene. I had assumed it was from the lamps, but then I saw the metal drums, and realized what he intended. 'Calvin, please, stop this. Don't.'

'You've got to be kidding. I couldn't live with myself.' He laughed without humor. 'Of course I won't be living . . . at all.'

'What are you saying?

'Look around, Lil, what do you see?'

'An incredible collection . . . Museum quality.' I tried to flatter him, to slow him down, but the look in his eyes made me realize he was beyond reason.

'You're right; it's the best collection of eighteenth-century American firearms in existence. And you're the only one who will ever see it. You see those barrels, Lil?'

'Yes.'

'One hundred twenty gallons of kerosene. We're about to give Grenville something to talk about.'

'But all of your beautiful antiques . . .'

'That's the point. What do you think would happen to my collection if I didn't destroy them? I had intended to leave it all to the town, as a museum. They could have had the house as well; I know it needs work, but it's a seventeen-twenties center hall colonial.'

'That's a wonderful idea.'

'Things change. I was willing to forgive a lot of things. But not that.'

'Wendy Conroy?' I asked, having moved past fear to clarity. Like a switch had been thrown I stopped shivering, my jaw unclenched and everything clicked in place.

'So you do know, or at least think you do. But it wasn't what you think. She was insane. She'd sit in the chair begging me to do it. How was I to know that each detail was being stored away? If she'd kept her filthy mouth shut, none of this would have happened.'

'I don't understand.' Struggling back against the wall, my rubber-soled shoes searched for purchase on the dirt floor as rivulets of rainwater squeezed from the thick wool and trickled down my neck and back.

'This.' He pulled a crumpled piece of torn notebook paper from his back pocket. 'Look at it.' He thrust it in front of me.

The light flickered across the wrinkled page making the words difficult to read.

> *Drill me now, my mid-day lover*
> *Drill me hard, make me bleed.*
> *Take me rough, away from mother*
> *Drill my teeth, spread my knees.*
> *How I long to feel you.*
> *Then swish and spit away our guilt*
> *Whisper soft; send me home.*

'It wasn't Bradley,' I whispered, knowing in my heart it couldn't have been, but relief nevertheless.

'It's crude,' he commented, 'and Conroy led me to believe there was more.'

'That's why you killed Philip?' I suggested, pretending a boldness I didn't feel.

'It's not what I'd intended. But you have to understand, I saw everything I'd worked for was about to come undone. The last things I had . . . my reputation and this . . . he was going to take them from me.'

'I don't understand.'

'He tried to blackmail me. Attach himself like a leech and suck away my collection piece by piece. "Retribution", he called it, for the damage I had done to his sister. What a joke. How many other men had a piece of his precious Wendy; she was no innocent. Of course, try telling that to Philip Conroy.' Calvin gazed at the wall above my head. 'And when he started to jab his finger into my chest. I couldn't stand that.'

'Couldn't you have gone to the police?' I asked, knowing it was a stupid thing to say, but desperate.

'And tell them what? They're just as bad. Did you ever wonder why my mother's lawsuit against Carl McElroy was dropped?'

'I thought there was a settlement.'

'Right, that's what we told everyone. He gave us twenty-five thousand lousy dollars in exchange for pieces that were hundreds of thousands, maybe more. Beautiful things; a Queen Anne lowboy and a pier mirror that had been in my family for centuries . . .

gone. Of course he couldn't get the prices he wanted for them here, so he faked a sale and had his buddies sell them in Manhattan. I'm sure they made a tidy sum and all the time my mother kept telling me, it was for the best. "Why do you want those old things?" she'd ask. "You don't have any children, what do you want them for?"'

'That must have hurt,' I offered, trying to break through to him.

'You have no idea. She couldn't understand; what I was creating was better than a family. I wanted to leave a legacy that would have lived for centuries, a collection of eighteenth-century life that would bring scholars and visitors from all over the world. I'd throw open the doors, and say, "Look at what I've put together."'

'It's a marvelous idea,' I said, encouraging him to go on. 'It's what the town needs. It's not too late.'

I could see passion in his eyes as he considered the possibility, but just as quickly, it passed. 'Too late . . . Too late for me, too late for you, and too late for Hank and all his busy-body friends.'

'Don't do this, Calvin,' I pleaded as I struggled to pull my legs under my body, the weight of my bound wrists making it treacherous.

'Sorry, Lil, I wish it could have been different. I'd even thought that with Bradley gone . . .' He paused. 'Ssssh . . . I hear them.'

He pressed his ear to the trick wall. A thin strip of denser black framed the entry; it wasn't fully closed.

With his attention momentarily off of me, I pushed back against the wall and using my legs for leverage struggled to my feet. My head throbbed; I felt faint from the kerosene fumes.

He glanced back and saw that I'd made it to my feet. He smiled. 'It's too late, Lil.' He reached toward a drum of kerosene, removed the lid, and, straining, spilled out a forty-gallon wave. The fluid sparkled yellow and blue as it washed across the floor, soaking the dirt and leaving puddles. The smell was overwhelming as he hurriedly opened can after can and dumped the contents. My shoes, already soaked from the rain, got splashed and the chemical further chilled the soles of my feet. I heard muffled voices from behind the hidden door. It was hard to breathe. And all I could think was: *I don't want to die.* I thought of my daughters and my grandchildren, but mostly I pictured Ada.

Calvin stumbled as he emptied the last barrel. With a flourish he threw a can top into the air, deliberately letting it clang as it bounced and rolled into a row of muskets.

I heard Hank Morgan shout in the distance.

Followed by Mattie's: 'There's something coming from behind that wall.'

Calvin turned to me. He smiled as he pulled the matches from his pocket. 'It's time,' he whispered, turning back to the door. 'Time to go.'

I edged away, realizing I was about to die. And then I heard another voice, Ada's. 'No!' I screamed as loud as I could. 'Get out of here! He's going to blow us up!'

Calvin turned and winked. 'Good girl, Lil. I knew you had it in you.'

'They're behind the wall,' Mattie yelled, and I saw specks of dirt land in the pools of kerosene as they pushed the trick panel, and it started to move, opening into Calvin's death trap.

'Go back!' I screamed, horrified that my words were having the opposite effect. 'Get out! Please!'

Calvin's hands shook. 'It's time. It's time.' He was practically dancing with the match in one hand and the box in the other.

As the wall moved, I ran toward him, my hands shackled behind me and the flaps of my coat catching between my legs. I didn't know what I was trying to do, but he saw me coming and stepped away. 'It's time,' he taunted, planting himself in front of the opening door.

'Go back!' I shrieked, changing directions and stumbling toward the hidden passageway.

'Lil!' Ada yelled.

'Go back! Get out!'

'Come on in!' Calvin shouted.

I caught the flicker of flashlights as the crack widened. With a final surge the door flew open. As it did, Calvin struck the match.

THIRTY-EIGHT

Time hung suspended as the horror of what he was about to do spread. I watched as Mattie struggled, revolver in hand, deciding whether or not she should shoot.

'Go ahead,' he taunted, 'shoot, it's better than a match.' He was clearly delighting in her predicament. 'No? Guess I'll have to do it after all.'

With a desperate surge, I lurched toward the door, the weight of my sodden coat slowing me down. 'Get out!' Moving like the Frankenstein monster toward Mattie, Hank, Kevin and Ada, whose eyes were fixed on mine. I couldn't see behind me, but, like Lot's wife, I knew that looking back was a terrible option. Still, from the corner of my eye I saw Calvin touch the lit match to his kerosene-soaked sleeve. A horrifying wave of blue rolled up his arm.

'Go back!' I screamed, and stumbled through the door, barreling into Mattie and Hank. 'Ada, run! Just run!' I pleaded as I caught the glimmer of orange flame. My shoes squished with rain and kerosene and I knew that one touch from the fire would send me up like a candle. *But maybe?* Realizing that I would not survive, but perhaps I could increase the chances that Ada and the others would. I knew about kerosene; I've been around it my entire life, from Girl Scout camping trips, to the stove in the house where I grew up before the town had installed gas lines on Main Street. Kerosene is relatively sluggish to ignite and I was soaked in water. These thoughts passed in an instant: *I can be a barrier – at least for a few seconds – between them and death*. On the floor a terrifying tongue of orange rippled past my feet. 'Move!' I screamed. 'Get out!'

Slouching into my coat, I managed to flop the wide hood over my head as I pushed behind them, and we stumbled en masse back down the uneven dirt passage. I imagined myself a giant green-wool mother duck herding her young to safety.

Waves of blinding smoke caught up with us and swirled over and past. My eyes teared as I struggled for breath.

Directly in front of me, through the dim flicker of flashlights,

I could see that Ada was lagging; *why is she even here?* She glanced back at me, her expression frozen with terror. Our eyes connected. 'Run faster,' I begged. I desperately wanted to grab her hand, which, considering mine were firmly bound behind my back and getting warm, was not possible. And I had an awful thought – *if we die, at least it's together.* 'Ada, faster!' I shrieked, gasping with the growing heat. *She's not going to die down here. That is not going to happen!*

'Keep your heads down! Smoke rises; stay low,' Mattie ordered as we hurried down the tunnel. I had the vaguest memory of being carried and then dragged down here by Calvin. *Was there a turn? Is it just straight? I don't remember it being this long. It's endless.*

Behind us the flames spread, lapping at the kerosene that had spilled into the tunnel. A wave of heat chased at our backs as the fire sought out oxygen to feed its mounting hunger. An unearthly scream followed us. 'Burnnnn!' It was Calvin, his voice high pitched, clearly in unbearable pain, but triumphant.

I focused on my feet, knowing that to fall would be the death of me, but worse, others would try to help me up, robbing them of precious seconds. The heat exploded into pain on the exposed flesh of my hands. The metal shackles throbbed around my wrists as they passed comfortably warm into something more like a branding iron. I bit the inside of my mouth to hold back the scream, wondering if the second had come where I too had caught on fire.

My heart pounded, and I heard Barbara's accusing voice in my head, and saw the face of Dr Doom and Gloom:

'She should never have left the hospital.'

'See, this is what happens to people who don't follow doctor's orders.'

I told myself: *keep moving, don't die down here, Lil. Tell Ada how you feel. Tell Ada you love her.* While trying to pull my hands turtle-like back up my wet sleeves.

And miraculously I was still moving, each awkward step a victory. Ada in front of me. I glanced up from under my hood at a different sound . . . The sound of hope. I caught the flicker of a flashlight and then light from above. Impossible to see, with the smoke so thick, and the heat like a furnace. But then I heard Mattie helping Ada up a flight of rough-hewn steps and then Hank's firm hand on my shoulder urging me upward. I heard Kevin cough, and someone grabbed my elbow as I nearly fell face first up the stairs. 'Let me help you, Lil. Careful.'

A wave of denser black rolled up behind us, and I held my breath as I cleared the last step. I'd been barely conscious when Calvin had carried me down, but I did remember this pewter-filled pantry. My eyes teared as I caught hazy glimpses of the priceless heirlooms, which had started to sag under the rising temperature. In seconds, I imagined they'd be little more than dull gray puddles. My lungs burned, and I turned my mouth into my hood and took a tiny sip of air through the cloth. In front of me I saw Ada's outline in the pantry door. She grabbed me by the coat, and gasped, 'Lil, come on!'

There were helmeted men and women at the door in black parkas with huge rifles. Someone was barking at us, 'GET OUT! GET OUT! GET OUT!'

I nearly toppled as I passed through the kitchen door and out into the driving rain. But Ada stopped my fall, and someone was holding my coat from behind. I heard a man shout out, 'She's injured! Where are the medics? We have wounded!'

I shuddered, praying that whoever was hurt it wasn't too bad. My eyes fixed on Ada. She stared back at me, her silver hair blackened, streaks of soot running down her nostrils and the corners of her mouth. 'Your eyebrows,' my voice croaked. 'They're gone.'

'Lil,' she said, tears running down her face, 'we have to get away from here.' She was sobbing.

I gasped, when she pulled at the sleeve of my coat. The pain was unlike anything in my memory. It shot from my fingertips and went screaming to my brain.

'What's wrong?' And then Mattie's voice: 'We need a medic, now!'

THIRTY-NINE

I tried to breathe through the pain as Ada and I were directed by Mattie to a relatively dry patch under an ancient red beech. 'Don't move!' Mattie instructed. 'I'm going to find medics and then you're both going to the hospital.' Her tone making it clear that this was not something to be discussed.

'It's your hands, Lil,' Ada said, her expression anguished. 'They're burned.'

'But we're alive,' I said, feeling like someone was holding my fingers to a lit stove. But if I stayed perfectly still, it was almost bearable.

Behind us, sirens blossomed through the driving rain. While we watched, flames and dense black smoke swept over the ancient house. Around us, Grenville came to life as crowds of rapt onlookers drank in the spectacle. Fire trucks and ambulances filled the air with deafening wails as they screamed down High Street.

My knees trembled, my hands felt like they were still on fire and my wrists – still cuffed – throbbed with every beat of my heart. My head swam with vivid images, Calvin striking the match, his screams and the very real fire before us. 'The poor man.'

I felt Ada's hand on my shoulder. 'Why did he do it, Lil?' Ada asked as the front wall of the upper floor seemed to shudder and then the whole top-floor facade gave way.

A gasp went through the gathering crowd as the front of the house collapsed, revealing rooms filled with Calvin's priceless antiques.

'A cherry highboy!' one of the local dealers shouted as a tongue of flame shot up the side of the nearly three-hundred-year-old piece of furniture.

Ada's question hung in the air. *Poor Calvin.* Rather than answer it, there was something I desperately needed to say. I turned to her, and despite the pain and the horror of what we'd just been through, I felt such certainty as the words came through my lips. 'I love you, Ada.'

She smiled, which, considering the lack of eyebrows gave her an oddly surprised expression, and before she could respond a pair of medics, led by Mattie, approached.

Tears fell as they gently separated us and started to ask questions. 'Can you walk?' one of the medics asked.

Considering I'd just run through hell it seemed odd, but I answered in the affirmative, never once taking my eyes off of Ada. They led us down the gently sloped side yard. In front of us, barriers were being erected and seemingly from nowhere there were news crews and swarms of locals taking pictures with whatever electronic device they happened to have. I saw cameras and cell phones pointed in my direction and then shifting back to the burning house, as though unable to snap up enough tragedy fast enough.

I let my body surrender as the earnest young medics eased me up on to their stretcher's orange mattress. Two others were with Ada in the ambulance parked directly in front of us. I watched as they placed an oxygen mask over her nose and mouth, and strapped her to their gurney before hoisting her into the back.

'I'd like to get these handcuffs off of you, before we get you into the ambulance,' the female medic said, her voice kind. 'I'll give you a shot of morphine. Do you have any allergies?'

'No,' I answered as her partner put an oxygen mask over my nose and mouth and he then proceeded to cut away my wonderful green wool coat. His red-handled utility shears struggled with the dense fabric. It reeked of kerosene, but there was still so much water trapped in the warp and the weave that it had saved my life.

The lights on Ada's ambulance sprang to life, and the siren blared as they pulled away. 'You need to take me to the same hospital where she's going,' I said.

'OK,' the medic said, and she peeled back the coat where her partner had cut it off around my shoulder and gave me a shot. I looked at the two medics, neither one more than thirty, both so earnest and focused. He'd put his shears back into his bright red kit and was now approaching with a pair of bolt cutters.

'This may hurt,' the woman said, her kind brown eyes focused on mine.

'It's OK,' I said, feeling the first warm glow of morphine. 'I'm alive.'

'Yes,' she said, a small smile breaking at the corners of her mouth as she gently gripped my elbows. 'You most certainly are.'

I heard the snap of metal, and my hands fell apart. The pain was horrific as the woman gently eased my arms from around my back to my lap, which she cushioned with gauze trauma pads. I did not want to look, imagining the very worst.

The medic stared down, her head nodded as though appraising the ripeness of a piece of fruit at the market. 'Jim, while you've got the cutters, do the wrists too.' She looked up. 'You'll feel better with them off. How's the pain?'

'Better,' I replied, feeling increasingly floaty.

'I've seen worse,' she said. 'I don't even know if you'll even need grafts.'

Comforted by her words, and the morphine, I hazarded a look. 'Boiled lobsters,' I said through the mask, but all the fingers were where they should be, albeit bright red with angry fluid-filled blisters.

By now her partner had stripped off my coat, which lay in sad pieces on the ground. They eased me back on to the stretcher, my hands swaddled in loose gauze. 'One, two, three,' she said, and I was up and into the back.

I don't remember much of the emergency room at Brattlebury Hospital. Just tremendous relief at seeing Ada in the curtained-off space next to mine. They cut away the rest of my clothes and ran tests, including a painful blood-gas measurement, where the technician jabbed into my damaged wrist taking blood from the artery. We both wore blue plastic oxygen masks and got hooked to cardiac monitors. It seemed that every fifteen minutes a nurse was showing me a pain scale with faces ranging from happy to very very sad, and I had to select one to indicate on a scale of ten how much pain I was in. It was definitely a tossup, yes, the pain was excruciating, but every time the morphine drip got pressed, I lost clarity. The worst was when the burn specialist came, and it wasn't so much the pain as my fear of what his conclusions would be. He was about my age, and had much of Bradley's quiet bedside manner. After he'd thoroughly examined my fingers, hands and wrists he spoke. 'The reason it hurts so much is a good thing. You have first and second degree burns. The skin is going to fall off, and we'll need to give you an ointment to protect against infection and they are going to hurt . . . a lot. But I don't see any full thickness burning. You are very lucky, Mrs Campbell.'

If I wasn't stoned out of my gourd, and hooked to multiple IVs and a cardiac monitor, I would have hugged him. 'They're going to be OK?' I asked, feeling tears track down my cheeks, and sounding like some bad soap-opera actress.

'You're going to be fine.' And he grabbed the clipboard off its hook by the end of my bed, scribbled a few lines and went to find my nurse.

I drifted into a half-dreaming state, which was frequently

interrupted by requests for me to point at one of the ten faces on the pain scale. More blood was taken, and at some point I was wheeled in and out of an x-ray suite. Finally, after a few hours of being poked and sedated, the ER physician determined we both needed to be admitted. Ada for observation, and me to insure I didn't go into shock from my wounds or have a repeat cardiac event.

With my daughters and a visibly shaken Aaron milling in the waiting room and popping back every few minutes to check in on me and Ada, I wasn't about to argue. At least they put us in the same room, our beds separated by three feet and a fall-leaf patterned plastic curtain.

In addition to my burns, we both had smoke inhalation and I had a throbbing bump on my forehead from the car accident. Ada had a racking cough that shook her frame each time she tried to clear her lungs.

Almost as soon as they'd settled us in our room my daughters appeared in the doorway with Aaron. 'United we stand,' Ada whispered as she fiddled with the controls of her hospital bed, raising the back as high as it would go.

I smiled dreamily at my children and whispered back, 'Divided we fall.' There was so much I needed to tell her.

'How are you feeling?' Barbara asked, planting a kiss on my cheek, and then looking at my two bandaged hands that looked like jumbo gauze-wrapped marshmallows.

'Tired,' I offered. 'I'll be better when this is all over and I'm home.'

'I bet.' Chris sat next to me on the bed.

There was a stretch of uncomfortable silence as the three of us sat.

'You guys are like heroes,' Aaron said.

'I suppose,' Ada said. 'Aaron, hand me those slipper things?' She carefully moved her legs to the side of the bed. As she got up a wave of coughing overtook her. She struggled to get control of her breath, her face turned bright red.

'You OK?' Aaron asked, standing beside her.

She nodded and placed a hand on her chest as tears squeezed from her eyes. 'I'm fine.' She took a careful breath. 'It's just going to take a while to clear the smoke, that's all.' She looked distracted.

'You sure you're OK?' I asked.

'I can't stop thinking about the fire,' she said, her eyes – like jewels – on mine. 'It keeps popping into my head.'

'Me too. It's strange . . . I'm thinking about something entirely different and suddenly I'm smelling smoke and having that awful feeling, like we're going to die.'

'That's normal,' Chris offered. 'You've both been through a trauma. It must have been awful. I can't imagine what I would have done. This whole thing is so scary.'

As she spoke, a heavyset man and a thin woman with a tightly curled mouse-brown permanent appeared in the door. While I'd never been introduced, I knew them: Ada's daughter, Susan, and son-in-law, Jack.

'Mother,' the woman said, going to Ada.

'Hello, dear,' Ada said, giving her a warm hug and kiss. 'Lil, I don't think you ever met my daughter, Susan . . . and that's her husband Jack.'

I smiled at Susan. 'Hi.' I looked into her face for traces of Ada's features; perhaps something around the mouth was the same. But she had a tentative expression, like she was waiting for something to taste bad. The man in the doorway, dressed in a navy suit, barely acknowledged my presence and didn't even look at his son.

With the arrival of his parents, Aaron grew sullen. His mother and he exchanged glances. Finally Susan spoke to him. 'How is school going?' she asked.

'Fine.' He looked at his hands.

'It's better than fine,' Ada said. 'He's going to make honor roll.'

'That's our Aaron,' Susan responded with a forced enthusiasm.

I stared at her husband, still in the doorway, his features obscured by shadows. 'Don't you want to sit?' I asked, curious for a closer look. 'There's an extra chair.'

'No thank you,' he replied curtly. 'We weren't planning to stay . . . Susan.'

'Right,' said Ada's daughter, standing at the sound of her husband's impatience. 'We really can't stay.'

'Of course,' said Ada. 'It's nice that you came at all.'

Susan looked at her mother; it was clear that she wanted to say more.

'Susan. Now!' her husband persisted.

'Coming.' She stopped a few feet from the door, turned and looked at her son and then at Ada. 'I'll come tomorrow.'

'That would be lovely,' Ada answered.

'Honey. Don't make us late . . . again.'

'Coming.' And with a twitch of her lips, which might have been a smile, she trailed after her husband.

I watched as Chris and Barbara threw each other glances.

'For the love of God –' Ada cut the silence – 'just say it.' And then she stopped, catching the sad expression on Aaron's face. 'I'm sorry, sweetie.'

'It's not your fault,' he brooded. 'I used to wish that she would leave him, but she never will.' He gritted his teeth as tears moistened his eyes. 'I hate it when he does that, and that was nothing. She just stands there and apologizes.'

'I know,' Ada tried to comfort him. 'But everyone makes their choices and it just kills you when someone you love makes the wrong ones.'

'You don't like him either,' Aaron stated.

'I don't. I never have.'

'Did you ever wish that they'd split up?'

She started to speak, and then she looked around the room. 'Oh, who am I kidding? Yes.'

'So it's not just me. You see it too.'

'Of course I do.'

'I don't want to go back there,' he stated. 'I know this sounds bad, with you in the hospital right now. But I can't go back there. It's like everything I do is wrong, and it becomes a big deal. At least with you and Lil, it's not like it's the end of the world or anything if I mess up.'

'We'll talk to your mother,' Ada said. 'You can stay with me as long as you'd like.'

'But if you move back to New York . . .'

'He's right,' I interjected. 'Oh who am *I* kidding?' *What is it about near-death experiences?* 'Ada –' and it was all I could do to keep from pulling out my IV and going to her – 'if you go to New York, I'm coming with you.' She stared back, something caught in my chest; I felt myself falling into the sapphire blue of her eyes. I could see her struggle. I'd crossed a line; *no going back, Lil.* I didn't care what my daughters were thinking; only Ada mattered.

She smiled, and held my gaze. 'We'll talk . . . later.' She glanced at my daughters, who seemed unnerved by my strange declaration, and were probably writing it off to the stress and the drugs. 'But I have to look after my mother.'

'I know.' I felt such horrible frustration, desperately wanting to let everyone know that I loved Ada Strauss. 'And if you go, I'm coming.' But as I glanced from my bed to hers, and then made a quick survey of the worried looks on Barbara and Chris, I realized: *not the time or place, Lil.* I gritted my teeth and stopped the words that were screaming in my head: *I love you, Ada Strauss.*

A knock at the door. Mattie Perez popped her head in. 'OK to come in?' She was carrying a pair of African violets, one purple and one magenta.

'How lovely,' Ada said, giving me a quick and reassuring wink.

'So, you want some news?' Mattie asked. 'Or would you rather wait?'

'Are you insane?' Ada said. 'What?'

'I thought you'd like to know, your friend Evie's painting was recovered.'

Ada sighed. 'Thank goodness, I think I've had enough crime . . . No offense. So where was it?'

'Tolliver found it. One of the workmen had . . . misplaced it.'

'Oh,' Ada responded. 'Misplaced?'

'Hank assures me there'll be an investigation. But frankly, not my job.'

'So where do you go now?' I asked, realizing that the detective's time in Grenville was coming to an end, and something about that was sad.

'Back to Hartford. I'm sure they'll have something new for me. Plus I have a mountain of paperwork to get through on this.'

'You'll be missed,' Ada said. 'Don't you want a career in calm and lovely Grenville?'

'Too much crime,' she joked.

'You have a point,' I agreed. 'I suppose we need to give some sort of report.'

'When you're feeling better.'

'I feel fine now.' I looked at Barbara. 'OK, I admit not one hundred percent. I just want to go home as soon as possible.'

'Hey,' Barbara said defensively, 'have I said a single word about that?'

'True, you've been good.'

'So what did happen?' Aaron blurted. 'Why did he do it? It was the dentist, right?'

I looked around the room. They all wanted to know what happened in that cellar, Aaron was just young enough to come right out and ask for it.

I looked at Mattie. 'Is it OK?'

'Go ahead. We'll still need to do it formally, but I'm itching to know.'

'Let's see . . . Parts of it are fuzzy. I remember driving in the rain and somewhere on the way to Shiloh he rammed me; I think I tried to get away . . .' Images tumbled as I pictured his eyes coming at me through the windshield, knowing we were going to crash and that I couldn't stop it. I remembered wondering if the airbag would work, and the sharp snap as it inflated. It blinded me and I had just wanted it out of my way. I could feel the car skidding. I thought I'd end up off the road sinking into the swamp.

'There was so much rain that I couldn't tell what he was doing and then I saw the gun. It's strange,' I went on, feeling giddy from the drugs. 'I knew he was going to kill me. At first I couldn't even feel afraid, just numb. He dragged me out; he must have carried me. I was pretty dazed.' I felt an itch in one of my fingers, and when I tried to move it, the scratch blossomed into sharp pain. I held my breath, and thought about pressing the pain pump, but in a couple of moments it eased. 'I was dripping blood. I feel so strange.'

Ada was watching me intently. 'Lil, you don't have to do this now. Maybe just rest.'

And I was caught in the warmth of her gaze. 'Did I tell you that I love you?' I couldn't stop myself.

'You did.' She didn't miss a beat. 'And you're the bravest person I know, Lil. I love you too. And when we get out of here, we've got some figuring out to do. But right now, maybe some rest?'

'No, I need to tell you what happened, and if going through this is what gave me the strength to tell you how I feel, then it lets me find something good, something wonderful inside so much ugliness and horror. Calvin was no monster, and yet, somehow he had become one. Like he'd figured a way to shut off the parts of him that were human and caring, as if there were two very different people living inside of him. When he handcuffed me and put me in the van I asked him what he planned to do. I've known – knew – Calvin most of my life. His mother and my mother had sat on committees together. I knew him when he was a little boy, I can even remember helping him dress up as a pirate one Halloween and then taking him around trick or treating. And later, he was our dentist. Even as he forced me into his van, he was polite . . . which is so strange, because he was clear that he was going to kill me. I remembered wondering about the other murders, and how the bodies had been found, that there seemed to be a purpose to it. Like Mildred's jewelry being sprinkled all over.'

'Did he say why he did that?' Ada interjected.

'They'd cheated him. They'd taken advantage of his mother, robbed her of her things, and Philip Conroy tried to blackmail him. What he did afterwards was poetic license.'

'I don't get it,' Chris said. 'To kill over antiques.'

'They were his life,' I explained. 'There was a fortune in that house. It was like a museum.'

'But still . . .' Chris persisted. 'There had to be something more.'

'There was.'

'Wendy Conroy?' Mattie prompted.

'Yes. The poem ripped from her notebook. Philip Conroy had confronted him with it; that's what started everything in motion. If that hadn't happened, all of this might have been averted. I think Calvin was always a little tightly wrapped and between his mother's death and Philip's accusation something made him snap.'

'So that's why he cut off Philip's finger?' Mattie stated.

'Huh?' Aaron said, missing the detective's point.

Mattie explained, 'The finger of blame; so he cut it off.'

'Not quite,' I said. 'It was more literal. When Philip confronted Calvin, apparently he was jabbing his finger into Calvin's chest. It upset him tremendously. I don't think Calvin liked to be touched.'

'Did he say why he planted it in the auction?' Ada asked.

'No, wish I'd asked. If you think about it, he really wanted to go out with a bang . . . literally. So the finger at McElroy's auction may have been his way of getting people to pay attention . . . scare them.'

'He was insane,' Barbara commented.

'Maybe,' I said. 'But the more he talked, it made sense. He'd spent his entire life taking care of his mother and collecting antiques. Other than that, what did he have? He never married, no kids. I think Calvin's love of antiques was how he defined himself, like a curator. And suddenly his mother starts to lose her mind and begins selling off the family heirlooms while he's at work.'

'Or molesting Wendy Conroy,' Chris interjected.

'Perhaps,' I said. 'But from his perspective, she was willing. Anyway, his mother clearly had Alzheimer's but all of the dealers were just too happy to accept her consignments or give her pennies on the dollar for priceless things.'

'So mostly revenge.' Mattie commented.

'Yes. In Calvin's mind, the murders were justified. Even the fire was planned. He was waiting for Hank to come down the tunnel.' I paused thinking about some of the things he'd hinted at around Hank, that my long-time friend and Bradley's golf buddy might have been in cahoots with the dealers. There was no proof, and at least for now I'd hold my tongue. But while Calvin may have been barking mad at the end, I knew in my gut there was mostly truth in what he'd told me.

'And?' Aaron asked.

'He wanted us all to die. And he wanted the whole town to witness the destruction of his things. Things that he had originally intended to bequeath to the Historic Society.'

'How childish,' Barbara said. 'If you won't play with me I'll take my toys.'

'It went deeper . . .' I struggled for the words but they all seemed inadequate.

'Tragic,' Ada said, and she gave me a questioning look. 'Was he in love with you, Lil? Was that the other piece? That day he fixed my tooth, the way he looked at you . . .'

'Yes,' I said, and a sob erupted from my throat. 'And I never knew. I don't think he had much love in his life. Just caring for his mother, and this fierce connection to his possessions. And now he's dead, and all his things burned up with him.' As I said that, an obvious realization took hold. 'That's why he came after me. Not because I'd cheated him like the others.' It was an awful thought. 'It's like I was another piece of Chippendale, and if he couldn't have me . . . Oh, God.'

Silence settled. I thought of Calvin and couldn't take my eyes off Ada. I was crying and felt guilty and simultaneously elated; not just to be alive, but this sense of new beginnings, a giddiness. *You're in love, Lil. And she said she feels the same. At least I think she did.*

'Well,' Mattie said, 'I think that answers the bulk of the questions. It's been an eye opener being in Grenville.'

I turned away from Ada. 'How so?' I asked.

'There's more here than what's on the surface. It's not just the antique capital of Connecticut. The real industry is old people, isn't it? There seems to be a systematic stripping away of a person's worldly goods; like cows being processed for slaughter. Not to whitewash any part of what he did, but Calvin Williams was fighting back. If I were on this police force, I'd say there are a number of loose ends worthy of investigation, like the business ties between Nillewaug and Pilgrim's Progress; something smells bad there. Anyway, on that note of conspiracy, I should head out.'

'Don't be a stranger,' Ada said, 'there'll always be a place for you at our table.'

'I may take you up on that,' Mattie said. 'Meeting the two of you has been without doubt the best part of coming here. While there may be something rotten below the surface, there's also a lot that's good.'

After she'd gone, I told Chris, Barbara and Aaron that I was feeling tired. But really, I wanted to be alone with Ada. Barbara's parting shot as she looked at Ada and me: 'I don't understand what's going on here.' She shrugged. 'I guess we need to talk.'

As the door closed behind them, Ada pushed her covers back and swung her legs over the side of the bed. She stared at her IV, and then pressed the clamp over the tubing and pulled the needle from her arm. She drew her arm in tight to her chest to stop the bleeding.

'What are you doing?' I asked, unable to take my eyes off hers.

Her monitor started to ding as she eased her feet to the floor and crossed the three feet that separated our beds. I turned my head against the pillow as her hand gently touched the side of my face. 'I wonder what she wants to talk about, Lil?'

And her lips found mine.

It was a perfect kiss.

When we separated, our lips still close, Ada chuckled. 'We've wasted a lot of time, Lil.'

'I know, but no . . . We've been together for a long time, none of that's wasted.' I desperately wanted to stroke the side of her cheek, but that would have to wait.

'I hope not,' she said, her expression clouding. 'I've never been so frightened. The thought of losing you. Lil, there's no way I'm moving back to New York.'

'I'll go with you.'

'No, it doesn't make sense. We'll figure this out. If Mom doesn't like Nillewaug we'll find someplace else, or maybe a live-in aide. I can afford it. But this is my home now, Aaron needs me . . . and I need you.'

'OK then.' I thought of Barbara's parting comment. 'Did we just come out?'

'I think we might have,' she said.

'Just checking.' And all I could think was of how much I loved Ada, how right it felt to be with her, and how much I wanted to kiss her again. And so I did.